STATE OF THE ORBIT

FIRST, A PIECE OF MINOR HOUSEKEEPING: where previously a volume of *Apsis Fiction* consisted of an Aphelion (July) issue and a Perihelion (December) issue, with *Perihelion 2016* we are moving right on to Volume 4, so that a given volume no longer spans two separate years. This leaves poor Volume 3 with its lone *Aphelion* issue, but that can't be helped. Volume 4 will consist of *Perihelion 2016* and *Aphelion 2016*, and the pattern will repeat for all subsequent foreseeable publications.

Besides, the perihelion of Earth occurs in the first week of January (in 2016, the Earth's orbit will bring it the nearest it ever gets to the sun on January 2), and this way the perihelion issues of *Apsis* will have a shot at being released more or less during Earth's perihelion—which was the whole point of their names in the first place.

Of course if you pay no attention to the issue/volume numbers of these books, and only their publication dates, you might not even notice. The stories in this book continue uninterrupted from *Aphelion* last July—though I can assure new readers that these stories stand on their own, and that I've included notes before each, so they may be read out of order without fear of confusion. These same notes will also tell you exactly where in their series a given story falls and where to find the rest, in case you wish to go back to the beginning and read them in order.

The lead story in *Perihelion 2016*, however, is solitary. "Violin Lessons for the Prince of Hell" was written to accompany this issue's cover illustration, but it is notable as part of a loose collection of tales featuring the exploits of the capricious Grimbald. The best thing I can do to describe Grimbald is say that her name is the two things she is not: grim and bald. In fact, she is their opposite. She first waltzed into my imagination some time in 2005 and has sat there, grinning, ever since. She was the namesake of my short-lived podcast, *Radio Grimbald*, the fiddler of "Fiddler's Dream" (*Fiddler's Dream and Other Stories*, self-published electronically in 2011), and has made cameos in many of my novellas. Perhaps most notably, she also appears in the second story of this issue of *Apsis*.

"The Goblin's Fiddle" takes us back to the world of the magician Bouragner Felpz and his friend and confidante Corianne Birch. This is the same world as all the stories involving Grimbald are set in, just in a more definite space and time. It had its beginnings in the first batch of ideas I sketched out when planning the various adventures of Felpz, and is one of the few that has remained virtually unchanged since that time. In the broad scheme of things, it comes tenth in the string of stories making up the second volume of Felpz's adventures.

"The Devil His Fiddle" is more of a poem than a short story, but in its defense it is a *short* poem. It is one last morsel of Grimbaldian meta-mythology and provides a suitable bookend to both "Violin Lessons" and "Goblin's Fiddle."

"The Silver Chimera" is the next Bouragner Felpz adventure, and is something of a sister-story to "The Last Dragon" from Volume I—being that it is Felpz recounting events from his past to Corianne, though he is honest about the exact dates this time.

With "Sons of Fire" we leave Felpz's world for the more realistic setting of *Driving Arcana*. I call it such not because the events which take place in it are any more plausible, but because it occurs in a place which actually exists in our world. Namely, Chicago. Do not be fooled, however: there is as much magic in *Arcana* as there is in *Felpz*, and of a darker, wilder variety. It is

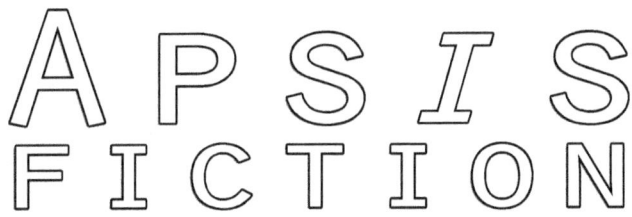

The Semi-Annual Anthology of Goldeen Ogawa

Volume 4, Issue 1 • Perihelion 2016

CONTENTS

author • illustrator • editor • book designer
GOLDEEN OGAWA

a HELIOPAUSE PRODUCTION

Apsis Fiction: The Semi-Annual Anthology of Goldeen Ogawa
Volume No. 4, Issue 1, Whole No. 6 (Perihelion 2016).
Published semi-annually by Heliopause Productions.

FICTION/Science Fiction/Short Stories

FICTION/Fantasy/General

First Edition 2016

ISBN: 978-06926086-1-6

the seventh story (or "spoke" as I artfully like to call them) in the first Wheel of the *Driving Arcana* saga.

"Chronostrophe" began as a word I invented to describe those gnarls in space-time that occur in many time-traveling stories in which the author has not sufficiently thought out the mechanics of temporal manipulation, and evolved into the eighth *Professor Odd* episode (which can also be thought of as the second episode of Season Two). Unsurprisingly, it has a few of these gnarls itself, due to this author *over*-thinking the mechanics behind the asynchronous temporal cartwheels the characters perform. It owes a great deal to *Doctor Who* (as does the entire *Professor Odd* series), but whether it owes a nod of thanks or a sincere apology I'll leave the reader to decide.

Wishing you a happy Terran Perihelion of 2016, and many happy hours of reading,

—*Goldeen Ogawa*
California
November 2015

"Violin Lessons for the Prince of Hell" accompanies this issue's cover illustration. Its protagonist, Grimbald, is a recurring character in many of my stories, and part of the meta-mythology of Antellonia—the universe which also houses Bouragner Felpz. Both story and picture were created in 2008.

VIOLIN LESSONS FOR THE PRINCE OF HELL

IN TIMES LONG PAST, the Prince of Hell was prone to fits of gloominess. He would mope about the inner circles of Hell, paying no heed to his business or duties, and be what we on Earth might call a wet blanket.

Then one day the Prince, in his gloominess, stepped upon a fiddle someone had left lying in the hall. When he picked it up it bit him, much to his surprise and consternation. And when he found the fiddle's owner you can be sure he had some stern words for her. But she only tweaked his nose and told him to stop moping so. It did not become a prince, she said, let alone the prince of such an important place as Hell.

Now the Prince of Hell had not had his nose tweaked in many thousands of years and did not know how to respond. The fiddle's owner, whose name was Grimbald, Queen of Dreams, took his silence as agreement and offered to teach him how to play the violin. And since Grimbald did not (and still doesn't) understand the concept of "No, thank you" that is exactly what she did. By the afternoon she had the Prince playing merrily and quite cured of his moping. His father complained that this ruined the atmosphere, but Grimbald didn't care.

Next she is planning on teaching him how to dance.

With "The Goblin's Fiddle" we return to the Adventures of Bouragner Felpz. *The story comes tenth in the second volume, following "The
Case of Countess Baronia" (*Apsis Fiction 3.1: Aphelion 2015, *from
Heliopause). The preceding tales of Volume II have been published individually in Apsis volumes 1, 2 and 3, and those of Volume I have their
own collection,* A Study of Magic *(Heliopause, 2013). "The Goblin's
Fiddle" was written in the early months of 2014.*

THE GOBLIN'S FIDDLE

Spring 2325

I T NOW COMES for me to tell of that most bizarre escapade con-
cerning the Goblin's Fiddle. Those of my readers who read the
Elgan papers in the Spring of 2325 may remember the sensa-
tional story of a passenger train inexplicably disappearing from
its tracks en route to Redling, and then just as inexplicably reap-
pearing in the middle of Hexenwald forest—forty miles from
where it had last been seen. No one on the train could give a
clear account of what had happened, save a particular magician
whose explanation was discounted on the grounds that it was
"too incredible to be believed."

Well, it should not surprise any of my readers to learn
that the magician in question was none other than my friend,
Bouragner Felpz, and that what he said was completely true. I
would have told the authorities the exact same story (having
also been a passenger on that train—the now infamous Rotgreif
Express) but none of them thought to ask me.

I shall tell the story now, in its entirety, and while some
may find it fantastical, to those familiar with the adventures of
Bouragner Felpz it should not be beyond the realms of credulity.

I unwittingly entangled myself in the affair—and, it followed, Felpz—by having the gall to take myself away on a foreign
holiday. I made the trek all the way to Milany before working

my way north around the Crowan Sea, visiting the grand old cities of Frazia and Amaris, and staying a spell in Schüle. It was entirely delightful and quite an adventure considering I did it all by myself—though my daughter flew down to visit me in Schüle at the end of my stay. We spent a enjoyable week taking in the sights of Elgany's brightest city, before we came to the end of our mutual vacations and turned homeward. My daughter, true to her nature, rode home on the back of the dragon that had carried her to Schüle in the first place, while I took what I thought at the time was the much safer route: that of the Rotgreif Express, which joined Schüle, Glossen, and Redling by way of reliable iron train tracks.

When I boarded the train on the evening of April 13th, I was in that exhausted but happy state that follows three weeks of travel and sightseeing, and was prepared to sleep the two days it would take for the train to reach Redling Central Station. My daughter, bless her, had insisted on buying me a first-class ticket, and so I treated myself to a decadent complimentary supper after seeing my luggage satisfactorily stowed.

I'll admit, I found my fellow travelers almost as interesting as the sights of those famous cities, and lingered over my coffee to indulge in a bit of innocent eavesdropping.

It appeared that my neighbor—a tiny old woman bedecked in pearls and heavily embroidered clothes—was an Aldonican countess, and she spent the entire meal deep in conversation with a statuesque Milanian woman with iron-gray hair heaped in an impressive bun. This woman, I gathered, was the mother of a young musical prodigy, whom the countess was most insistent give her a private performance while we were en route.

I sipped my coffee, both amused by the Milanian's attempts to politely decline the countess's request, and also sympathetic when it appeared the countess would not be put off. She was a woman of that pointed, wiry variety who asked for things by making it sound as though whatever it was she wanted was actually in her target's best interests.

"He should be a *star,*" she said, her Aldonican brogue barely noticeable under the authority and force with which she spoke. "It would be a wonderful opportunity for him to perform in front of a peer of the land—and before he ever reached it, no less. That way, when you get to Redling, you can tell everyone that he is Elzarino Cappofazi, charmer of royalty!"

Mrs Cappofazi made dubiously appreciative noises, and by an inspired maneuver managed to turn things around on the countess by stressing that her son was very tired and would likely not give a good performance while traveling.

"I would not wish you to hear him at anything but his most magnificent," she assured the countess, who was forced to accept the implied honor by dropping the matter.

I chuckled inwardly to myself over this, and after I returned to my compartment I made a note of the young man's name—so that I might, if he was indeed bound for Redling, attend one of his scheduled performances.

Then, feeling the effects of the stress of traveling and the generous meal I'd recently consumed, I curled into my bunk and went fast to sleep, lulled by the gentle clacking and rattling of the train as it hurtled on through the night.

I was woken sometime in the wee hours of the morning by the sound of music, soft and mournful, emanating from somewhere down the carriage. It followed no clear path or melody, and yet I was certain the tune had meaning. In my somnolent state I believed it had a great deal more meaning than any music I had ever heard. In some ways it reminded me of the song of the firestones I had heard in my youth. Loyal readers may recall this song, which when sung properly became a door to another world. This music had a similar quality, though what its purpose was I could not tell. Wondering on this, I fell back to sleep and did not wake again until I heard someone rapping on my door.

I awoke to find light full upon my face—not the warm, golden light of dawn, but the cool, bleached light of the moon. And the tapping, I saw when I blinked the sand out of my eyes, was coming from my window, not my door.

Light poured in from a crack in the curtains and lay in a pale stripe across my bunk. Pulling my dressing gown more tightly around myself as I sat up, I noticed with alarm that the gentle rocking of the train had ceased; we were apparently stopped.

Going to the window I pulled back the curtain and felt my heart leap to my throat at what I saw on the other side.

A huge face, like something between a lizard and a bird of prey, gazed back at me. The face was ringed with feathers and had a short, hooked sort of beak—which had been the source of the tapping. Its eyes were very dark and green, and blinked slowly at the sight of me.

"*Need help?*" the face asked, its voice light and chirping, like a parrot's, though faintly muffled by the glass separating us.

I was so surprised that it took me a moment to realize what it had said.

"I am fine, thank you," I told the face, firmly. I knew that many strange creatures lived in the Hexenwald, which lay not far from the tracks, and supposed that the stopped train had attracted attention from one of its residents.

"*I'll stay near,*" the face said. "*Just in case.*" Then it peeled away from the window, and I caught a glimpse of a long, snake-like body twisting through the air as it writhed away. Its absence revealed the landscape beyond, and I felt my jaw drop open at the sight of it.

We were no longer in the forested mountains of northern Elgany, but on a wide, flat plain of bluish-green grass. It stretched away to a distant horizon where steep, spiky mountains capped with white, like rows of sharp teeth, cut into a deep, dark blue sky. In this sky was no sun, but a huge ivory moon that shone with a soft brilliance. It lit the plain like daytime, but was dim enough that I could look directly at it, and saw there a range of mountains that formed the shape of a dragon wrapped across its surface.

I staggered back from my window, shook my head violently, and questioned whether I was really awake. This was certainly strange enough to be a dream, but as I stood there and felt the cold air clinging to my ankles, and heard on the other side of my door the shocked gasps of my fellow passengers, I began to realize that I was very much awake, and something very strange had happened indeed.

Seeing that I would likely get no more sleep that night, I dressed with the intention of going out to see what my companions had to say, only to find when I slid my door open that the corridor was jammed with people, making it impossible for me to leave my compartment.

This makes it sound as though there were more people than there actually were: the corridor was sufficiently narrow that it was difficult for two people to pass one another, and so what first appeared to be a crowd was in fact a line of about twenty people making their way slowly past my door. They were all in their nightclothes, and appeared understandably worried.

"Excuse me," I said, catching a young man by the sleeve of his nightshirt as he inched by. "Can you tell me what is going on?"

"That's the question we've all been asking, hasn't it, mum?" he said dryly. "The conductor's just opened up the dining car, and we're hoping he'll have an explanation."

I doubted that, but I joined in the line at the next opportunity, and so made my way with the rest of first class back to the carriage I had so recently quitted.

The conductor was a tall, dark man with a fine white mustache and a snowy head of hair. Upon first impression I had taken him to be the sort of steadfast, unflappable man who would remain calm in any situation. This impression was borne out now, when he stood at the head of the dining car, very neat and composed in his blue-and-gold uniform, and ponderously cleared his throat.

"Ladies and gentlemen," he said, inclining his head ever so slightly in the direction of the countess. "It appears we have lost our way in the night. I beg you all to remain calm and patient while the captain and I attempt to get us back on the right track."

The room exploded with questions. *Where* were we? made up the bulk of these, but I also heard a few voices, raised in alarm over the others, asking *how would we get back?* and *how did we get to wherever* here *was?*

The conductor raised an implacable hand for silence and waited stoically until the clamor died down.

"I wish I had answers for you," he said. "At the moment, we cannot be certain *where* we are, though it seems to be some sort of alternate dimension. We have no knowledge of how we came here, but we have several ideas for how we might return. Our primary concern, however, is your safety. Which is why we ask you to return to your quarters and to not, on any account, step outside the train. Thank you, that will be all."

This only caused more clamor, but seeing I would learn nothing of value I turned to leave. In doing so I caught a glimpse of the Milanian woman, Mrs Cappofazi. She was standing behind me, near the door, clutching herself tightly around the midsection, and staring with stricken horror out the nearest window. Sensing my gaze upon her she turned her face to mine, and I saw her eyes were wide with despair and horror. Then she shook her head and darted off through the door and down the passage.

I chose not to pursue her but returned instead to my own compartment, hoping that I might find something in my belongings which I could utilize to contact Felpz, or perhaps Abharus, who would likely have better luck sorting us out than the poor conductor.

I had not yet managed to get my trunk down, when I heard the soft thump and slither of something on the roof of the car. At first I worried it was some sinister monster, but then my mind went to the odd feathered serpent that I had first seen upon waking.

Bearing in mind the conductor's sensible instruction not to set foot outside the train, I opened my window as far as it would go and pressed my face to the resulting aperture.

"Hello?" I called. "Is that you?"

Immediately the light from the ivory moon was cut off as something dark dropped between my window and the sky. Green eyes glittered and a beaky mouth smiled.

"It *is* me," the creature chirped. "Do you want my help? I could fetch my mistress."

"No, thank you," I said, as I had no idea *who* would be mistress of such a creature and did not wish to find out under current circumstances. "But do you think you could fetch someone *else*? A friend of mine, he is a magician. He is called Bouragner Felpz. Or Felpass, sometimes," I added, in case the creature might know my friend by his older name.

The face twisted almost upside-down, like an owl, and frowned.

"He is also called the Purple Magician," I added, a little desperately.

At once the expression on the birdlike face cleared, and its eyes twinkled.

"Oh, I *know* the Purple Magician," it said. "I will fetch him. Fetch him at once!"

"You needn't," I said hastily. "Just tell him Corianne is stuck on the train, and the train is . . . well, wherever *here* is. Do *you* know where we are?" I asked, struck by a sudden inspiration.

"Corianne is stuck on the train, which is lost between the teeth and the throat," recited the creature. "I will tell him!" And with a flick of its long tail the creature was twisting up through the pale sky, and I was left pondering its last words. I only hoped Felpz would be able to make more sense of them than I.

Having done all that I could towards resolving my predicament, I settled myself to wait, but found I could not sit still for the shivering excitement that continued to rush through my veins. Though the walls and furniture of my little compartment were perfectly unchanged, in this strange moonlight everything took on a slight shimmer, as if seen through a pane of lightly smoked glass. The light was also strange in that it penetrated even the darkest shadows, and so in a way I could see things rather better than I had by the ordinary lamplight. It gave the world a dreamlike, uncertain feeling, which led me to feel similarly uneasy.

Then I felt a curious shiver, like a breath of cold air on the back of my neck, and a moment later I heard a faint sound, high and mournful, like the whine of an injured animal. This slowly grew and strengthened, until it finally lifted to become the haunting melody from the night before. Distant at first, it soon penetrated my compartment, and it was only by assuring myself that I was still alone could I convince myself that the player was not in the room with me.

The music had not been playing for more than a minute when the train surged into motion again. Glancing out my window I saw the vast field of blue-green grass creeping by, and it appeared the spiky mountains were drawing slowly nearer.

Rising carefully I opened my door and put my head into the corridor, only to have it nearly taken off by one of the porters flying past. In his wake I saw my neighbors emerging, some shouting questions, others looking around for the source of the music.

This now seemed to be coming from all around us, and was growing loud enough to be uncomfortable. Before it became unbearable, however, it was cut off in an abrupt screeching, and a moment later the train slowed and came once again to a halt.

"What in the great beyond is going on?" came a shrill voice from the direction of the countess's compartment.

"That *is* a pertinent question, my lady, but I'm afraid the answer is somewhat beyond me," came the reply, almost at once, from the shadows at the end of the carriage. Though the speaker was yet invisible, I felt my whole body relax, and a warm feeling of reassurance swelled in my breast: for I recognized that voice immediately as belonging to my friend Bouragner Felpz.

The door to the dining car was flung open, and there was the conductor—rather more ruffled than the last time I had seen him—with the porter behind him, gazing timidly from under one elbow. They stood there, struck still as the tall form of Bouragner Felpz, his coat vividly purple even in the washed-out light of the ivory moon, emerged from the shadows at the far end of the corridor. His eyes found mine immediately, and he smiled jovially.

"Corianne, how happy I am to see you—even if it is rather earlier than I expected. I confess, you were right to worry about losing your way on your travels, though you've managed to do it in an entirely unique way."

"Do you know this person, ma'am?" the conductor said, and I turned to find myself face-to-face with his humorless gaze.

I refused to be intimidated, however, and drew myself up proudly before I answered.

"This is no ordinary person," I told him. "This is the renowned magician Bouragner Felpz. As he is a *particular* friend of mine, I thought it would do us all good if he lent us some assistance in getting out of our current . . . predicament. So I called him."

The conductor looked at me, disbelieving, but was forced to turn his attention away when the countess's door slid open and her voice could be heard echoing into the passage.

"—magician? Bring him here at *once*. He'll be much more useful than these mundane blue-sleeves. Perhaps *he* can tell us where we are."

I saw the porter wince, and the conductor turned a stormy glare upon the countess's poor maid, who was just shutting the door behind her, her face dark with shame.

Felpz had already raised a hand and was shaking his head.

"All in good time," he said. "*Where* you are is no mystery. The problem will be getting you all *back* to more or less the right place."

"Felpz," I said, reaching out to tug his sleeve. "*We* still have no idea where we are. The odd creature I sent to fetch you said it was somewhere between the teeth and the throat, but I'm afraid that means nothing to me."

Felpz turned a surprised look at me. "Really? Do you not recognize it? All of you?" He looked around at us, apparently astonished at our universal ignorance. He gestured expansively. "You are in *Dream,* my friends. Between the teeth and the throat of it, to be precise. Now, it will be impossible for me to get you back to where you belong without knowing what brought you here in the first place. You, conductor . . . ?"

"Jamison," said the conductor stiffly.

"Jamison," said Felpz. "If you would, gather the crew in the . . . have you got a dining car? Oh good. Yes, the dining car. I suppose you have too many passengers to fit them all at once . . . better have them brought in one at a time. But first, I must speak to your crew. And have a look at the engine. I take it you will want to come, Corianne? Just so. How was Schüle? No doubt you wrote to me of it, but your letter had not yet arrived when I was called away."

Staggered by this abrupt change of topic, I endeavored to dredge up some of the memories of my visit as we made our way slowly down the passage—squeezing past the countess's maid—and once more into the dining car.

Felpz listened attentively as we were then shown into the galley beyond, and thence to the foremost reaches of the train: the little cabin where the staff would squeeze themselves when not on duty. Here my words petered out, and just as well, for

Felpz strode forward and opened the door that would lead us out of the train—it being the only way to reach the engine.

I saw the conductor give an involuntary twitch, though the man clearly thought better of warning a magician off his job.

"You may step out as well," Felpz assured us as he climbed down. "This is a singularly benign section of Dream; as long as you remain in sight of the train I anticipate no problems."

"Felpz you really must explain better than that," I said, following him out the door. "Do you mean to say we are *dreaming?*"

"Nothing of the kind," said Felpz, who had reached the ground and was inspecting the wheels of the coach. "When I say Dream, I mean the *place.* That wondrous, maddening, inscrutable place where conscious and unconscious thought take form. Where stories exist as islands, and the foundations of history lie sunk in the sea of memory. If you'll remember, our adventure with the withered hand of Asterly Hall introduced us to one of its residents: the lamphra Badgrave."

I did indeed remember those events, and the singular character of Badgrave, and paused to wonder whether that had anything to do with current events, but I was distracted when I reached the ground and saw why Felpz had been examining the wheels.

There were no iron tracks beneath the heavy metal rims, and they were sunk deep in the lush green grass. Tracks of another sort—crushed stems and gouged earth—stretched out behind them, clearly the marks of the train's recent journey.

Raising my eyes I saw we stood in view of the engine. When last I had seen it, this impressive boiler on wheels had been belching steam and smoke, its headlamp blazing proudly, its huge steel form vibrating with power.

Now it was dark and cold and silent, a lump of metal crouched on that surreal landscape. The only movement was a flicker of denim as the enginemaster put first his head, then his upper body, out of the little window to the driver's cabin and called down to us in Elgan.

Felpz's head went up at once, and he answered the driver in kind. They conversed thus for some minutes, and since I had only the crudest grasp of the language I soon gave up following the thread of their conversation and turned my attention to our surroundings.

Now that we were out in the open air, the feeling of looking through a pane of frosted glass had evaporated, and I could see clearly every blade of that wondrous, blue-green grass. The mountains in the distance appeared more jagged and sharp than ever, and a faint breeze wafted down from their direction. It smelled of old, dry, unopened books, but that was almost overpowered by the fresh, pungent smell of the damp grass.

Felpz, meanwhile, had progressed down the engine, inspecting the driving wheels and eventually the cowcatcher. I drifted after him, not wanting to let even the smallest distance grow between us—for I felt this was a place where things could easily be lost or forgotten. Indeed, since I had been out in the air I had felt a deep calm come over me, a complacency similar to the feeling of drifting off to sleep, and I worried that if I did not keep moving I might stand there, ankle deep in the blue-green grass, forever.

At the very least, Felpz was easy to keep track of: his purple coat seemed to glow in the light of the huge ivory moon, and I could find him even out of the corner of my eye. When he finished with the train and came marching back down its length I saw his brows were furrowed in thought. He waved at the enginemaster and offered a few words of reassurance, but spoke no more until we had climbed back into the coach.

"This is most remarkable," were the first words out of his mouth. The conductor, the porter and I were pressed into the small free space around him, and our anticipation must have been palpable. "You can absolve your engine of any wrongdoing. There is nothing about it to suggest that the machine is under any direct enchantment. Although the good *motormeister* tells me the train ran smoothly into this realm, and they were only able to stop it by dousing the engines and applying all the brakes. Even so, moments before I arrived, they said the train moved of its own accord."

"Yes," we all cried at once. "I felt it," I added.

"It seems to have stopped at the first hint of my arrival," Felpz murmured with an amused quirk of his lips. "This suggests to me that there *is* something facilitating your journey, but it is certainly not based in the engine. How are the passengers, Mr Jamison? I think it is time I spoke to them. I shall start with you three here, if you don't mind."

"It was a little past midnight that we noticed the change," the conductor volunteered. "Though I can't say when it actually happened. It being night we weren't exactly glued to the windows."

"Of course," said Felpz, nodding encouragingly.

"I was first aware of the light. The moonlight. Knowing we were still in the first quarter, when it suddenly came blazing in through the windows it was a shock. It was about that time that all the gas lamps went out as well."

"And the train continued to run smoothly?"

"For a bit, sir, for a bit. We began to decelerate immediately, however, as the engineers noticed the change as well and got the train to stop."

"Yes, that tallies with what the *motormeister* told me," Felpz said. "And you, mister . . . ?"

The porter, a young freckled lad, jerked himself to attention. "Sterngarten," he offered. "It is just as *Herr* Jamison says."

"And you noticed nothing out of the ordinary in the hours previous? How was the run from Amaris to Schüle?"

"Our journey up until now has been perfectly ordinary," said Jamison stiffly. "No disturbances."

"Except the music," I put in.

"You heard it?" Young Sterngarten said, his eyes very large and bright with something like relief.

"We do have a violinist on board," Jamison allowed, but Felpz had already turned away from him to concentrate on me.

"What music?" he asked, very intent, and I knew I had not been wrong to speak up.

"When I first woke—" I began, but Felpz interrupted almost at once:

"This would be at what time?"

"Oh, I don't know. It must have been after midnight, as we had already left our iron rails. Anyway, I heard music. Fiddle music, to be precise." I proceeded to describe in detail my impression of the music, helped along by Sterngarten's encouraging nods. Jamison, however, only frowned more and more as

I went on. I would have found it off-putting, but my experience with Felpz told me that this would likely prove critical to finding a solution, and so I forged on.

"You say the sounds held meaning?" Felpz echoed.

"I would not have dared put it that way," Sterngarten said. "But now that she says it so, I have to agree."

"And you have not heard this music since?" Felpz asked.

"In fact I *did*," I said, feeling triumphant. "Just before the train began to move again. I heard it stronger than ever."

"I did hear complaints of a noise," Jamison allowed. "But was somewhat distracted at the time, you understand."

"It stopped with your arrival," I added.

"Ah," said Felpz with a sage nod. "That is very helpful, thank you, Corianne. Mr Jamison, I believe you mentioned something about having a violinist on board?"

"Just so, sir," said the conductor. "A Mr Cappofazi, traveling with his mother. Something of a child prodigy, I understand."

"Would it be possible to interview him *sans* maternal interference? No? No, I suppose not. Then I will interview them together. *Herr* Sterngarten, would you be so kind as to fetch them? I don't think we need disturb the other passengers, but if they ask, tell them they need not worry. We should—*should*—be able to set all to rights by morning. And in the meantime, Corianne, this will prove to be a most memorable finale to your holiday. Now come, let us leave these cramped quarters."

The drama of the night was not yet over, however. Once we had installed ourselves in the dining car we had to wait for some time before the efforts of young Sterngarten produced Mrs Cappofazi and her son. Far from being in their bedclothes—as all but the staff, myself, and Felpz were—the mother and son were dressed in finer clothes than they had dined in, though these were now somewhat rumpled. But while Mrs Cappofazi strode imperiously into the car with the air of one about to conduct an interview rather than be the subject of one, her son merely drifted in her wake. A small, pale boy with lank dark hair, he had a nose that would have been striking on a marble statue but on a child seemed cumbersome and out of place.

Mrs Cappofazi appeared ready to take command of the proceedings, but Felpz spoke before she had time to open her mouth.

"It is good of you to come, madam. Please believe, had I been able to rectify our situation without rousing you from your . . . " he paused to take in her evening gown and neat calfskin boots, " . . . rest. But I have discovered, through my investigations, that you and your son are partly responsible for the current state of affairs."

I could see the woman's breast swell indignantly at this, but her son tugged earnestly at her sleeve and spoke softly, causing her to deflate a little. She turned to him, and spoke very quickly and quietly in Milanian. Despite my recent immersion in that language I caught little of her meaning, but by the way Felpz's eyes followed them, and by the twitching of his brow, I guessed he had little trouble surmounting the language barrier.

"It is not *our* fault," Mrs Cappofazi said at length, her manner having softened somewhat. "It is his *violino* . . . "

"Fiddle," provided the boy.

"I thought it might be," said Felpz. "I don't suppose you have it with you?"

The young boy shook his head vigorously, his dark hair flapping. "It flies away," he said. "Somewhere on the *treno*, er, the train."

"How do you know it is still on the train?" Felpz asked.

"Because I hear the music, *mago*. Don't you?" The boy asked this, his eyes very wide and open and innocent, but I felt a shiver run down my spine as I realized the train was not as silent as I thought it had been.

Beneath our voices, beneath the rustling of Mrs Cappofazi's dress, was a faint hum. A whine, like a lost animal. It seemed to resonate up from the floorboards, and only by holding my breath was I able to make out the haunting melody that had crept into the sound.

Sterngarten muttered a curse in Elgan, and the conductor, Jamison, turned around very sharply, as if he expected to find the source of the music around his feet.

"What in the blazes is that infernal thing?" he cried.

"Nothing infernal," Felpz said mildly. "Though . . . I understand it was well received by the Prince of Hell. No, I believe you somehow managed to lay your hands upon a most extraordinary instrument. I should like to have the story, if only for my own satisfaction, but first I believe we had best get it back to its rightful owner.

"I am speaking, of course, of your violin, Mr Cappofazi. Tell me, what does it look like?"

The boy appeared taken aback by this question, but his mother stepped up promptly and began to explain:

"It is a very old instrument. Dark mahogany in color, with a unique carving upon its surface."

"Does it not have teeth?" asked Felpz.

"Teeth?" cried the woman. "I should think not. No violin has teeth!"

"I know of one that does," Felpz said. "And it is the only violin—nay, the only *thing* that could possibly cause the kind of trouble we are currently experiencing."

For once Mrs Cappofazi was silent. By her side her son had gone even paler than before and looked ready to topple over.

"You saw it," Felpz stated, but gently, and he stepped over and guided the boy into a chair.

"I thought it was a dream," moaned the boy, and finally the whole picture snapped into focus.

"Good gracious, Felpz," I said. "It's the *Goblin's Fiddle,* isn't it?"

Felpz looked up and positively beamed at me. "*Very* good, Corianne. You'll be able to start your own consulting business at this rate."

"The Goblin's *what?*" said Jamison, and the Cappofazis looked at me in confusion.

"Is it anything to do with the *Wichtelschneider?*" Sterngarten asked.

"Corianne," Felpz said, standing up abruptly, "you may explain."

"It's a bit of a misleading name," I admitted, as Felpz went over to the door and began feeling around the frame. "It doesn't belong to a goblin, nor was it made by one—to my knowledge no one knows who made it. It is the instrument of . . . well, this is going to sound downright fanciful, but it's the instrument of

Grimbald, the Queen of Dreams. Surely you've heard of her . . . "
I trailed off. My audience was rather more interested in Felpz,
who had now moved his examination to cover the coach wall.
Sliding around the windows and inspecting the floor in places,
he made for a distracting sight.

"As such, it is a powerful part of Dream itself," Felpz said, no
doubt sensing that the tide of attention had turned to him. "It
would be completely within its power to transport a train—nay,
an entire city—into Dream. All it would need is a player. Someone to unlock its power." He shot a glance at Elzarino Cappofazi,
and the boy hung his head.

"No, do not be ashamed," Felpz assured him. "Worse things
have befallen those who played the Goblin's Fiddle. Count yourself lucky."

"But how on earth did it fall into the hands of a human?"
I asked, feeling a little frustrated. "From all the stories I read,
Grimbald was quite attached to it."

"She was—is," Felpz corrected himself, gently coaxing Sterngarten and Jamison aside so he could examine the wall behind
them. "But she is also easily distracted. She has a habit of leaving it in odd places—sometimes I think she does it on purpose
just to see what happens."

"How did you come by this violin?" I asked, turning to the
Cappofazis.

To my surprise Mrs Cappofazi colored, and cast her eyes
downward as she answered:

"My family was not rich," she explained. "When Elzarino
wanted to play the violin we had no money for lessons, but I
thought, if he had at least a toy violin then he could pretend to
play. But I had not the money even for that. Then I found this
old *violino* at the *avanzo negozio*—er, what you would call a junk
shop? So I bought it for my son and bring it home. And we put
some cotton strings on it and made him a bow out of a piece of
old broom handle and some more string. And he played with it,
and to our astonishment it made music! We took to standing
on the street corner every *Sabato*, and in time he earned enough
money to buy a real bow. Later, we put real strings on the violin,
and cleaned it and polished it, and to our surprise we find out
it is actually a very good old violin. He gives performances, and

people like his music because it is like no music they have ever heard. It has never done anything like this before," she finished earnestly.

"Except," said Felpz from the other end of the coach, "make music with cotton strings. That should have been your first clue. But do you mean to say you noticed nothing out of the ordinary tonight?"

The boy went red in the face at that, and his mother looked indignant. Eventually, however, he explained:

"I take the violin out to practice. I always play a little before I go to bed. But when I have it out and tuned I was suddenly tired, and I sit down to rest. The next thing I know, I am waking up on my bunk, and the violin is gone. I hear it playing, though, and the music is so strange I can do nothing but listen. Then it stops, and I get up to tell Mamma—and that is when I notice that the outside is gone wrong."

"And you did not alert anyone to the fact that your violin had gone missing?" Felpz asked. He was now wandering back and forth along the coach, apparently at random. Yet I couldn't help be reminded of a cat, casually herding its pray into a corner, and felt my heart begin to beat a little faster.

"We tried!" protested Mrs Cappofazi. "But all they say is, 'go back to your compartment, madam. We are doing everything we can, madam.'"

"Also," her son put in, quietly, "we began to suspect my violin was being . . . used somehow. I kept hearing it play. Sometimes it sounded like it was in the room with us."

"No doubt it has been moving all over this train," Felpz said tiredly, "trying to find a way to get the thing started again. Now I am here, however, its options are limited. Would you just take a step to the side, Madam Cappofazi, and I think I shall be able to put a face on tonight's troubles."

So saying he made a little dart past the Milanian lady, nearly clipped one of the tables, and sent a chair crashing to the side. Ignoring it, he dove into a shadowy corner and, after a slight scuffle and some grunting, re-emerged, triumphantly carrying something at the end of his outstretched arm.

"There," he said, pausing to nurse his free hand. "Is this not your violin, Master Elzarino?"

To say it was a violin would be to put entirely the wrong idea into my readers' heads. In general size and shape it was quite like a fiddle, but around its edge were studded horns and curving claws, and in place of gracefully curving F holes was a gaping mouth lined with teeth. There were little stones set on either side of the fingerboard, and what with these and the toothy mouth it was easy to see a face on the instrument—and it was not a pleasant one. Across the body were carved runes— some large and angular, some small and curling, like the trails an insect larva makes as it bores through wood. The whole thing was of a dark, radiant wood, with a faint reddish tinge around the corners. What was left of its strings hung limply below the scroll, for they had all been cleanly severed.

What made us recoil, however, was the violent snapping of the violin's toothy mouth. So vigorous was it that I saw how Felpz's shoulder jerked as he held it.

"Mr Cappofazi," he said, a little out of breath. "Correct me if I am wrong, but this *is* that same violin, is it not?"

The boy, half hidden behind his mother's skirts, nodded shakily.

"It is not meant to have teeth, though," he said in a small voice.

"You mean it never bit you?" Felpz asked in some surprise.

Elzarino Cappofazi shook his head.

Felpz laughed ruefully. "Count yourself lucky, then. Count all of you lucky, in fact, that Corianne had the wits to summon *me*. I shudder to think what would have become of you had this . . . artifact . . . been allowed free roam. But that is all speculation; now we should have little difficulty in summoning its master—which may bring about its own set of problems, but I am optimistic as to our prospects."

"Its master?" I repeated. "Didn't you say it belonged to the Queen of Dreams herself?"

"Indeed I did," said Felpz. "A little room, please. Mind your fingers. Yes," he said, edging his way towards the door, "I said the Queen of Dream, and that is who I intend to summon. It is *her* fiddle, after all, and the only right thing to do with it—as with so many objects of power—is to return it to its rightful owner."

He had reached the door by this time and, holding the snapping violin well clear of it, pushed it open with one hand.

"I should mention, for those present, not to try to attract attention to yourselves. Above all do not try to be clever. Grimbald likes clever people, and if she likes you, it will be much more difficult for you to return to your normal lives."

So speaking he carefully stepped off the train and hopped to the ground. As one we crowded 'round the little aperture and peered out, only to see him wading away through the blue-green sea of grass, the violin—now thrashing vigorously—still held safely at arm's length.

When he was easily ten yards from the train he stopped, turned around in a slow circle, and then, very calmly and politely, said:

"Grimbald?"

Nothing happened. All was silent.

"Grimbald?" A little louder this time, but still nothing.

Taking a deep breath, Felpz raised his head to the huge ivory moon and shouted "*GRIMBALD!*" into the dim blue sky.

At first, I thought nothing had come of it this time as well. Then someone behind me, whose voice I did not recognize, said:

"Oh, *this* is interesting."

Slowly, we turned our heads and found someone new had joined our number. In height she was half a head shorter than I—shorter even than young Elzarino—with a bush of wildly curling dark brown hair. In the uncertain light of the ivory moon this appeared to twist and curl around her face as though it were alive. This face was not one I would soon forget: round as an apple with a soft nose and dimples, it was made subtly sinister for being the color of the deepest blue sky, with dark blue shadows—like patches of midnight—around the eyes. These shone like little glass orbs, and it was difficult to tell where their gaze fell, as they had neither pupil nor iris. The unsettling effect was compounded by the wide smile that stretched from cheek to azure cheek, indigo lips drawn thin across bright, white, square teeth.

It was an odd sensation; for I have confronted demons, fairies, ghosts and dragons, and though each of these pressed their presence upon my consciousness in different and discomfiting ways, this person presented nothing more than an unusual sight. Yet she was all the more frightening because of this, for I had no idea what her intent could be. Was she malevolent? Kind? Did her presence portend nightmares or salvation? As her face, with its blank, colorless eyes, rotated slowly towards each of us in turn, I was put in mind of a wildcat—something that appeared benign enough, but could at a moment's notice turn into a fierce force of chaos.

"Yesssssss . . . " said the little blue woman, the *s* trailing off into a soft hiss, and I caught a flick of her shiny, dark blue tongue between the white teeth. "This is *very* interesting."

"Grimbald," said Felpz, warningly, and I heard the rustle as he waded back towards the train through the grass. "Come away from them. I have what you want."

The woman took no notice. Her black dress, which hung snugly over her squat, plump figure, fluttered around her blue knees as she took a step towards us. She wore heavy, brown leather boots, and their soles looked as though they had dried mud on them.

We drew back, and Grimbald laughed.

I thought at first the laugh echoed, back and forth until there were three or four voices laughing. Then I noticed that they all differed in pitch, tone, and pattern. One was a chuckle, one a guffaw, one a sinister cackle, and one a disarming giggle. But they were all unmistakably the voice of the blue woman in the black dress.

"Sorry, Felpass," she said with a grin, even as the other laughing voices faded away. "This is *too* much fun to pass up. Now—what have we here . . . "

All at once I found myself staring into milk-white eyes—they reminded me of twin moons of the kind one saw on winter nights—and I felt a tickle as a tendril of Grimbald's curling hair brushed across my brow.

"*You're* a bit early," she said. "I'll leave you . . . for now. And *you* . . . "

She whirled away, crouching before Elzarino Cappofazi. "*You'd* best learn to think for yourself, young man. Can't have mothers and fiddles running your life. Why, it'd be all the wrong sort of play, day *in* and day *out* . . . " She swung out her bare, blue arms, waving them back and forth as she spoke. "Carpe noctis, and so on. You've got a deep well, see you don't poison it."

"Grimbald!" Felpz said abruptly, now standing directly outside our door. "Will you have the decency to take your trouble-mongering fiddle *back* now? It's giving my arm a dreadful ache."

"It's only because you haven't been *polite* to it," Grimbald said, not turning to look. "You should have taken me up on violin lessons when you had the chance."

Felpz let out a heavy sigh. "Grimbald," he said, in the tones of one trying to coax a cat down from a tree.

Grimbald, however, was patently not listening. She had straightened up and was sniffing the air, dog-like, while she turned in a slow circle.

"Pearls?" she said, slow and disbelieving. "Sterling silver . . . oh, and *pale* gold. Very nice . . . most of the diamonds are glass, but one is real. Why . . . that is *lovely* . . . "

"Grimbald," Felpz said sharply. "Do not. Don't you *dare* . . . "

At last Grimbald turned to regard the magician, and her eyes fairly blazed.

"I never dare!" she cried, still grinning cheek to cheek. "I am *Grimbald!*"

The air around her blurred, her dress flared, billowing like smoke, and when it cleared, the space she had occupied was empty.

"Felpz," I said, a little shakily. "What did she mean going on about pearls and silver and gold?"

Felpz let out a frustrated groan. "It is one of her favorite . . . *hobbies* . . . " he said disgustedly. "To steal crowns. Comes of not having one herself—though she *could* if she ever spared a thought to it. GRIMBALD!" he shouted, his voice amplified so that we all put our hands over our ears.

"The countess!" gasped Sterngarten, and Jamison cried, "She will never ride with us again if we allow her crown to be stolen!" And in a tumble of uniformed limbs the two men went running off down the coach.

What they hoped to do against the Queen of Dreams herself I could not fathom, but from the expression on Felpz's face I guessed he foresaw some dire fate. Taking a step back from the door he angled himself down the train—towards the countess's compartment—and holding the fiddle high above his head he spoke, with perfect composure and gravity:

"Grimbald, if you do not take your fiddle back *this instant* so help me I will . . . I will *feed it to the Arkengal.*"

Another blur of blue and black, a puff of smoke and a wriggle of hair, and Grimbald was standing directly in front of Felpz. There was a thin circlet of silver set with glimmering pearls and glinting stones tucked crookedly amongst her dark curls, and though she stood up straight the highest of these barely cleared Felpz's chest.

"You wouldn't," she hissed.

"I would," Felpz whispered back.

Grimbald snorted. "You're no fun. Who put ice in your bed this night?"

"And I'll take the countess's coronet back," Felpz said, extending a hand.

Grimbald glared up at Felpz, and for a moment I held my breath, certain something unexpected and awful would befall him.

Then Grimbald laughed. Not her eerie, multi-voice cacophony, but a simple, good-natured laugh.

"It's not *hers,* though," she said. "It was given to her by a not very nice man who stole it from a princess of Carndül. I'm just *returning* it."

"Then why are you wearing it?" Felpz asked tiredly.

"Because!" said Grimbald, raising a hand, one finger extended. "I *need* both my hands . . . to *play* with!" And with these words she reached out, and though Felpz was holding the fiddle high above his head, she somehow managed to snatch it from his hand.

Felpz let his arm drop in relief, just as Jamison and Sterngarten came bursting back into the dining coach. A shrill cry from behind them heralded the appearance of the countess, and the stunned Cappofazis found themselves pushed aside by the wiry little woman.

"*You!* I'll have your neck, you blue, thieving *tart!*" cried the countess, red in the face and bristling with anger.

Felpz turned a truly horrified expression upon the woman, but Grimbald only smiled. Slapping her hip with one hand, she tucked the belly of the fiddle—now quiet and docile—under her chin, and drew a bow out of thin air.

"Dreams, my little lady lord," she said. "Get too deep in them, and you can lose things. But consider it payment—and a bargain at that—for the violin performance you were so set on having! And never say Grimbald takes without giving *back!* You've heard my fiddle whine, and you've heard it moan, but count yourselves among the lucky few to have ever heard it *sing.*"

She raised her bow. Felpz nearly tripped over his own feet as he darted back to the train, half stepping onto the running board.

"What do we do?" I whispered to my friend.

"The only thing one can do when Grimbald plays," he said with a wry grin. "*Listen.*"

"You can also *dance!*" Grimbald called, beginning to tap out a beat with the tip of her bow. "*I* intend to!"

It should not, by rights, have been possible for that stringless fiddle with a gaping mouth full of teeth to make a sound— yet in the way of that strange place it not only happened, but made perfect sense.

Grimbald drew her bow across the fiddle and it produced a deep, resonant chord—more akin to a 'cello than a violin— which hung in the air, vibrating, long after the melody had moved on. It swooped and soared, dipped and scattered into countless notes that fell on us like a gentle rain. Around her in the grass little balls of light winked into existence, and as she played they slowly rose and hung in the air around her, gently bobbing to the tune of the music.

And how shall I describe such music? It was not meant to *be* described, I think, but I can give my reader some idea of it by describing how it affected me.

It was the sort of music that stirred feelings of excitement and anticipation deep within my heart—similar to the feeling of sitting down with a good book. It put me in mind of dark, beautiful and mysterious places, of lonely towers where magical things lived, and vast cities underwater that spread out like a filigree of golden light.

At the same time it filled my limbs with a bright, white-hot energy, and without any conscious thought I found myself nodding and bouncing in place. I was appalled when I discovered this, until I noticed that everyone else in the train was doing likewise. Young Elzarino was fairly capering about, and his mother did nothing to stop him. The only person who seemed (literally) unmoved was Felpz, but I noticed how the knuckles of his hand, where he gripped the doorframe, had gone white, and I guessed it was taking an immense effort to hold himself still.

Out in the field, under the huge ivory moon—which seemed to have gotten bigger while Grimbald played—the cloud of lights had risen into the air and begun swirling around her. She laughed and threw up her leg, beginning to stamp and kick even as she played. Her black dress swirled and her hair twisted out, catching the orbs of light like dew in a spider's web.

The music grew faster and faster, the visions it conjured swimming before my eyes, and at a certain point Grimbald tossed her fiddle and bow clean into the air, where they hung suspended, playing themselves as if by some invisible hand. Meanwhile, on the ground, Grimbald began to twist and jump, her strange laughter joining in with the music.

At the sound of her laugh, the land began to change. The moon retreated, growing paler, and the sky grew darker, darker, until it was almost pitch-black. Columns of darkness erupted from the sea of green grass, putting out thorns and bushy leaves. The smell of pine sap and oak, wet moss and earth overpowered the gentle scents of Dream, yet still I could see Grimbald—she seemed to occupy a separate level of reality from the dark forest springing up all around us—dancing and laughing, her violin playing itself in the air above her head.

"What is she *doing?*" I hissed at Felpz.

Felpz groaned, looking a little green. "She is sending us *back,*" he said. "I was *afraid* of this—who *knows* where we'll end up!"

His words were drowned out, however, as Grimbald took her fiddle back and changed the tune. Now the music was gently receding, the tempo slowing, but her laugh remained.

One of her laughing voices spoke then, and its words wove in and out of the laughter like a strain of music.

"*Dreams take and leave you, little earthlings,*" said the voice. "*Before the beginning, and after the end, Dream will have you. Go out, go* out, go out into the day. But you will come back, come back, night after night, until the great endless night swallows you all. Dream will have you, before the beginning, and after the end."

And when the voice had finished speaking I found I could no longer see Grimbald, or her fiddle, or the moon, or the distant mountains—and the sea of blue-green grass had been replaced by an impenetrable forest, dark and damp and smelling sharply of sap and moss.

I felt myself come awake then, the mist clearing from before my eyes, and I realized the music had ended—it only echoed like a fading memory in my head—to be replaced with the real sound of crickets in a wet wood at night. Soon these noises were joined by a clamor of voices as my fellow passengers realized what happened—and that we had *still* not been returned to our proper place.

"Now this," said Felpz tiredly. "*This* is what I was afraid of. Do your best to calm them down, won't you Corianne? And I will see about divining where in the world we are."

Despite Felpz's doubts, and as my readers no doubt remember, it turned out we were still in Elgany—a mere forty miles from the nearest train tracks. We were also, however, deep in the Hexenwald Forest, with no conventional way of obtaining help. It might have evolved into something terribly ugly had not Felpz expedited our rescue by sending an obliging owl to the nearest village with a message. The bird returned at the first light of dawn, bringing with it a stout Elgan matron on a broomstick. Apparently there was no pre-existing task force devoted to putting wayward trains back on their tracks, but after some consultation with the staff of the train it was decided the witch would muster her colleagues, and return with a means to airlift the passengers to her village—from whence coaches could be arranged to rejoin them with the Rotgreif Express.

Sadly, I was not present for this spectacle—though I heard it involved several enchanted hot-air balloons and was most impressive—for Felpz and I left as soon as the witch returned at the head of a flock of reinforcements.

This was in the early afternoon, however, and we waited out the morning—after an improvised breakfast—by keeping the Cappofazis company.

Mrs Cappofazi seemed understandably contrite, but her son was downright despondent.

"What shall become of us now?" he moaned, propping his elbows on the window of their compartment and staring out into the trees. "I thought I was an excellent *violinista,* but it was the instrument all along, not me."

"Not necessarily," Felpz said, crossing his legs and folding his hands over his knees. He leaned back against the headrest, his eyes closed. "Did you have a dream, Signor Cappofazi? Any ambition of your own?"

The boy drew his eyes away from the window and frowned at Felpz. "Dreams? Yes, I dreamed of making music. Making music for people to dance to, sing to, weep to. But how am I to know that was me at all and not the *violino?*"

"Because of the nature of the Goblin's Fiddle," Felpz said, still with his eyes shut. "It does not put ideas into people's heads— merely brings out what is already there. Did you not read what was written on it? The runes were quite clear."

I nudged my friend gently with my elbow. "Not all of us are as astute as you in those matters," I reminded him.

Felpz cracked an eye open at us, raised an eyebrow, and sighed. Lifting one hand he traced a pattern through the air as he spoke:

"*I am the Fiddle of Grimbald,*" he said. "Those are the big ones across its face. But if you read the fine print near the bottom, you'll find it says, *by the power of my voice, let dreams conquer all.* The fiddle is remarkably perceptive. If it brought something extraordinary out of you, Signor Cappofazi, it is only because there was something extraordinary within you to begin with. You've been given quite the leg up, really. And though you may find your natural talents lie along different lines than that of the violin, have no doubt that you are capable of remarkable things— magic fiddle or no."

"Do you really think she might have left her fiddle in that shop on *purpose?*" I asked him. "I mean, *anything* could have happened!"

"Precisely," said Felpz, closing his eyes once more. "That is one of the quirks of Grimbald—she revels in the unknown. In *possibility*. But is it not true of dreams as well? They intrude upon our ordered lives, show us possibilities we might never have thought of on our own, and in time they vanish as we drag ourselves back to wakefulness—or when they have run their course. Is it not fitting, then, that an instrument of Dream should behave in a similar way?"

As none of our company could come up with a satisfactory answer to this question, the compartment fell into silence as the remainder of the morning dragged by.

The brigade of witches arrived just before one in the afternoon, and in the chaos and confusion of flying robes, voices yelling in Elgan, and the frantic passengers, Felpz took me by the elbow and led me off into the forest.

"I have every faith in *Frau* Schwarzstamm. She is quite a powerful and resourceful witch," he explained. "They have no real need of us anymore, and to be honest I am tired. I took the liberty of arranging for your luggage to meet us in Redling—I hope you don't mind—for I think we can make our own way home from here."

So it was that I missed the spectacle of the witches and their hot-air balloons, as Felpz and I walked through the Hexenwald Forest, our way truncated by Felpz's magic, until we reached Lundberge. There we caught the first train to Redling, upon which Felpz announced he was finished for the day and promptly fell asleep.

My readers will be glad to know the remainder of our journey passed in perfect peace, and the rescue efforts by the witches of Hexenwald were entirely successful—though I understand their largesse extended only to the crew, passengers and their effects; the train itself they left in the wood where Grimbald put it. It is still there, for all I know, the great green expanse of the Elgan forest having swallowed it up like the sea swallows a sunken ship.

As for Elzarino Cappofazi, he never made it to Redling. He turned around and went straight back to Milany, where he promptly gave up the violin and turned his hand instead to composing. Though there were some rough years early on, lately I hear he has been meeting with increasing success.

One of the many songs that are sung (or recited) about Grimbald, the capricious Queen of Dream. It would have been from "The Devil His Fiddle" and others like it that Corianne recognized her name and understood why Felpz was concerned about what she might do.

THE DEVIL HIS FIDDLE

A Song of Grimbald

Do you know who taught the Cat to fiddle?
The Cat to fiddle
The Cat to fiddle
It was the Devil who diddle, he did, he did!
It was the Devil who taught the Cat to fiddle.

Do you know who taught the Trickster to fiddle?
The Trickster to fiddle
The Trickster to fiddle
It was the Devil who diddle, he did, he did!
It was the Devil who taught the Trickster to fiddle.

Do you know who taught the Fairy to fiddle?
The Fairy to fiddle
The Fairy to fiddle
It was the Devil who diddle, he did, he did!
It was the Devil who taught the Fairy to fiddle.

But who on earth taught the Devil to fiddle?
No one on earth!
Above or below!
Who was it taught the Devil to fiddle?
It was Grimbald who did it! She did, she did!
It was Grimbald who taught the Devil to fiddle.

Singing Grimby, Dancing Grimby
Blue and black beneath the moon!
Whirling Grimby, Wild Grimby
Make the Devil dance your tune!
Grimbald! Grimbald!
The Queen of Dream!

"The Silver Chimera," though it comes immediately after "The Goblin's Fiddle" within the second volume of The Adventures of Bouragner Felpz, *actually takes place hundreds of years earlier. In this regard it mirrors "The Last Dragon" from Volume I, but this time there is a real historical figure to give us some idea of the period. It is the penultimate story in Volume II, and was written in the spring of 2014.*

THE SILVER CHIMERA

Late Summer 2327

FOR ALL THE LONG YEARS we spent living in close proximity, I seldom heard my friend, Mr Bouragner Felpz, voluntarily speak of events from his youth. The fact that his youth was shrouded in the mists of the distant past led me to imagine many reasons for this reticence: a distaste for dragging up events so long gone, sorrow at the memories of lost friends, or plain and simple forgetfulness. I never questioned his cause, however, nor asked him to share his memories, and I do believe this was one reason for the strength of our friendship. I did not even try to determine his exact age, though I guessed he had seen more centuries than many of us see decades. Just how many centuries I had no way of knowing, until one summer evening in the late 2320's, when to my surprise and excitement, he began to talk of King Arell.

It was brought on, prosaically enough, by a play we had seen that afternoon in which the nineteenth-century monarch had a supporting role. It was a good piece of dramatic fiction, performed by an enthusiastic group of actors in Griffinsgate Park, and the setting—open air with strong, slanting sunlight—had served the story perfectly. Afterwards, as we walked back through the long summer twilight, I could not stop singing its virtues. And as to one who has enjoyed something there is no greater delight than in sharing that joy with another, my happiness was punctured by Felpz's distinctly sour attitude; he walked in silence, barely responding to my words, with a pinched look on his face, as though he had bitten into a pear and found it a lemon instead.

"Whatever is the matter, my friend?" I asked him. "Did you not like the story?"

"The story was serviceable, with a predictable but satisfying ending," he allowed.

"Did you not like the actors?"

"The actors were delightful."

"The costumes, then? The choreography? Was there someone in the audience who distracted you?"

"The costumes were ingenious," Felpz said briskly. "The choreography was charming, and the audience singularly well behaved."

"Then what pebble has gotten into your shoe?" I asked. "For you look as though the characters had done nothing the whole time but insult your mother."

That at least caused his grimace to break as he let out an involuntary laugh. He quickly sobered again, however, his face settling into an expression of dissatisfied contemplation.

"It is nothing so much to do with the *play* but with *history*, and this country's blatant disrespect for the accuracy of the latter," he said.

"Felpz," I said, biting back my own annoyance. "It is a work of *fiction*. You can't expect the writers to slavishly serve events from over five hundred years ago."

"No, but I would have wished they had the decency to *respect* them. Respect them for what they *were*, not paint it over with pretty pastels."

"I'm afraid you've lost me," I admitted. "What *was* it that bothered you so?"

"Their choice of actor to play King Arell," he admitted at last, "looked *nothing* like him."

I found myself a little taken aback by this. First by the implication that Felpz had seen Arell the Great in life, and second by the sheer ridiculousness.

"Felpz," I said gently. "You cannot expect a modern actor to look exactly like a historical figure—or anyone else, for that matter."

"Nor do I," Felpz announced. "But there are characteristics, Corianne, that become intrinsically linked to one's person. Imagine, for example, if I were a character in a play and the director was thoughtless enough to cast someone with *blond* hair for the part. Why, it would be laughable. Bouragner Felpz does *not* have blond hair, save when it serves me as a disguise."

"Is *that* your problem?" I asked, for indeed the actor playing Arell had been a handsome, blond man. "Is it so important Arell not have yellow hair?"

"Goodness, *yes*," sighed Felpz, his whole being seeming to shudder. "He had black hair. Black as coal and ink, *and*"—he raised a finger and wagged it at me—"his skin was not much lighter!"

This made my step falter, it came as such a surprise, but Felpz did not notice. Now he had begun, he seemed unable to stop.

"And he was not some willowy, graceful boy. It's true he was quite young when he was crowned, but he was already a head taller than me and twice as wide across the shoulders. Yet for all that he was gentle as a lamb, no malice in him, and his honesty was so blunt you could use it to hammer nails. There was a reason I simply handed my kingdom over to him when the time came."

If the first revelation had made my feet falter, this one nearly tripped me.

"You had a *kingdom*?" I stammered.

Felpz glanced down at me in vague surprise, as if confused why this should startle me. Then his face softened, and he smiled.

"Only a very small one, a long time ago. Many people did, in those days. Anyone with enough power, in one form or another, could take a piece of land and call him or herself monarch of it. And I had more power than most. I flatter myself I took to ruling out of concern for the people of my birth country, who I found beset by all manner of troubles. I'd even go so far as to say I improved things a little. In truth, however, I fear I was as intoxicated with power as any, and it wasn't until I met someone frighteningly sober that I realized what had happened to me. Then, in disgust, I threw away all the fine things I had acquired during my short reign, and might have thrown my magic away too had Arell not convinced me otherwise."

He fell silent, and I, holding my breath in anticipation of more, could barely contain an outburst of frustration.

We walked on, and I noticed Felpz was not shortening our journey by magic, as he was wont to do, but taking us the long way home, as though his legs were restless and needed the exercise. We were nearing our street at last when my patience was rewarded.

"He gave me a silver chimera, out of gratitude for my services," Felpz said, his voice quiet and his eyes distant, gazing off over the steep roofs of the city houses, with their fat, squat chimneys like pots, to some place beyond the pale pink-and-yellow sky. "A token, really, but a meaningful one. I wonder if I still have it." He fell silent again, and I resigned myself to wonder what story might lie behind this reference, but upon our return he spent the next two hours turning his study inside-out, searching for the elusive keepsake. And as he searched, he began to talk.

Settling myself innocently in a corner, I organized the detritus cast aside by the whirlwind that was my friend, and I listened.

"Of all the things he gave me, it was one people never mentioned. The importance was all between the two of us," he said, picking up where he had left off. "Do you know Arell's coat of arms? They are unlike any other Kyrish monarch—either before or after. Only his bear the chimera volant above the crown."

"I seem to remember something to that effect," said I, recalling with difficulty my knowledge of the Norumblanain dynasty. "It is because Arell owned a chimera, did he not?"

Felpz paused in his search to shoot me an arch look. "No, he did not own her. He never owned her. In fact, the whole point was that he did precisely the opposite. I see there are still some holes in your education that need filling, so make yourself comfortable; this may take a little time. Yes, you may take notes, if you must," he added, seeing my hands dart involuntarily for the pocket in which I kept my notebook and pen.

"It was in winter," Felpz began, leaning back on his heels and casting his eyes up to the ceiling, "some years after I ceded what authority I held over the northwestern corner of this country to King Arell. That much I remember clearly. It followed some unpleasant business with the half-dragon Machalion—he was my rival in many ways, and I believe a large part of my decision to hand over my power to Arell was so I wouldn't have to deal with *him* anymore—so it must have been some time during the eighteen-seventies. Yes, that seems about right. It was when Arell came to Kyremouth and began building what is now Kingstower. You may have seen illustrations or even photographs of it and know it as the towering monument that stands over the Kyre delta—part colossus, part lighthouse—signifying the northern extent of his country. When I arrived, however, on a muddy winter day so very long ago, that bustling city was still in its infancy, a collection of timber houses that had been hastily thrown together in advance of the king's court, and as likely to burn down as they were to get swept away in a mudslide. And the tower was two scaffolds tied together with string, a mere placeholder amongst the rush of buildings.

"I came out of a sort of morbid curiosity, if I came for any reason at all. I was in a very low state at the time; I had become disillusioned with things I once held in high esteem, and I still bore an emotional wound from the loss of Machalion. It is an odd thing, Corianne, how having some form of consistency in one's life—even if it is only the consistency of a rival—can provide a much needed anchor. My volatile relationship with Machalion had been such an anchor for the better part of the previous hundred years, and the loss of it left me adrift in a swiftly changing sea. Worse, I had become disgusted by my own magic, and took to excising it from my person—akin to an animal that develops a nervous habit of pulling out its own feathers or hair. As a result I was but a pale shade of myself, hardly recognizable, when a cold wind blew me into Kyremouth.

"I did not go down to the King's Docks, as they were called then, but stayed up on the western swell where the old village of Kyremouth—built sensibly of stone and populated by hardy fishermen—used to stand. Since wind and water magic were some of the few things that still felt clean and good to me, I quickly made myself useful as a weatherman, and once people grew to trust me enough, I was even allowed out on the boats. I pride myself that I never let a ship run afoul, nor by my workings did I cause anyone else trouble, and it seemed the people liked me for it—though I believe my habit of standing at the stern, in nothing but my tunic and short leggings, letting the frigid winter wind whip through me, was unsettling to them.

"It was by chance that I found myself on the King's Docks one day, having been attached to a boat whose duties brought her there. It turned out the crew's business would keep them all day, and I was given leave for the duration to take what joy from the new town as I could find.

"I did not expect to find much. The streets were all of mud and the buildings damp and cold. The population had been whittled into hard, sharp people who seldom smiled and went about their work with a grim determination which, though admirable, was not conducive to good humor. Finding the people unwelcoming I allowed myself to drift through the town, letting my feet choose which path to take. This eventually led me to the little headland where a patch of ground had been cordoned off, and the foundations of the Kingstower were just being laid.

"I wandered around the perimeter of this, taking in with dull curiosity the piles of timber under canvas sheets, the immense coils of ropes, and the shipments of stone which were slowly but steadily being carted in, and wondered at the audacity of the young king, who thought he could build a tower in such a place.

"Having satisfied my curiosity, I made to leave, only to find my way blocked by a huddle of people. These were no common townsfolk, nor were they my local seamen: two wore arms openly, and one was very tall and cloaked in a fine fur cape and hood. They appeared to be arguing over something, but I knew they could not help but notice me. This being the very last thing I desired, I dragged up some of my vestigial skill and attempted to slip by them in the form of a fine mist.

"It must have been a very poor attempt, for I had barely passed the group when the tall figure in the cloak reached out a hand and hooked me neatly by the elbow, causing the illusion to drop, and I found myself wheeled round to stare up into the great black, bearded face of none other than King Arell himself.

"How shall I describe him? None of the portraits do him justice. The best I can say is he looked like a polished, black stone that glowed faintly with a reddish blush. His hair, which had been a great black mane the last time I'd seen him, had been neatly plaited into countless rope-like braids which fell in a thick tumble around his face, disappearing into the collar of his cloak. Extraordinarily, his eyes, though they appeared as black as his skin, were in actuality an abyssal indigo, and sapphire sparks would flicker in them if the light was right. I could see those flecks of blue from where I stood gazing up at him, and found myself—as I believe many were—rendered immobile at the sight.

"'How now, it is the Purple Magician, is it not?' he said, his eyes widening in surprise. 'What winds have whipped you, mage? For you look closer to the lavandil than the iris.'

"In this I could not argue, for in my desolation even my color had weakened, my clothes bleached to the palest hues of mauve and gray-lavender. Combined with my ragged appearance, it must have reminded Arell of that rare form of daffodil, sometimes called a lavandil, that is pale lavender instead of gold, with a heavily serrated trumpet. In response I could only shrug and nod toward the foundation of the tower.

"'The winds brought news, and I wished to see,' I told him simply, wanting only to get away. His knights, whom I did not recognize, were eyeing me suspiciously—and though I feared little from them, the last thing I desired was to draw attention to myself, and attention I would surely receive if I continued to hold that of the king.

"But Arell seemed particularly interested in me, and as I could not in good grace run from him, I was forced to stand and suffer his piercing gaze. Eventually he seemed to come to an internal decision, for he drew back, putting his hands on his hips, and nodded to himself—causing his beard to jut slightly.

"'Well, your eyes may be sated, lavandil, but it appears to me your material appetite is still wanting. My cook has slaughtered a bullock this morning, and we are having the tongue tonight.

Join us, for I have a matter I wish to discuss with you, and I would not inflict it upon you with an empty stomach.'

"It is something I detest, Corianne, to be ordered about, but the spark of irritation in my gut at the king's words was the first warm feeling I had felt for a long time, and as he was my king besides, I could hardly refuse. So I was obliged to send my boat home with a well-wishing spell, and pushed my appearance into something less reminiscent of a vagabond before presenting myself at the king's door ten minutes before the appointed time.

"I think it says something for the quality of man Arell was, that as his newly arrived subjects were living in timber houses, so was he—though his dwelling was, perforce, the largest and best-supplied. I remember I was received with disconcerting familiarity, and shown with very little fanfare into the main room where the king dined when receiving guests. There a brave fire cast a glad warmth over me, and without thought I went to it and warmed my chilled hands at its hearth.

"In time the two knights I had seen before arrived, along with a white-haired man and—to my surprise—a small young woman with curly dark hair and thick spectacles wired onto her face. These were introduced as . . . oh dear, I cannot for the lives of me remember the knights! Corein and Athelwood, I *think*. But I may have confused their names with knights I met later. But the *man*, the man was Eutrus Njoorüd, and the young woman his daughter Ottasca, and together they served as the architects and chief engineers of Arell's ambitious tower. You'll have heard of Dame Njoorüd—she went on to build a great many interesting things in service to Arell—but this was still in the dawn of her career, when she labored in the shadow of her aging father.

"I do not think any of them had much regard for me, though Master Njoorüd had the good grace to be polite. His daughter, however, stared rather, and the knights were downright cold. So it was a relief when the king arrived and I could distract myself with food.

"I do not believe I had eaten so much in a single sitting before. Though I entered the room with no great appetite—as food had lost much of its appeal—once I had a taste I found myself possessed of a great hunger, and ate as long as I was permitted. It was a curious aspect of etiquette in those days: one was not allowed to eat past the person who sat in the highest place of honor at the table. As this was almost invariably the person who was the best fed in other regards, it was the cause of some rather uncomfortable meals. In this instance, however, Arell seemed to sense my desperation, and kept calling for his, and therefore *our,* plates to be refilled. I wonder if we did not eat through the better half of that bullock by the end of the meal.

"'Now that I have you satisfied in a corporeal manner,' King Arell said when he at last called for the plates to be cleared. 'I desire your insight into a distressing matter that has recently arisen regarding the construction of my tower.'

"Regretfully I leaned back in my chair, reaching absently for a fold of my cloak—before remembering the cloth that had been supplied to me for that purpose, and used it to clean my face.

"'I am, as I swore, at your majesty's service,' I replied dutifully, though most of my being rebelled. 'As far as my powers can assist you.'

"Arell nodded, and gestured to Master Njoorüd, who in turn looked to his daughter, who drew from a satchel she carried at her side a long roll of parchment, which she spread upon the recently cleared table. It was on that parchment that I saw for the first time the completed Kingstower, impressive even as a sketch of ink upon a flat sheet. But it was to the foundation, anchored deep in the underlying bedrock, that young Njoorüd drew our attention.

"'This tower,' she explained in brief, clipped words. 'It is so high, and the winds so strong, we cannot build it as a rigid being. It would snap and break. So we look to trees, how they bend in the wind and spring back into shape. To support this, we need deep roots. Complicated. Much digging. Here is where we have problem.' She pointed with a thick, callused finger at the dark scheme comprising the bottom third of the paper.

"'The excavating team encountered a seam of rock,' Master Njoorüd took over. 'Harder and paler. Took many days to drill through, and when they had done so they discovered the space within riddled with cavities—some large enough for a man to walk through erect. At first we thought this a boon, but now it appears it came with a terrible price. Since these catacombs have been uncovered we have lost ten men—six to attacks of madness, and three to incapacitating injury, and one has disappeared completely. No sight, no sound, no sign of anything living we have found besides what we leave ourselves. We have determined it must be some demon living within the rock.'

"'I have many brave knights,' Arell said, with a glance at Corein and Athelwood. 'But none with experience hunting demons. Further, what proof have we that it is indeed a demon? I wish to know for certain, and I know I need a magician to tell me so. We would be grateful if you could lend us your expertise, so that we may see this matter reconciled.'

"'And if I find it is a demon?' I asked dryly, pulling the parchment toward me to get a closer look.

"'Then we shall have to build the tower somewhere else,' Arell said with a shrug. 'But I'll not uproot my charges without good reason. You must understand.'

"I did, too, though I did not love him for it. Despite his moderate words I knew that to refuse even such a polite request from the monarch would be tantamount to treason. Besides, if I did not go into those catacombs and flush out whatever was hiding within, the knights—not to mention Maid Njoorüd— would never forgive me. And although I did feel some small flush of curiosity, I confess my overall mood of apathy still held sway. But my king had expressed a wish, and it was my duty to grant it. So I inclined my head in acquiescence, and it was arranged I would be shown into the pit the following day.

"That day was pale, as I recall, with the sort of high, bright clouds that do nothing to dim the light of the sun. I saw little of it, however, for as soon as I had broken my fast I found Maid Njoorüd at my elbow, an unlit torch in one hand and a box of flints in the other.

"'As you requested,' she said, and I heard the misgiving in her voice.

"I took the tools and thanked her, for indeed I had asked for them. I did not like to say it was because I didn't trust my own magelight, however, and left her unspoken question hanging in the air behind me when I left.

"'Do you not wish to see the survivors?' the young woman asked me as we made the short walk through the town from the King's hall and up the knoll to the site of the tower.

"These days I would have leapt at the chance, of course, but back then I had less of a care for my work, and only wished to get the ordeal over with so that I would be left alone. I shook my head, therefore, and bade her lead me to the mouth of the tunnel where these unfortunate accidents had been occurring.

"This turned out to be many tunnels, for the foundation of the tower radiated eight passages from the main body—just a big, damp hole in the ground—and Maid Njoorüd explained how they had lost workers down all of them. I stood there, up to my ankles in mud, and tentatively pushed out a piece of my mind to probe the tunnels.

"At first they all seemed equally cold, dark, and damp, but the further I pushed the more I sensed something—so faint it was like the echo of a sound, or a taste at the tip of one's tongue. It put me in mind of something sharp and metallic, and strange beyond reckoning. Whatever was in those tunnels was like nothing I had seen before—and I had seen many things, even in those distant days.

"I took the torch and the flints and went down the tunnel where the echo seemed strongest, but I waited until I judged I was out of sight of Njoorüd's curious eyes before I summoned fire to it, with help from the flint.

"I cannot tell you how irritating it is, to one accustomed to the even, diffuse glow cast by magelight, to manage by the flaring and flickering glare of a torch. Every shadow so sharp and black it seemed to portend some evil beast, and moving with the faintest gust that disturbed the flame. It was so very irritating that I stopped, threw down the torch in disgust, and summoned up magelight for the first time in years. To my surprise, far from feeling like a thread pulling a boulder—as most magic had felt recently—it was as though the thread had been attached to a plug, and I had just uncorked it.

"One thing you must understand about magelight, Corianne, is that it is not simply *light*. It is *awareness*. To a non-magic user, that awareness is conveyed by light. But to the one doing the magic, the awareness can be cast much further, and by more subtle means.

"When I cast magelight, it radiated through the tunnels, bathing them not only in light, but also in my *awareness*. For a brilliant, glimmering moment I could see the entire network of tunnels laid out inside my mind, and what I saw astounded me.

"There were far more tunnels than shown on Njoorüd's map. There were tunnels that stretched out in directions no ordinary person could take, let alone see. From these twisted corridors breathed the stale smell of an ancient magic of a kind I had only encountered once before—in similar circumstances. It was a sobering realization that, whether by some arcane fortune or plain mad chance, King Arell had chosen as the site for his tower an ancient goblin grave.

"A thing you may not know about goblins, Corianne. They are in their way quite as magical as any elf or fairy, but at the same time perfectly unique. Their magic is the magic of stone, of darkness and of twisted space. They thrive where no other life thrives, deep beneath the surface of the earth. It is painful for them to walk under the open sky, which is why they are considered such hideous, unpleasant creatures: very few have seen them in their natural habitat. To a goblin, the surface and open air is as frightening as a deep dark pit is to us. And as we put our dead, and our prisoners, in holes in the ground, so do goblins place their dungeons and graves near the surface.

"As I stood in the dark and damp and sensed the old goblin tunnels stretching out around me, I assumed that this must be the latter, for it felt as though it had not been occupied in many a long year. Then, as I probed deeper, I noticed several odd features that set it apart from the goblin graves I'd seen in the past:

"There were no catacombs, no chambers where the dead could rest. Rather, all the passages led, by one twisting way or another, to a single chamber not far from the foundation of the tower. This chamber interested me, in that it appeared to have once been accessed by a single shaft that led down—to what I could only suppose would be the goblins' city—but that had been filled in with rock and gravel as far down as my magelight could reach.

"I was on the edge of an isolated flower of goblin architecture. Whether it had been abandoned because of its proximity to the surface or for some other reason I did not yet know.

"My natural curiosity, which had been rendered latent by my recent bout of apathy, came to the fore with a rush, and abandoning the now-useless torch, I set off down the goblin tunnels. These were both the material tunnels that Njoorüd's workers had discovered, and also the tunnels that stretched sideways, into the realm of space peculiar to goblins. From these I caught another taste of that strange, metallic magic, and with a little spiritual wriggling I was able to crawl along one of these twisted passages, feeling my way with one hand held out, forcing the magelight ahead of me.

"It was a good thing I did, for I encountered traps along the way. These were the sort clearly laid to deter intruders—but goblin intruders, for whom the darkness held no mystery. A human with a simple flaming branch had no hope of perceiving them, and judging by how many had been sprung, I guessed here was the reason for the injuries to Njoorüd's men. For although it had taken me some work to crawl into these tunnels on purpose, goblin architecture is so mercurial that it will sometimes lure humans into it rather than keep them out. I did not envy those poor people, who must have been quite lucky to escape with their lives.

"At last I came across a trap that had not been sprung, but *disabled*. This was surprising, since I doubted any ordinary human could have done such a thing. Then, upon closer examination, I discovered that the trap—which involved a nasty device like a spiked hammer—had been disabled from the *inside*. That is, from the direction of the single chamber with the filled-in shaft. To do so, someone must have come from that chamber, though how they could have reached it in the first place was a mystery.

"Edging my way around the trap, I was immediately struck by the metallic magic—this time no echo, but a full-on cacophony. It was so strong I had to pause and pull in much of my own magic that had been stretched out to feel my way ahead— as one might pull one's hand out of a bowl of hot water—and cower there until I could adjust to this new magic.

"It is a curious thing, but when you have gone off magic for a long time, when you return you are much more sensitive. Coming on so strongly, and after such a sabbatical, I was nearly overcome. I had to call upon some little-used skills to make a sort of magical bandage for myself, so I could continue down the tunnel.

"You may be surprised that I still wanted to explore: in truth I wonder at it myself now I look back. I can only imagine I was overcome with curiosity. That, and I got the distinct impression from the tone of this new magic—as it were—that whatever owned it was in great distress. And like someone hearing the cry of a wounded animal I followed it to its source."

Felpz, who had so far been relating this story from a rather uncomfortable position on the floor, paused long enough to stretch, and crawled over to his bench where he settled himself again. He idly lifted the lid of a nearby box, then let it fall closed with a sigh.

"What I found, there in the dark . . . was like nothing I had yet seen or have seen since. The size of a small dragon it was, with a tail that lay in coils, filling most of the chamber. It had no hind legs, but two powerful arms like that of a lion and a pair of feathered wings folded tight along its back. You will laugh when you hear this, but at first I thought it had no head! Then, as I approached further into the room, there was a twitch along its neck and I found a wide, feline face assessing me from the midst of a bushy mane of silver hair.

"I say feline, but it was like no ordinary cat. Not even the exotic beasts from Saffara or the Beranicas. It had a wide forehead in the center of which was set a gleaming blue stone, piercing blue eyes, and behind each ear, partly buried in its mane, was a tightly curling horn—like that of a ram. It was, from the tip of its fine whiskers to the end of its scaled tail, a brilliant, gleaming silver—shimmering with scattered reflections in my weak magelight.

"I think we stood for some time, each regarding the other with apprehension, when the silence was broken by a soft moan from the center of its coiled tail.

"This was no half-heard sound of magic, but a real noise from a very real human throat, and it galvanized me into action. Now

I looked, I could see a swatch of rumpled brown hair and a thick, pink arm protruding from the coils, and as I came forward I saw it move, feebly.

"No sooner had I begun to approach, however, than the creature withdrew further, the end of its tail snaking around to come up in front of me, blocking my way. There was a further disturbance of the mane around the creature's face, and two more heads appeared. Poking out from the mass of silvery fur, they trained two more pairs of sapphire eyes upon me. I regret to say that it wasn't until I saw these two other heads that I recognized the creature for what it was: a *chimera*, one of the many species of extraordinary animals best known for the Crowan monster whose name they now bear. This chimera had the heads of an owl and a feathered snake, in addition to the horned lion, the former two being significantly smaller, and mostly hidden in the mane.

"Now all three heads were alert and staring at me, and that alone gave me pause. Then the beast spoke to me, in words audible to my ears, but strangely distorted by the fact that they came from three different mouths at once.

"'*No harm,*' said the chimera in a strange chorus. The snake hissed, the lion growled, and the owl—who was the clearest— hooted softly.

"'I assure you I mean anything but harm,' I replied at once, for aside from the creature's remarkable size, I could sense its huge, metallic magic piling up around it, and knew I would be hard pressed to overpower such a beast even at my peak condition, and in my weakened state I had no wish to offend it.

"'I come on behalf of the king above ground, whose subject you appear to hold. He wishes him returned and begs you not to torment the workers whose business it is to build his tower here.'

"'*No torment,*' replied the triple voice. '*No harm. Men come. Men go. They run from me. Sometimes they fall. Their lights fail. This one is hurt. I help him. I heal. No harm.*'

"'That is most generous of you,' I assured the chimera, daring to take another step. The tail's end—which was decorated with a small frill of stiff, mirror-like feathers—did not move to block me further, nor did it get out of my way. 'However, if you would allow me, I will take responsibility for him. He is a creature of the surface, and it will not do to keep him here. Allow me to return him to his king.'

"*No harm,*' repeated the chimera, its coils tightening protectively around the poor man. '*So alone. So long. No one to care for. No one to comfort. No wish to be alone.*'

"'Am I to understand you are trapped here?' I asked, peering around the end of the tail. The three faces still looked at me, and in each I read clearly such a sadness that I was taken aback. This was no sinister monster but a much misunderstood creature.

"*Not trapped. Never trapped. Imprisoned. Goblins found me. Goblins hatched me. But I grew too big. Too fierce. They built this dungeon for me, buried me next to the sky, and forgot about me.*'

"'You mean to say you have never seen the open air?' I asked in surprise, eyeing the chimera's wings.

"*I see things in my dreams. Everything is open and blue. No walls, no stone, no darkness . . . but big white stones that do not hurt, but swallow you. They shed tears upon a faraway land.*'

"'Then you were clearly not meant to live your life underground!' I cried, horrified to think of how long the chimera must have spent in its prison, longing for a sky that was so relatively near. 'Come,' I told it. 'Follow me, and I will lead you out of this maze. For the men you see have breached your prison wall, and the way to the sky is clear for you. We may bring your foundling, as well, and you may return him to the king yourself.'

"*I do not like kings,*' said the chimera gravely. '*Kings chain you. Kings keep you. Kings throw you in prison when they do not want you any more.*'

"'This king is different,' I said, and realized as I did so that I would be put to some serious difficulty if what I said was not true—for I knew I could not let Arell keep this beast as a pet.

"*How do you know this? What are my reasons for trust? Who are you?*'

"I admit these questions unsettled me somewhat. I had long since given up the use of my name—it having become associated with all the most distasteful forms of my magic—and though I was becoming more comfortable using magic again, I was not yet ready to reclaim that name. So I fell back on a title that was equally my own, but which held no such connotations.

"'I am the Purple Magician,' I told the chimera. 'And I swear upon my color you will have the sky, with no king to hold you.'

"At last the chimera lowered its tail, and walking forward on its arms, it peered at me with all six of its eyes. It inhaled, deeply, and I felt a little of my magic get sucked in, turned over, and then blown back at me. It was an odd feeling; like hearing an echo of your own voice and not recognizing it right away. I was surprised at how strange and terrifying it felt, and realized why such a powerful creature would recoil from me at first sight. That, and I began to believe that the chimera did not quite understand the extent of its own powers.

"'*This is not a color I am familiar with,*' admitted the chimera. '*But you smell of wind and sky-tears and something open and . . . wet.*'

"'The sea,' I offered.

"'*The sea . . .*' echoed the chimera. "'*It sounds like something that should be seen. Lead me, purple man. Lead me to the sea.*'

"'This was, more or less, what I proceeded to do. It was something of a task getting the chimera out of the goblin tunnels—they had been built to keep it in, after all. For its part, the chimera insisted on carrying the unconscious man in its arms while it slithered behind me like a giant, gleaming snake. It was slow going, since I had to stop several times to pull the tunnels into place so we could pass through. When I found myself in the human excavation once again, it was only to lose the chimera somewhere in the dark. I had to go back in, where I found it searching for me in distress. At the last I led it out of the tunnels, one hand clamped firmly on a silver elbow. Passing into Njoorüd's corridor felt like pulling a great weight uphill, until the chimera suddenly figured out what was happening, and then it was all I could do to keep up as it surged forward, slithering easily over the uneven ground.

"We very nearly got lost all over again, in the perfectly mundane way one does in a dark pit underground, but eventually I caught sight of a pale glow that could only be daylight, and made for it with relief.

"We emerged into a crowd of expectant faces—royal knights, workers, and townsfolk alike—who gave out a collective gasp as the chimera slunk from the dark tunnel into the comparatively blinding light of day. For not only were they presented with the sight of a strange and frightening beast, but even in the weak sunlight the chimera shone and glittered, the scales on its long tail reflecting the light like countless, tiny mirrors, and its wings flashing sharply. Had it been an ordinary animal such as a dog or horse it would have been just as blinding. As it was our audience was hard put to stare as much as they wanted while at the same time shielding their eyes from the glare.

"At sight of the crowd I felt the chimera tense at my side, and I got ready to cast a stiff stasis over the lot of them should they turn hostile. When nobody so much as moved, however, I sought out Master Njoorüd and beckoned to him.

"'I have found your missing man,' I told him as he approached, with many fearful glances at the chimera—in whose arms the unconscious man still lay. 'Your demon, as it turns out, is nothing of the kind. Any misfortune that befell your men in the tunnels below was due to an unhappy misunderstanding. Now take this poor fellow and see he's properly cared for, and let your king know I have returned.'

"'There is no need for that,' came the prompt reply, and I looked up to find Arell standing on the lip of the pit, his hands resting on his hips, and surveying the scene with an unreadable expression. The crowd cleared instantly, dragging Njoorüd and the unconscious man away with them. I saw the chimera watch them go with concern, so I put a hand on its shoulder and led the way up the ramp to where the king waited.

"I shall not soon forget that sight, for the two of them— Arell with his impenetrable black face and rich robes of red and ochre, and the chimera with its gleaming silver pelt and glittering scales—made quite a contrast as they stood regarding one another. Though Arell held himself with all the regality of his office, the chimera seemed imbued with its own alien majesty, and in truth I thought they looked like two monarchs meeting for the first time—and I held my breath, knowing from personal experience how easily such meetings could turn sour.

"But then Arell laughed mightily, his white teeth flashing, and held out a hand to the chimera, which it took gingerly in one paw, and for a moment black skin and silver fur were joined in a small embrace. Then Arell was turning to me and saying:

"'There must be some good story behind this, lavandil, for never in all my years have I seen such a creature.'

"Briefly I relayed my experiences in the tunnels, my discovery of the old goblin dungeon, and the chimera within.

"'*He leads me to the sea,*' the chimera explained, when I was finished.

"To his credit Arell hardly batted an eye at hearing the chimera's triple voice, and nodded firmly. 'Though you hardly need a guide at this point, my lady. Take your wings and let them bear you north, and you shall find all the sea—why as far as you *can* see," and he laughed in that expansive, good-humored way which had already endeared him to so many.

"And the chimera—who I believe had no gender as you or I would understand it, but because of Arell's words people took to thinking of as female—shook out her blade-like wings, which when unfurled stretched clear across the pit and cast a diffuse shadow over us, and beat them experimentally against the air. She coiled her long, snakelike body beneath her, and then sprang upwards, her wings a blur, flashing in the distant sunlight.

"She made quite a sight climbing up into the sky, glinting like a mirror, and as she streaked towards the ocean a ragged cheer went up from the crowd still clumped around the pit. I saw her as a flash of silver on the gray-and-white sky, and then she was lost to my vision.

"And that, Corianne, would have made a perfect end to my little escapade, but as it turned out, it was nothing of the kind. For the chimera came back that very evening, exhausted and hungry, and Arell took one look at his panicked knights and put *me* in charge of her.

"I will not bore you with the details of feeding and tending to a large and very magical animal—she ate a great deal, which made her ill, and it wasn't until I figured out she fed on energy directly, as dragons do, that she recovered. I took her on long walks over the headlands, where she could feed on the buffeting wind, and down on the beaches where she delighted in the breaking waves. She grew stronger daily, and after about a month, she took to assisting Arell's men in placing some of the larger stones in the tower—whose construction, no longer delayed, was well underway by this time.

"Eventually, however, she tired of this, and would spend more and more of her time flying around the coast. Then one night she did not return—though we continued to see her in the distance, keeping an eye on the construction of the tower. When at last this was complete the sightings became fewer and fewer, until finally she was seen no more. I do not doubt she is still out there—chimeras like herself are not vulnerable to the ravages of time as mundane animals are—and you can find her likeness all over Kyremouth even today. Most noticeably, a coiled chimera, wings outstretched as if to take flight, rests above the main entrance to the Kingstower—though only a few locals still remember the reason for it.

"As for myself, the whole enterprise took up a year of my life and culminated with King Arell sitting me down one evening, after the chimera had vanished and the tower had been completed, and saying to me in his blunt, honest way;

"'This affair with the silver chimera, lavandil, it brings to light a shortcoming I have when it comes to the specialities of my staff. That is to say, I have no one I can trust in matters relating to magic and its peripheral troubles—the succoring of ill chimeras, for example. I therefore offer you the position of Royal Magician to the Monarchs of Kyreland for however long you deem fit to hold the title.'

"I stared back at the man in horror. I'm afraid all my propriety deserted me, and I burst out at once: 'No, my king, I beg do not ask that of me. It is everything I despise about magic, and precisely what I wished to avoid by handing my kingdom over to you.'

"'Your reluctance does you credit, lavandil,' Arell replied good-naturedly. 'It is one of the traits I find renders you most desirable as an advisor. But if you worry about being given too much nobility and power, perhaps you would consent to advising me personally on matters of magic that pertain to my dominion? You would hold no rank, no title, save that of friend to the King. Though I would ask you to choose a name by which I and others might address you.'

"This gave me some pause. I liked Arell, and that he was willing to compromise on the nature of my service spoke to how highly he regarded me. It felt mean spirited, and a bit cowardly, to refuse.

"I would not give him my name, however. I was not ready to be Bouragner d'Felpass again—in many respects I doubt I will ever be.

"'My king,' I said, 'I do not think I can improve upon the name you have yourself given me. Call me Lavandil, and let that satisfy all wants.'"

Felpz turned and looked at me then, and I saw a mischievous smile spreading across his face at what must have been a flab-bergasted expression on my own.

"Do not tell me you didn't put the pieces together before now?" he asked.

"*You* were Lord Lavandil?" I cried, my mind finally connect-ing the meaning of that curious name I had so often seen linked to Arell's in my history books. To think that I had been learning about my friend as child—by reading about an historical figure I thought at the time to be long since as dead as the king he served—came as such a surprise it rendered me momentarily speechless.

"Ah yes, the *lord* bit came later," Felpz said, wrinkling his nose in distaste. "A common man with the ear of the king would not do. They made me take a title, eventually, when one was freed up by the execution of an earl. I promptly gave management of the estate over to the late man's poor daughter, and I understand her family keeps it still. There was some bother over that, as women holding titles in their own right was a new thing at the time, but it allowed me to be styled as Lord Lavandil, Magician Commander, and people were satisfied with that—if not exactly happy. Great griffins, that reminds me!"

My friend sprang from his seat at the bench and darted out the door.

Unfolding myself more slowly, I followed him, only to find he had disappeared into my bedroom of all places.

"Felpz!" I cried in protest as I entered to find him pulling aside my nightstand to look behind it. The blue demonic lamp—the result of a hair-raising adventure I had endured when still a maid—rocked precariously as Felpz threw himself to the floor and felt around under my bed. Putting a hand out to steady it

I bent over the purple bulge of his back to peer at him. "Felpz, what in the heavens are you doing?"

"This room used to be my second storeroom, before I took you as my ward," Felpz explained. He had thrust one arm completely under my bed, turning his head sideways so part of his shoulder could follow. "Not everything got moved during the preparations, and I just remembered I left Lavandil's paraphernalia in a box . . . *here.*"

He removed the shoulder and arm, now brown with dust, at the end of which was clasped an old leather case. Cracked and fairly matted with dust, it was no wonder I had never noticed it before—it must have been jammed right into the far corner under my bed. It had no visible seam or lock, but after Felpz had wiped off the worst of the dust (with a handkerchief I handed him before he could use his sleeve) he blew on it, stroked his fingers along the sides, and the box sprang open.

I caught a glimpse of a fold of pale, gray-lavender cloth before that was thrown aside. There was a heavy clunk as a tarnished metal chain followed it, then a brocaded belt, and a small ornamental knife. I scooped these gently off the floor and marveled at them. They were true examples of exquisite, rich Arellian fashion. The knife's hilt was set with stones and elegantly cast in the form of a griffin, while the sheath was similarly encrusted. The brocaded belt was sorely worn, but enough pearls still clung to their threads that I could discern the delicate pattern of swoops and spirals they must have once formed. And the metal chain, upon closer inspection, turned out to be heavily tarnished silver and quite delicate—the sort of chain that was worn by Norumblanain nobles over their shoulders as signs of office.

"Felpz," I said in quiet awe. "These are your regalia . . . "

"Signs of indentured servitude," Felpz muttered, pulling out a crumbling velvet bag and dumping the contents into his palm. "Arell knew exactly what he was doing when he gave his councilors those chains. The man had a wicked sense of humor under all that—*ha!*" he broke off, having cast aside a battered signet ring (which I hastily caught up and added to the pile in front of me), and now he held, dangling by a thin chain from his fingers, a single pendant half the size of my thumb.

At first it looked like a misshapen lump of tarnished silver, but then Felpz rubbed it on his cuff, and it came back flashing and brilliant.

"There you are," Felpz said, as if greeting an old friend, and offered the little figure to me.

I found myself holding a tiny replica of the chimera Felpz had described—with a long, serpentine body, the chest and forelegs of a lion, and three heads: a maned lion with an owl and feathered snake at its sides. The chimera had been posed with its tail cast in an arc, framing its outstretched wings, the tip meeting with its torso and blending into it somewhat, from the wear. Three tiny sapphires glittered in the lion's face, but only dark holes showed where the eyes of the owl and snake had once been. Though not battered, I could tell the pendant had seen much wear, and had at one time been well loved.

"It is very beautiful," I said, handing the chimera back with reverence.

Felpz took the pendant by the chain and held it up to the light—which, since it came from my demonic blue lamp, made the silver glimmer and the sapphires shine even brighter.

"He gave this to me near the end," Felpz said, softly now, almost as if speaking to himself. "We had something of a falling out, as can happen in any relationship. He, being the better man, had the sense to let me go gracefully. He gave me this chimera as a symbol: just as he had set the chimera free, so I was free as well." Felpz got an odd look on his face then, a strange mixture of sadness, anger, and longing. It was only visible because he was holding the little pendant up to the light, and his face was raised to gaze upon it. It was such a private expression that I looked away, feeling as though I had accidentally caught a glimpse of a personal memory that I was not meant to see.

"It was an immensely handsome gesture," Felpz went on, his voice sounding more normal. "I was so touched by it that I came right back and stayed with him until the end of his life. It got a bit rough there at the end, but I am glad I stayed. It would have been selfish of me not to."

When I again chanced to look at him, my friend had lowered his hand and was now gazing around my room, as if he had forgotten where he was. He took in the curtains, the carpet beneath us, my own neatly made bed, the writing desk overflowing with journals and loose papers, and the overstuffed bookshelf. His gaze lingered a while on the eerie blue lamp, and I saw a small smile budding at the corner of his mouth.

"Time is such an odd thing," he said after a while. "There is at once too much of it, and not enough. I've heard it postulated that, to an immortal, life can become one long, dull road with no end in sight. That we become *weary* of life; worn out by it." He snorted. "It has been, to my certain knowledge, only *mortals* who say things like this. I cannot tell you, Corianne, how precious I find my continued existence. Indeed there are times when, far from being overwhelmed by the vastness of eternity, I wish to *stay*. To have a small eternity contained in a single moment. But the river of time moves ever onward, and though we may ride it for different lengths, we must all ride it just the same."

He smiled at me, and shrugged. Then he gathered up all that remained of Lord Lavandil and put it back in the box, which in turn he took into his study, and I never saw it again.

The silver chimera, however, he hung by its chain over the lamp on his desk, where it glimmered and glittered, even in the faintest light. And to my knowledge, it hangs there still.

Bouragner Felpz will return in
"The Hidden Road"

In "Sons of Fire" we return to the saga of Driving Arcana, *set in a world only slightly modified from our own. Within its series it comes seventh in the first volume, or Wheel, following "Missionary Man."* *Preceding stories have been published individually in* Apsis *volumes 1, 2 and 3, and they also appear in their own collections:* Driving Arcana: Rotation One *(Heliopause, 2014) and* Driving Arcana: Rotation Two *(Heliopause, 2015). It was written in the late summer of 2014.*

SONS OF FIRE

The suburbs of Kansas City

THE MOTEL ROOM was quiet and dark, despite the lateness of the morning. The thick curtains which had been drawn against the harsh streetlight now served to keep out the piercing sun. While the temperature steadily climbed in the asphalt parking lot outside, inside the little room all was dim shadow and vague, lumpy shapes. The only light came from Jill Hamilton's computer screen, which she hunched over guiltily, trying to block as much of its glow as possible.

Though most of the time her bodyguards took it in turns to keep watch through the night, with the rising of the sun Selene had declared herself done, and fell into the bed not occupied by Clara. Now their sleeping forms were but a rumpled twist of blankets in the shadows, and Jill—who was the only one who had slept through the whole night—after breakfasting in the motel's cafeteria, had muted her computer and silenced her phone and now sat, trying to type as quietly as possible, while she listened to the two women peacefully breathing.

There was an ear-splitting, tooth-grinding chime, followed by an insipid melody rendered with all the musical acumen of a nineteen-eighties arcade game. It blared out of nowhere, filling the room, and beneath it was a soft, and accordingly aggravating, buzzing noise.

It was unmistakably the ring of a cell phone, but not any that Jill knew. With some of the money brought in by the sale of her childhood home she'd bought both her employees smartphones which, in addition to allowing her better access to them when they were out and about, had a far more pleasing selection of ringtones. This was not any of them.

"Y'all realize this means *bloodshed,*" Selene gasped, rising out of her cocoon of blankets like a monster from Greek mythology. With her thick, tightly curling hair half-pulled from its ponytail and pushed out in all directions she did look a little Medusan, and though she had not yet managed to open her eyes, her teeth were bared in an awful grimace. She flailed, shedding blankets, and began feeling around the bedside table for the source of the noise.

Jill shut her laptop at once and began homing in on it. Being more awake than Selene, she soon figured out it was coming from the dark pile of leather panniers that Clara had left in a corner by the door.

That gave her pause. Clara fiercely valued—and guarded—her privacy. Also, having seen some of the things to have come out of those panniers (magic rings, armor, special knives) Jill was reluctant to begin pawing through them—even to silence such an awful noise.

As it happened, however, she didn't have to. Clara turned over and, without ever actually sitting up, crawled over the end of her bed, and then over a good three feet of floor, until she could reach the topmost pannier and flip it open. She was so tall her hips and legs still rested on the bed, while her torso stretched out over the floor as she began rifling through the contents of the satchel.

"Clara, you make that noise stop—or I *will* kill something!" Selene cried, crumpling back into her bed and mashing the pillows into her face, from which further threatening murmurs continued to emanate.

Clara said nothing, but single-mindedly dug through her pannier until her hand came out holding a small, battered, and very much outdated cell phone. It was the simplest, cheapest kind of phone—just a keypad and a small digital display—and it looked like it had been sat on at one point.

Clara, her face illuminated by the glowing screen, blinked at it, read the number displayed, and then she answered.

"What is it?" she asked, sounding both irritated and strangely fragile. As Jill watched, however, her face darkened, and something like fear flashed in her cold blue eyes—though this was quickly pushed down and hidden.

"*Who* is this?" she asked, her tone suddenly changing. Now she sounded angry. "How did you get this number? How did you get his *phone?* . . . You are *what?* Oh. *Oh.* Why are you calling me?"

A silence stretched on after this last question, and Jill saw Clara's eyes widen briefly, her nostrils flare, and her already thin mouth tighten.

"When did you last see him?" she asked. Now she sounded tense, and a little shocked.

"Oh. I see. Yes, that's to be expected. Look, have you tried . . . *oh.* Oh. No, I understand. Listen, you *stay where you are.* Where are you?"

Silently, Jill passed Clara a pad of the motel's complimentary notepaper and a ballpoint pen. Clara, collapsing to sit on the floor, took them both with her free hand and began to jot down an address.

"Okay, I have it. Thank you. I can be there in . . . " Clara's eyes went to the ceiling; she frowned, and then looked back down at the paper, " . . . seven hours. I will call his phone if there are any delays. If you notice anything . . . suspicious . . . call me at . . . " she fumbled in her pocket for her other phone. Jill took pity on her and looked up the number on her own phone before holding it out for Clara to read. " . . . 7803, area code 831," Clara finished. "Do you have that? No, area code eight three *one,* like a one dollar bill. Yes. What?"

Clara paused and looked past Jill. Selene, who had gradually re-emerged from her fortress of blankets and pillows as she listened to the phone call, blinked at them owlishly. Clara looked past her as well; to Jill it almost seemed like she was looking out of the motel room entirely, to a very different place.

"I'm his sister," Clara said at last. "I'll see you soon." She ended the call and lowered the hand holding the phone. Finding both Jill and Selene staring at her with the obvious question printed bold across both their faces, she merely shrugged.

"I have to go to Chicago," she said simply.

"You have a *brother?*" Selene said incredulously. Jill could almost see what she was thinking, too: what someone with Clara's genetics, but with a Y chromosome, would have to look like. He was probably a bonafide titan. Then her analytical brain caught up with her imagination, and she came down off her cloud with a thump.

"What's happened?" she asked. "Is he all right?"

"I don't know," Clara said. She was repacking the pannier, glancing at the clock by the bed. "He's missing. Has been for three days. His ... his *girlfriend* just called me. Using *his* phone— apparently he had my private number listed as 'Emergency.'"

"How come we don't got your private number?" Selene asked, brazenly.

"Because I have not given it to you," Clara replied, without rancor. She moved over to the bed and reached down, drawing out her heavy, leather biking boots.

"Three days is more than long enough to file a missing person report," Jill pointed out. "Shouldn't she call the police?"

Clara paused with one boot on, the other held poised over her foot. Her face worked into a grimace and then out again. "She did. They aren't ... Flammard's not ... " she sighed, finished putting on her boot, and shrugged into her leather jacket. "The kind of person he is . . . any trouble he can't get himself out of, the police wouldn't be able to help—even if they wanted to." She reached for the leather harness that held her namesake—a two-handed claymore broadsword—and buckled it on. She turned to Jill.

"I apologize," she said. "But I must request some ... time off. I will meet you in five days, wherever you wish."

Jill blinked dumbly at her, but fortunately Selene spoke for both of them.

"Hell with that, we're coming with you!" she said, bouncing out of bed and fumbling around for her own boots.

Jill looked around at the disaster area that was their motel room. She frowned.

"There's no way we can be in Chicago in seven hours. It's more like eight, and that's if we leave *right now*. Which we can't," she pointed out.

Clara nodded. "Precisely," she said, slinging her panniers over one giant shoulder and making for the door.

"So give us the address, at least!" Jill shouted, starting after her. "We'll meet you there!"

Clara stopped, ponderous, turned around, and glared at them. "This is personal," she said, quiet and deadly.

"It's common *sense*," said Selene. "Look, girlfriend, I get it. He's family. And family is complicated—good *lord* I know that— but if he's anything like you, and *he's* in *trouble*, then, I'm just saying you might want yourself some backup is all."

Clara's nostrils flared, but she did not open her mouth and spit fire at them—which Jill had thought looked ready to happen a moment ago.

"Fine," she said, digging in her pocket and pulling out the notepad on which she'd scribbled the address, and flung it at Jill. "I will see you there," she said, and pulled open the door.

"Don't you need a copy?" Jill called after her.

"I've memorized it already," Clara replied, not even bothering to turn her head. The door slammed behind her, and a minute later they heard the muffled roar of her motorbike, Unicorn, coming to life and tearing out of the parking lot.

There was one stunned moment of silence in the room after her departure, and then Selene whipped into action, pulling back the curtains and turning on all the lights so she could see to pack. Jill carefully entered the address—a residential on the north side of Chicago—into her phone, and went to help Selene.

They found Clara's toothbrush and sharpening kit in the bathroom, as well as a pair of her socks hung over the towel rack to dry.

"See, *see*?" Selene said, waving a brown hand at the articles. "She hasn't even barely *started* yet, and she needs our help!" She carefully packed the toothbrush in a clean plastic bag, and put it and the rest of Clara's possessions in a corner of her backpack. "*See you there,* my fine ass. Jill, you let me drive. We'll make it in *six!*"

* * *

The stone was cold and a little damp under his cheek, though that might have been condensation from his body heat. Somewhere in the distance was the sound of a generator; it was dull enough that he guessed it was in a different room. There was light, that much he could tell even through closed eyelids, and he kept them closed as he listened with all his might for any clue as to where he was.

Waking up from a drugged sleep was not the most pleasant experience at the best of times. Waking up from a drugged sleep in an unknown location without the use of one's hands—his were bound tightly behind his back—was even more disconcerting. To Flammard Nordstern it brought back a flood of memories, most of which were associated with extremely unpleasant events in his life, but with the memories came old habits, reawakened with the rising tide of adrenaline in his system.

He reached out with his senses—the regular kind like hearing and smell and touch, but also that particular *sense* that belonged to him alone. It was the sense that could tell him, for example, if that soft *patting* sound was a flap of cloth in a breeze, or the footsteps of his captor.

It turned out to be the latter. Flammard held himself dead still, relaxed and hardly breathing, until the owner of the footsteps retreated out of earshot.

Only then did he dare crack open an eye and look around.

He was wedged into a tiny cell; four feet long and high, and barely wide enough for him to turn around in. There was a bucket in one corner and a drain in the floor; the grate was digging painfully into his thigh. The only light shone in weak beams through the bars at the front, where there was a door of the sort found on animal cages, secured with a heavy chain. Beyond the bars he could glimpse another wall of similar cages; some dark and still, others with their doors hanging open. In the one directly across from him were visible a pair of feet in worn sneakers, which twitched periodically.

The first thing Flammard did was free his hands. This was easy enough, though he had to cheat a bit. He felt a pang of regret at having to do so—he'd sworn off cheating in *that* way when he'd moved in with Lalai—but he figured the situation warranted it.

With his hands he gave himself a thorough check; discovered bruises on his neck and shoulders consistent with being carried, but none in the more vulnerable areas of his body. He also found a circular band-aid at the base of his neck—impossible to reach with bound hands—and he ripped it off at once. There was a little patch of gel underneath, and this he carefully wiped away with the hem of his shirt—and then wiped the excess on the bars with a shudder.

The bare necessities done, he retreated to the farthest corner of his cell, curled his knees into his chest, and assessed the situation.

The lock on the chain would give him no problem, if cheating was back on the table. Where he went from there, however, was less certain. Judging by the temperature (dangerously cold if Flammard had been an ordinary person) and the sound of the generator, he guessed he was somewhere underground. That could be problematic, especially if there were guards. Which there most likely were. People who knew how to incapacitate someone like Flammard and take him somewhere he couldn't easily locate probably knew better than to leave him unattended. It was surprising, though, that they hadn't thought to lock him up properly. It made him suspicious.

No, things did not look good.

And that was *before* the screaming started.

Chicago, Illinois

M ALALAI AHMADZAI HEARD THE ROAR of a motorcycle distantly from where she sat at the kitchen table. She'd been sitting there ever since Satsuki had dropped her off after grocery shopping—all but the milk and eggs still sitting out on the counter. Lalai hadn't had the energy to put them away.

The roar of the engine intensified, but instead of retreating down the street it came to a stop. There were footsteps on the walk, and from the window Lalai looked down to the front door and saw it open for a tall—was that a woman? It was hard to tell. She was tall for a woman, if she was one, her head a bright, bald orb perched atop black, leather-clad shoulders. It bent, and Lalai caught a snatch of conversation. Gem had intercepted the visitor. That was a relief.

Then there was a step on the stair that started Stirling barking in the apartment below, and then a knock on her own door that sent butterflies up to Lalai's throat and down her arms. It had been over seven hours since that strange phone call in the morning, and she'd all but written off the harsh voice of Leonard's sister—if it was his sister at all.

Another knock. Not exactly impatient, but sharper this time. It spurred Lalai to action, and she dragged herself from the little kitchen to the door and cracked it open—leaving the chain in place.

She was met by the sight of a snugly zipped leather jacket and a gloved hand raised to perform a third knock. Readjusting her gaze to point upwards, Lalai at last found the face attached to this impressive body. It was a plain, roundish face, with ice-cold blue eyes and a thin, unfriendly mouth, but there was an angular jut about the cheekbones and a concerned wrinkle between the fine, platinum eyebrows that was achingly familiar. Lalai felt her mouth fall open slightly.

"My god," she whispered. "He *does* have a sister."

The concerned face frowned. "He has two, actually," the woman said. "I am the only one . . . available. I am Clara Nordstern. May I come in?"

Lalai took a deep breath and undid the chain. Clara didn't move, however, until she'd opened the door the whole way, stepped back, and ushered her in.

It was almost like watching a robot, or a particularly well-disguised alien, walk into the room. Clara was so tall her head nearly brushed against the slanting ceiling (one of the charms of living in an attic apartment, but as neither Lalai nor Leonard were above five and a half feet it had never bothered them), and her wide shoulders were made even wider by the hilt of the sword she wore strapped to her back, which jutted out to the right of her neck. She was dressed from head to toe in black motorcycle leathers, with matching black gloves. The only thing not black was the harness that held her sword, which consisted of crisscrossing brown leather straps that buckled around her waist.

For someone so big she moved softly and with an assurance that radiated stability. If someone tried to punch her, Lalai thought, they would probably bounce off.

Icy blue eyes found her, harsh as a searchlight. Not at all like Leonard's gentle hazel ones, but the expression behind them was like enough for Lalai to see the resemblance. Perhaps not a full sister, though. A half-sister, maybe?

"And you are?" Clara asked. Her voice was light, but clipped.

"Malalai Ahmadzai," she said, feeling the butterflies rise in her arms again. "Lalai for short. I, uh . . . I appreciate you coming so . . . fast."

Clara shrugged. She had a funny sort of shrug: first lowering her shoulders and then raising them again. She moved further into the little apartment, taking in the carefully stacked bookcases, picture-lined walls, and the old *rubab* hung in a place of honor between the two wide windows.

"Flam—er, *Leonard,* lives here?" she asked. There was a curious fragility in her voice, and Lalai noticed the flub over his name. She didn't remark on it, however.

"Yes," she said simply.

"How long?"

Lalai found she had to think about that a moment. "Three years?" she said. Had it only been that long? That wasn't long enough. The butterflies were lumping in her throat now, and she had to fight to keep them down. "We moved in—together—when he got his job with the fire department."

"The *fire department?*" Clara said sharply, sounding a little alarmed.

"He's an EMT," Lalai reassured her. "Just made paramedic."

"Oh," said Clara, and a small, bitter smile flitted across her face. "Good for him." She unclipped her sword from the harness and leaned it carefully next to their oldest, most battered armchair. It had a very long hilt with downward-sloping—what were they called? Quillions?—with four little rings arranged like the leaves of a four-leafed clover at the ends. It was an impressive, businesslike sword.

"May I?" Clara asked, indicating the chair.

"Yes, oh yes, of course," Lalai said, realizing what a poor host she was being. "Can I get you anything? Coffee? Lemonade?"

"No, thank you," Clara said. "Please, just sit down, and tell me what happened."

Lalai took a deep breath, and went and got a chair from the kitchen. The only other seat in the little living room was the loveseat under the window, and sitting in *it* only made Lalai miss Leonard even more. It was sitting in that seat, one rainy afternoon in April three years ago, that they had curled around each other and Lalai had realized that *yes,* this—the house, her career, his job, *their relationship*—was going to work.

Now she pushed the chair between her legs and sat, leaning her chest against the backrest. "Where do you want me to start?" she asked.

Clara had been interested to find the musical, intelligent voice belonged to a diminutive brown woman with smokey black hair and dark, red-rimmed eyes. Dressed in a flowing silk shirt and a neat black-and-red floral print skirt with stockinged legs in sensible flat sandals, she looked like a well formed, stylish person gone a little off the rails. Which was understandable. What had surprised Clara was moving into the space of their little attic apartment. To her it felt cramped, but she was sure this was due entirely to her size. It was clearly a comfortable, well loved and well lived-in place. The walls were covered with bright, colorful watercolors depicting flowing, flowery animals. There was half a week's worth of mail and two grocery bags on the kitchen table, and the sink was filled with dirty dishes, but these seemed to be symptoms of the calamity that had just occurred, not indicative of the regular state of affairs.

It was with a small pang—both of loneliness and jealousy—that Clara realized the reason she hadn't heard from Flammard in four years was because he'd been busy building himself a life. A happy one with the name Leonard and a brilliant woman named Lalai.

Clara ground her teeth and resolved to do her best not to ruin it.

"When was the last time you saw him?" she asked.

"Tuesday," Lalai replied, as if she'd answered this question before. "He had—was supposed to have—night shift at the station, so we got dinner together. He went to work, I went to bed . . . I heard him come in around seven in the morning—at least, I thought it was him. I didn't actually *see* anyone. But it must have been him, because when I got up, his phone and keys were on the table. But he wasn't." Lalai swallowed visibly. "He wasn't *anywhere.*"

"Did you hear anything?" Clara asked, patiently.

"Outside? No . . . well, I mean, nothing unusual. I heard Stirling bark—that's the dog on the second floor—but it was her friendly, hello bark. That's why I thought it was Leonard."

Clara frowned, rubbing her chin with one hand.

"How had he been acting . . . lately?" she asked. "Anything . . . seem to be bothering him?"

Lalai shook her head, tears welling up under her big dark eyes. She was the opposite of Flammard in so many ways, and yet Clara could imagine how they complemented each other.

"No . . . everything was . . . everything was *fine.* More than fine, *good.* He was . . . we were . . . he got a double break this weekend, and we were going to go downtown and do the museum walk—can you believe we've lived in Chicago three years and never been to Millennium Park? He was *happy.*"

To Clara, Flammard being openly happy usually meant he was up to something—and it wouldn't always be pleasant. On the other hand, that was ten years ago. Now things might be different, as they obviously were in so many other respects.

"What have you done, in the meantime? You mentioned you already tried the police."

"Yeah," said Lalai, with a roll of her eyes. "The minute forty-eight hours were up. They weren't . . . well, he's *your* brother. You know."

"I know," Clara said. And she did know. More than Lalai did, if she thought Flammard had been abducted by ordinary humans.

"It's *ridiculous,*" Lalai hissed, clearly trying not to scream. "He's an *EMT.* He works with the fire department! You'd think a whole crew wanting to know what's become of their paramedic would, maybe, you know, *motivate* them? But *nooo* . . . as soon as they found out about, well, *that,* it was suddenly . . . 'we see this a lot, Miss Ah-mad-zai. That kind go missing all the time, Miss Ah-mad-zai.' *That kind.*" She wrinkled her nose in disgust. "That's what they called him. Sorry." Lalai reached up to wipe her streaming eyes with the sleeve of her shirt, but paused before moving on to her nose. "Excuse me," she choked, and moved into the kitchen, from which she emerged a moment later, blowing her nose on a hand towel.

"Anyway, that's where I've been the past three days. Just this morning I woke up around two, and after trying for hours I couldn't sleep, so I just started going through all of Leonard's contacts, calling them and asking if they'd seen him. Then I got to an entry labeled 'Emergency' and that was *your* number."

Clara nodded. "That is probably because I told him to call it if there was one. May I see it? His phone, I mean."

"Oh yes, yes, of course."

Lalai produced a sleek black smartphone in a rubbery case with little birds on it. Clara took it, but didn't wake it up. She held it in her hand, trying to get a sense of Flammard from it. But either it was a new phone, or he hadn't cared for it very much. Even after she took her glove off she felt nothing but cold, hard glass and metal.

In the distance, from the street below, came a rumble of an engine. Not the soft purr of the small city cars that coasted down the quiet, residential street, but a big, gutsy growl.

Arcana crept down Dayton Street like a self-conscious bull in a china shop. He stopped in front of a tall house made of cheerful red bricks while Jill squinted at the address.

"This is it," she told Selene after a moment.

"Nice digs," Selene murmured appreciatively.

And they were. The house was large, the type that had an extra floor in place of a basement, with a scooped out yard in front, out of which peeked the crowns of little trees. Stairs led up to the recessed front door, which stood beside two narrow, arched windows. Above that was a second floor, and above that a terrace and what looked like an attic floor—the kind where the shakes of the roof bent over and came down in a wall around bright windows reflecting sky.

Most of the house was in shade from the vigorous trees that lined the street, and there was a black metal fence surrounding the front yard, with a simple latch gate leading to the front path. There was a well-chewed dog toy lying in the middle of it.

They had to go on past the house a little ways before Selene found a place where she could squeeze Arcana. On their way they passed Unicorn, which had been defiantly walked up onto the curb and parked next to a tree.

Jill had to get out and spot her as she parked, the street was so tightly packed with small cars, and it was a wonder they found a parking space at all. Even hugging the curb, Arcana's rear wheels bulged out into the street, and his red coat stood out against the pervasive grays, blacks, silvers and blues of the other vehicles.

As they approached the house its front door opened, and Clara walked out, followed by a small, middle-eastern looking woman in a loud print skirt, stockings, and a loose shirt. She looked like she had been crying, but Clara was as blank and composed as ever.

"Selene," she said, by way of greeting. "I need your ring."

"I'm sorry?"

"The one I gave you," Clara said, and gave Selene a meaningful look.

"*Oh,*" said Selene. "*That* ring. Righto, you got it." She turned on her heel and headed back to Arcana, returning a moment later with a small cloth bundle. She shot Jill a look as she passed her a second time. *See? Hopeless,* the look seemed to say. Jill rolled her eyes.

Selene dropped the bundle into Clara's waiting, ungloved hand, and stepped back.The other woman's long fingers closed around it, and she shut her eyes, concentrating.

"Are you ... friends of Clara?" the little woman asked timidly.

Jill and Selene exchanged looks.

"You could say that," Selene began cautiously.

"They work for me," Jill said frankly. "Jill Hamilton," she said, extending a hand. "This here is Selene. Um ... Clara left us in a bit of a rush this morning. You are ... ?"

"Lalai," said the woman. "I'm her brother's girlfriend. But you, er . . . probably knew that."

"Honestly," said Selene, watching as Clara began turning in a slow circle, the hand that held the little cloth-wrapped ring stretched out in front of her like the needle of a compass. "We didn't even know she *had* a brother, before this morning."

Clara's eyes flew open and her nostrils flared. She said nothing, but began to walk . . . off the path that led from the sidewalk to the front door, past the sunken yard, and around the side of the house.

The other three women followed in a confused line, with Jill bringing up the rear. They found Clara in the tiny backyard, staring down at a patch of curly grass as though she could bore through the earth with her eyes and see what was beneath.

"Clara, what—" Jill began.

"Shovel," said Clara, not looking up. "I need a shovel."

Selene turned to Lalai, who pointed mutely at a tiny shed wedged into a corner of the yard. Stepping over a pot of tulips Selene opened the door and found a mildewy shovel tucked between a rake and a moldy tarp. She returned, bearing the desired implement, and presented it to Clara.

Clara looked up, surprised, and took the shovel gently.

"Thank you," she said quietly.

"Clara, what on earth is going on?" Selene asked.

Clara dug the shovel into the dirt and began prying away the grass. "My brother, Flam—*Leonard*—is missing. I believe he has been abducted. I am looking to see if that is indeed the case."

"By digging up Lalai's yard?" Jill asked, shooting her an apologetic look.

Clara turned over a mat of grass and, laying aside the shovel, began scooping the soft, brown earth away with her gloved hand.

"There are some things we Nordsterns always take with us, wherever we go," Clara said by way of explanation. She glanced over at Lalai, her eyes narrowing. "They are not our wallets and cell phones," she said. Then her expression changed as her hand caught on something that was not earth or rock. She began pulling at the soil, excavating a long, narrow strip that revealed what looked like a cloth-wrapped bundle.

"What *do* you take, then?" Jill asked.

For answer, Clara gripped one end of the bundle and pulled, dislodging more dirt, and raised up on end a long, stick-like package. Having pocketed the ring, she used her free hand to brush away the last few clinging clods of dirt, and began teasing at one end, where there was a free strip of cloth.

The cloth, half rotted already, came off in pieces, revealing what was to Jill and Selene an already familiar object.

Lalai let out a gasp of consternation.

"What," she said, "is a *sword* doing buried in our backyard?"

Clara turned to her, holding what was indeed a sheathed sword. It had an intricately carved pommel with red leather around the long grip, loops of metal sprouting around the guard, and a further stretch of leather-wrapped metal that ended in a downward-facing crescent—after which the blade disappeared into the sheath, which was wide and heavy and wrapped in a complicated pattern of straps and buckles that, Jill guessed, would translate into something like the harness Clara wore if they were untangled. It was considerably shorter than her own massive claymore, despite the impressive hilt—though Jill imagined it would still be too big and heavy for herself.

"He chose to leave his old life behind four years ago," Clara explained, grimly. "But he would never, *ever* leave his sword."

Flammard was beginning to wish he'd kept his sword strapped to his back, the way Claymore did. But they probably wouldn't let him drive the ambulance if he did that—let alone treat patients. And his captors would have taken it away first chance they got. No, Flammard thought as he watched a pair of men—their heads hidden by black hoods—drag a third man between them back to a cell and throw him inside, what he really wanted was to have Feuermann in his hand *right now*. With Feuermann, he could slip out of his cell and calmly walk out of whatever torture chamber he was trapped in. Feuermann had that effect on people.

But he was alone, and empty-handed. Oh well. Time to use what he did have. This consisted of the jeans and shirt he was

wearing (they'd taken away his shoes) and—this was the important part—his *wits*.

The men in black hoods had been in and out many times
over the last few hours. Each time they were either dragging
someone out of their cell, or dragging someone back into one.
In between there was screaming—awful screaming—and a particularly horrible smell that anyone else might have been hard
pressed to identify, but Flammard knew to be that of burning
human flesh. It was difficult to see the state of the people when
the men dragged them back in, but they were silent. That didn't
bode well.

Now the men were coming back, and one of them was knock-
ing a stick against the fronts of the cells as he went.

"Check number five," his partner said, and the two forms
paused in front of Flammard's door.

Flammard squished himself as far back into the darkest corner as he could, and cheated as hard as he could.

The door opened.

The hooded head which gazed in had a perplexed air about
it. A thick arm reached up and shined a flashlight into the little
area. Flammard shut his eyes as the beam passed over his face,
and held his breath.

"What the ever-lovin' Christ," said a voice from under the
hood. "There's no one in here!"

"What the hell?"

"The door was locked—bolted. But there's no one in here.
Someone's been having a laugh." Their tone suggested they knew
exactly who this *someone* was, and that *someone* was going to get
some rather unpleasant payback.

"Give it a rest, Charlie," said their partner. "We'll take the
one in six. I think he's good to go."

The hooded head disappeared, letting the door swing closed.
It hit the wall of the cell and bounced, twice, before coming to a
rest about an inch from the doorframe. They hadn't even bothered to latch it.

In the shadows at the back of the cell, Flammard dared to
breathe.

His breath caught almost at once as he heard the man in the cell next to his—unlucky cell six—begin to shout and cry as he was dragged out.

"No, man—*no!* Don't take me—I got—I got—*no!*"

"Listen, bucko," one of the men in hoods growled. "You know how it goes. You come quiet, or Charlie here takes his stick and *makes* you quiet."

A strangled gulping sound. Another clang of a cell door. Whimpering, and the whisper of cloth on stone as the unfortunate man was dragged away.

Flammard waited. He waited until the noises had faded away entirely, and then—ever so slowly—he crawled forward and gently pushed his cell door open, and slipped out.

Immediately the room around him erupted into surprised shouts.

"What are *you* doing?"

"How did you get out?"

"Hey, kid! Hey *kid!* Let me out!"

"Yeah, man, let us out!"

"You can't leave us here!"

"*Please* be *quiet!*" Flammard hissed. "They'll *hear* you!"

This got exactly one cell to quiet down. The rest were too agitated, and the cacophony of voices continued to rise.

"They'll *kill* us!"

"I don't want to die here!"

They had a point. Flammard sighed, and went over to the one cell that had fallen silent. The man on the other side of the bars stared back at him, tight-lipped, but said nothing.

"Hi," whispered Flammard. "I'm . . . call me Leonard."

"Hey, Leonard," the man replied softly. "I'm Marcus. Listen—could you? I mean, *can* you?"

"Yeah," said Flammard. It was more cheating that he strictly wanted, but at this rate, if he was using his powers, he might as well make them *really* useful. "Just stay quiet."

Marcus nodded, and Flammard turned his attention to the lock. This was the good kind, and would have been almost impossible to pick from the inside. From the outside, however, Flammard was able to get it at the angle he needed, and a moment later he was helping Marcus out of the tiny cell.

Marcus turned out to be a large black man with an improbable halo of carroty curls framing his face. He stood up—and up and up and *up*—*almost as tall as Claymore,* Flammard thought— and the noise in the room redoubled.

It must have been partly from seeing another of their number released, but also, Flammard realized, behind the shouting in the room, the screaming had started up again. He felt his heart twinge at the thought of the man who had gone in his place, but at the same time he knew this would give them that much more cover.

"I'm only letting you out if you can *be quiet!*" Flammard shouted.

A few more cells grudgingly fell silent, but a couple shrill voices continued to cry out.

"All y'all shut *up!*" Marcus bellowed. He had a good, deep bellow, and the noise of it knocked the room into a brief quiet.

"I'll let you out, but only if you can *keep* quiet," Flammard explained quickly. "If you can't, then we'll *all* get it."

Silence. Flammard took that as a go-ahead, and got to work on the other locks.

All in all, he found nine more occupied cells. Seven of which divulged similarly agitated young men. And two of which . . .

Flammard braced himself in the doorway so that the growing crowd couldn't see inside. He'd felt obligated to check on the men who had been brought back, but after the second one he decided to spare himself the pain.

It only made him more determined to upset what was happening to the man who had recently occupied cell six.

Closing the door to the ninth cell—shutting out the sight but not the smell of burnt flesh—he turned to survey the crowd that had grown in the center of the room.

They were of every size and shape, from small and lithe, like Flammard, to huge and hulking, like Marcus. The only thing they had in common was that they were all male, and their hair was all some shade of red. He was not the only one to notice.

"Dude, what *is* this?" one of them asked. "Some sicko with a League of Red-Headed Men fixation?"

Flammard said nothing. He'd noticed something else they all had in common, but it was so subtle, and so weak in some cases, that he was fairly certain only he was aware of it.

Every single one of them had a faint, flame-like aura—when Flammard forced his eyes to look for it. None of them were as strong as his own—which he was aware of as a sort of orange glow on the edge of his vision—though Marcus's was fairly distinct. In fact, apart from Flammard, Marcus was probably the only one who might have picked up on it.

"We need to get out of here," he began.

"Ya *think* so, Sherlock?" said the man who had spoken before. Marcus hushed him.

"Mostly, *you* need to get out of here," Flammard went on, turning to Marcus. "I think I might know what they have in store for us, and after me, you're the one most at risk. Think you can lead them out?"

Marcus stared at Flammard. "I got no idea what you're talkin' about, man," he said. "But yeah, I'm ready to blow this joint. Which way is out, though?"

"You'll have to figure that out for yourself, I'm afraid," Flammard said. "But I think anywhere that goes *up* would be a good idea."

"Where are *you* going?" someone asked as Flammard fought his way through the press of bodies toward the door.

Flammard paused, and in the ensuing quiet they all heard, faint but distinct, a strangled, anguished sob.

"I'm gonna go find out what *that* is," he said.

"Dude, you *crazy*?"

"Old habit," Flammard snapped. "Marcus, get them going!" And he ran. Before his courage ran out. Before he lost the tenuous conviction singing in his veins. He ran. Behind him he heard the commotion as the crowd erupted in argument, with Marcus booming over them all. But Flammard ran, down unfamiliar corridors, bare feet stinging on the cold stone, and he did not look back.

Lalai frowned at Clara. "Is there something about Leonard you're not telling me?" she asked, a little accusingly.

"Many things," Clara said, dusting off the scabbard. "Now is not the time, however. When I return . . . with him. Then you may . . . talk. Or not. I know there are things that he would rather remain buried, like his sword. Now I must go . . . "

"Oh whoa, whoa there," Selene said, stepping into Clara's path as she tried to stride away. "Keep in mind some of us aren't exactly up to speed yet. Which we *want* to be," she added, earnestly, to Lalai, "We're here to help."

"I believe you," the woman replied, smiling shakily. "I . . . um . . . appreciate it."

Clara seemed torn. She groaned softly and looked up at the sky for a few moments. "I need to find an open area. No houses."

"Oz Park is just a few blocks from here," Lalai offered. "I can show you . . . "

"No," Clara cut her off, then continued, more gently. "No, thank you. Directions. We'll walk. I'll explain on the way," she added to Selene.

Lalai looked disappointed, but she gave the directions to Jill, who pulled up a map on her phone and led the way.

They left the red brick house with Lalai standing in the walk-way, hugging herself miserably. Jill felt a stab of sympathy for the woman, and wished there was some reassurance she could offer—but she knew from agonizing experience that maybe the only thing they brought back to her would be a terrible sort of closure.

"All right," Selene said, punching Clara lightly on the arm. "What's the scoop? I take it you're convinced your bro didn't just take off for Belize or something . . . so what happened?"

Clara sighed and recounted what Lalai had already told her. When she had finished, Selene frowned and scratched under her ponytail.

"So . . . " said Jill, also frowning. "Did I miss something? Why aren't the police involved? Did Lalai even *call* them?"

"She did," Clara replied bluntly. "They wouldn't help."

"Wouldn't . . . or *couldn't?*" Selene pried.

"Most likely, they looked at the type of man my brother is, and decided he wasn't worth their time. It's happened before." There was a note of bitterness in Clara's voice, and under that, a softly boiling rage.

Selene wrinkled her nose and frowned. "That doesn't follow. What's he like, this brother of yours? To borrow a phrase from his girl: *is there something about Leonard you're not telling us?*"

"Many things," Clara replied. Selene groaned.

"Some of them may prove relevant," Clara admitted. "Some not. I will inform you of the relevant information as soon as it becomes so. For now, understand that, for many years, my brother was—like me, and our sister—a warrior. A hunter of monsters. A guard against the ancient night. He . . . has skills. No ordinary person would be a threat to him. Whoever took him must have extraordinary powers. This will be a dangerous situation, and I do not wish to put you in unnecessary peril."

"Sister, you know we deal with *tons* of peril every time she gets some harebrained idea," Selene pointed out.

"It's for *science*," Jill protested. "Oh, we go right here."

Turning right necessitated crossing the street, which they did in a line. Jill wondered what the car that stopped at the intersection thought of them. Clara especially, in her biking leathers and carrying two swords.

"You *know* what I mean," Selene said as they crossed. "Point is, it'd be crappy of us to bow out of a little extra peril when your very own *brother* is in the stink."

Clara smiled, briefly, harshly, like she didn't quite believe it. "That's very . . . " she began, then stopped. "Thank you," she finished, quietly.

They walked in silence for a while, passing more brick-and-plaster houses, speckled with shade from the leafy trees lining the streets and lit in golden, sideways light from the setting sun. Up ahead a break in the buildings, with the crowns of larger trees encroaching on the skyline, heralded their approach to the park.

"His name is Flammard, not Leonard," Clara said eventually. "That will be important for you to know, if you are to help me find him. Flammard. Leonard is just what he calls himself . . . back there."

"Sort of the way your name's Claymore, but everyone calls you Clara?" Selene asked.

"Sort of," Clara allowed, and said no more.

* * *

The road they were on bent to the right, and from there a pedestrian path led off between a baseball diamond on the left and a wide, grass-covered swell on the right. Chattering from the diamond announced the presence of a woman's softball team getting in some evening practice, and Clara made instead for the swell, which was perfectly deserted.

"So . . . what are we doing, exactly?" Jill asked as Clara paced around, testing the ground with her foot.

"Locating Flammard," Clara replied shortly. She had found a place that was relatively flat, and holding the exhumed sword out in front of her, she gently drew the blade from its scabbard. It was silvery and clean, with an extraordinary wavy pattern down the length, which made the edges ripple. Jill had seen a sword like that, once, in an animated film. It had been the villain's sword. But this sword, while sinister, also had an elegance about it that was enchanting. With its long hilt, looped cross guard, crescent prongs, and wavy blade, it almost looked more like a decorative ornament than a weapon.

Clara twirled it expertly in her hand, causing the evening sunlight to dance along the blade. Because of the ripples, it almost looked like the thing caught fire for a moment.

"Uh . . . Clara? You're not gonna go all Inigo Montoya on us, are you?" Selene asked.

Clara shot the other woman a confused look, then she turned the sword down, plunging it abruptly into the earth, where it sunk in by almost a foot.

"What *are* you doing?" Jill asked.

"*Shh,*" said Clara. She had sunk to her knee, one hand on the hilt of the sword and the other resting on her bent leg, her head bowed. She stayed that way, perfectly still, for almost a minute. In that time Jill looked questioningly at Selene, who shrugged expressively. They waited.

After a while Clara began to speak, but in a whisper, as if to herself.

"We are our swords, and our swords are us. Find yourself, *foyaman.* Find yourself."

To Jill and Selene it appeared nothing happened, but to Clara it felt as though the sword turned under her hand. Its blade warmed, causing the damp roots of the grass surrounding it to hiss as the water turned to steam, and a bright, hot speck appeared in her mind.

It was such a relief that she nearly let go of the sword, which would have been disastrous. Clenching her hand around the rapidly warming hilt, she focused on that speck until she could sense its location in relationship to her own.

Flammard was still in this world. He was still alive, and all things considered, he was not so very far away.

Clara looked up. To her companions her eyes appeared a little glassy and far off, but she sounded perfectly normal when she said:

"I know where he is . . . I can't tell you where, but I *know*."

She stood up, drawing the blade out of the earth as she went. Jill took a step back when she saw its tip, which was glowing orange-hot.

"Clara . . . " she said, uncertainly.

Clara felt the hot speck in her mind fade to a warm glow as the sword left the earth, and she shut her eyes to hold it there.

"I cannot let go of the sword, otherwise I'll lose him," she said, hoping for once Jill would take her words literally.

Selene understood, at least.

"Let's take Arcana then, all three of us. I'll drive. Here, I'll carry that scabbard—you probably shouldn't sheathe it anyway, even once its cooled."

Clara nodded, and together the three of them climbed down off the swell and began retracing their steps.

One of the women on the diamond saw them go out of the corner of her eye, and was so distracted by the sight of Clara and the wavy, red-hot sword, that she nearly got brained by an incoming ball. It bounced and rolled off into some bushes, and by the time it had been recovered the three women were gone, and none of her friends believed her when she told them about it.

At first it was easy. All Flammard had to do was follow the screams. These eventually died down to a low moaning, and when that stopped altogether he had to pause and consider his position.

He was definitely underground. The air was cold, and the passages were all carved out of stone with sections of concrete to shore them up. Furthermore, he could feel the weight of all that earth pressing down around him, closing in tightly, holding him in thick, gnarled hands as strong as time and darkness.

He was cheating again, quite by accident this time, which was unsettling. He checked himself over to make sure he wasn't actually *glowing*—he wasn't—and leaned against the wall to catch his breath.

What bothered him most about his predicament was that he had no idea how he had been taken. He remembered coming home from his shift, leaving his things on the kitchen table, and noticing that the recycling needed to be taken out. He'd pulled the box out from its niche by the refrigerator, walked it down the stairs, out the front door, and around to the side where the wheelie-bins were kept. He remembered lifting the heavy, plastic lid . . .

And there it cut out. Sight, smell, touch, and memory. Only the sound of a word remained, faint and unrecognizable. And the voice . . .

Thinking of voices made him perk his ears up, which was how he caught the sound of actual voices speaking in the immediate present. He couldn't tell if any of them were the voice from his memory, but he edged his way softly down the corridor so he could hear them better.

There were three voices: two deep and rough, one high and sharp. Probably female. That one was easier to understand, and so for a while it was liking listening to one side of a three-way telephone conversation.

"That one was even more pathetic than the last. Are you even *checking* their auras before you take them?"

A rumbly, indignant answer.

"Yes, yes, he was a Son of Fire, but so are *you*, remember? Do *you* want to have a go at it?"

Indistinct speaking. The female voice laughed, humorlessly.

More rumbling. A question, this time.

"No, gut him and throw him back in with the others. I need a rest. We'll try again in an hour or so."

Flammard inched closer, exerting a tremendous effort not to be heard. Now he could understand one of the gruff voices when it said, "Yes, Mistress," and the shuffle of feet that followed.

Flammard just had time to press himself back against the wall of the passage as torchlight flared around the corner, and the two hooded men came through it, dragging a limp object behind them. Flammard caught a glimpse of an arm, a naked torso with blood on it, and in one unfortunate flare from the torch, a ruined face.

He'd seen worse. Once. When the fire crew had rescued a woman from a burning car. The burns had been all over her face and neck and chest, and he'd had to cheat to keep her alive on the way to the hospital.

Flammard wasn't sure if it made it better or worse that he couldn't do anything for the man. The turmoil of emotions in his chest made him shudder, and he hung in the corridor for a long moment after the sound of footsteps and dead weight being dragged over stone had faded into the distance. Then he jerked into action.

How long until they noticed the empty chamber? Well, that depended on how long it took them to "gut" someone. He could try to double back—meet up with Marcus and make a break for the surface—but something about what was going on rubbed him the wrong way. It was wrong beyond just the empirical wrongness of killing someone—it was *wrong* in that something was trying to happen that *should not* happen. And that passing reference to the Sons of Fire ... that couldn't possibly mean what Flammard thought it meant ... except it probably *did,* considering the way all those men had auras and red hair. In which case, Flammard had to stop them.

He rounded a corner and was nearly blinded by the blaze of light pouring out from the room beyond. Light and *heat,* he realized as he crept forward, for the illumination came from a solid wall of fire that took up one side of the room.

Concentrating *very hard* on not being seen, Flammard entered the room and looked around.

It was a long, rectangular chamber—the wall of fire taking up the far, narrower side, opposite from the door Flammard had entered by—with a rough sort of daïs halfway down that had a high-backed chair on it. The walls were lined with coarse hangings with rudimentary figures woven into them. Flammard caught an odd tingle from these, as though they did not wholly belong to this world.

The long sides of the room were also lined with narrow tables, on top of which were an assortment of clay pots, bleached bones, and some nasty looking knives. Flammard gave them a wide berth as he crept toward the wall of fire.

As he moved forward around the daïs and throne, a crude altar hove into view in front of the fire. It consisted of a lumpy, cold, gray stone twice the size of his kitchen table, with iron rings hung from posts driven into either side. Charred remains of something limp and reddish hung from those rings, and the whole thing gave out a feeling of terrible menace.

This stone did not do bad things to you, Flammard realized, but bad things happened on it. It breathed off coolness, even in the face of the fire, whose angry orange light did not touch it. If the hangings were not entirely part of this world, then the stone was completely alien.

Flammard came right up to it, reached out a hand to touch it experimentally, and then recognized what the charred remains hanging from iron rings actually were.

He'd seen intestines, once, outside the victim of a particularly brutal car crash. The sight had stayed with him longer than he'd liked, and now the memory rose up again, matching perfectly the ten or so inches of reddish-black wrinkly tubing tied off neatly to the iron ring.

Flammard took his hand away.

"I thought you'd be an interesting one," said a voice from behind him.

At the sound, Flammard felt all the hairs on his body stand on end, and his heart speed up. But he forced himself to turn, slowly, and face the high-backed chair—which he now could see was occupied.

There was a woman sitting in it. She was wearing a long, belted tunic made of black velvet, with supple leggings and knee-high boots with lots of buckles. Her legs were crossed, one foot kicking idly, and she had her hands knitted together over her chest, her elbows on the armrests of the chair. Her bright red nails gleamed in the firelight. She had dark red hair and dark brown eyes and very pale skin. Her lips had been painted red to match her nails, and they stood out vividly against the white oval of her face.

What struck Flammard the most, however, was her aura: it was a bright, angry flame that surrounded her whole body, with tongues of fire licking upwards, spitting and arcing. Like the corona of the sun. Her aura was hardly bigger than Marcus's, really, but it was so fierce and violent Flammard rather thought she was holding it back.

"I know you're there," the woman said, her mouth twitching in the suggestion of a smile. "You're good, though. I still can't see you—not really. But a bit rusty, maybe? I'm surprised you didn't notice me. Do come forward, so I can see you properly."

She uncrossed her legs in a whisper of cloth, resting her boots—which had impressive, four-inch heels—on the stone slab in front of her. She smiled briefly, her yellow teeth like a flicker of flame in her red mouth.

Flammard's heart was hammering in his chest. Beyond his recognition of her superficial appearance as a conventionally attractive woman, he was also feeling a subconscious longing plucking at the core of his being. A sinuous, insidious desire to take, to conquer, to devour.

It was such a foreign feeling to him that he recognized it at once as a cheat of the very worst sort. He blinked and shook his head.

"Stop that," he said, giving the intruding sensation a metaphorical kick in the muzzle.

The woman actually jerked back physically in her seat, a look of surprise crossing her face.

"Don't you like that?" she asked, sounding genuinely confused.

"No," Flammard ground out. "I really don't. I also don't like what you're doing here. You need to stop."

"Are you a submissive, then?" the woman asked, and a whole different set of feelings assaulted Flammard's mind. A desire to serve, to get down on his knees and crawl up the steps of the daïs. To lay himself out at her feet, open, exposed . . .

"I said *stop* that," he ground out through gritted teeth.

"Let me *see* you then," said the woman, with an annoyed flick of a finger. "I'm even more curious now; you're not like any man I've met before. There's something . . . *different* . . . about you."

Oh gods, she could tell, Flammard thought frantically. Mostly, people who said they could sense male and female energy were full of baloney—energies were so much more diverse and complex than just male and female, saying so only proved one's ignorance—but if she could sense him to that extent through his strongest invisibility cheat, who knew what else she could see?

Unless she was picking up on the *other* thing that set him apart from most men. He almost hoped it was that. That, he knew he could deal with.

His fear only made him shrink further away, backing around the horrible stone altar and its grisly decorations, until he could feel the warmth of the fire against his back. It felt . . . oddly comforting. Unlike the fire of this world, which was angry and wild, this fire recognized him. It knew him. Knew him and welcomed him. That alone was unsettling, but Flammard tried to draw strength from it. He wasn't sure why he was so *frightened* of this woman finding out about his heritage—she clearly suspected it already, that was why he'd been grabbed—except that from what he'd seen it could only make his situation worse.

She had gotten to her feet and stepped down off the altar to follow him, her hands resting on her hips and her head cocked to one side. Her dark eyes sparkled in the firelight as a slow smile curved up one side of her face.

"Interesting," she said, and began slinking toward him around the stone.

Flammard was backed so close to the fire now he could smell his clothes beginning to burn, but the flames were licking comfortingly at his neck, and he didn't pull away.

Heedless of the fire, the woman walked right up to him—in her heels she was a good two inches taller than he, and when she thrust an arm into the flames to block his escape, the fire surged forward and welcomed her as well.

Smiling widely, the woman raised her other hand to cup his face, and while one part of Flammard screamed in protest and began putting up mental barricades, another, treacherous part of him sang for joy at contact with a kindred spirit.

For they were kindred. As close, in fact, as he was to Clara and Schiavona.

"Oh my dear boy," whispered the woman, her eyes blazing in the light of the fire. They were both well into it by now, and Flammard could feel a hard stone wall at his back, from which the flames sprung. "You're no ordinary Son of Fire," she went on, stroking his cheek with a finger. "You are like *me*." She smiled hugely, and reminded Flammard of nothing so much as a dragon. "You're a *first generation* Child of Fire. A child of Loki himself!"

So she could tell, Flammard thought despairingly, wishing he could disappear into the flames.

They made good time once they got onto 41. They were apparently counter-commute, if the solid wall of headlights in the northbound lanes was any indication, and they headed along the lakefront at a good clip, until—as they were nearing Millennium Park—Clara shouted from the back seat, "Take the next right!"

The next right took them away from the lake and toward the city, passing brightly lit skyscrapers on one side and a large, green park on the other. There was something like an amphitheater set up in the middle of this, and the road was choked with cars. Arcana slowed to a crawl, and in the back seat Clara growled impatiently.

"Easy there, sister," said Selene, who was driving. "We are, quite literally, *not* in Kansas anymore. I can't go any faster on account of the car in front of me. Now, it's one of those dinky convertibles, but if I were to run her over—like I'm sure Arcana *could*—the maggie up ahead *might* take exception, and that's a barrel full of monkeys we do not want to play with tonight."

"Maggie?" Jill whispered from the passenger seat.

Selene flicked her hand over the steering wheel to the police cruiser two cars ahead.

"I don't suppose . . . " Jill began hopefully.

"*No,*" both other women said at the same time.

Somewhere a light changed. The traffic crept forward. On their left, the park opened up and Jill glimpsed, through some trees, a flash of something huge that reflected the lights of the city and the lights of the park around it. Like a giant mirror. Ahead of them, above the traffic, a train hurtled between the buildings—some fifteen feet off the ground—its wheels flashing on the elevated rails, whining as it slowed to a stop.

They crossed an intersection, passed under the tracks, and Clara shouted "Stop! Here!"

Of course, Selene couldn't stop there, but she turned down the next alley and squeezed Arcana between a couple of dumpsters.

"Close enough?" she asked, twisting around in the driver's seat.

Clara was already kicking the back door open and sliding out of the truck, the sword held out in front of her as though it were a glowing brand. Jill and Selene were a little slower to follow—the latter retrieving her trench gun, Freddie, from under driver's seat before going after the other two.

Clara was pacing up and down the alley, the wavy sword held aloft, and sweeping the air in front of her like it was a torch and she needed to illuminate their surroundings.

Evening had crept over the city, and it was darker in the alley with the high buildings looming overhead and cutting out all but a thin strip of quickly fading blue. At the same time lights were coming on in the upper windows, and from a sunken door the steady thrum of a bass could be felt, reverberating up through the brick and concrete.

Clara led them past this door, to another whose window was shuttered and dark. Drawing aside the screen Clara tried the handle. It was locked.

"I got my picks," Selene began, but the next moment Clara had pushed the door open, the frame shattering as the deadbolt tore through the wood.

"Oookay," said Selene, glancing around nervously.

"What is this building?" Jill asked, automatically reaching for her phone.

"The building doesn't matter," Clara said. "He is not here, but this is the way to him." She disappeared through the door, and Jill didn't wait for Selene's impatient nod to follow her in.

The door led them to what appeared to be the back room of a bakery. Jill caught sight of shadowy rolling shelves stocked with bread and pastry boxes. There was a smell of flour and sugar, and a single light flickered in an adjacent room.

The place was deserted.

"Down," said Clara, and Jill instinctively ducked. But it was a description, not a warning, as she looked and saw Clara pointing to a set of stairs leading to the basement.

"Charming," said Selene, and reached into her pocket for the flashlight that clipped to Freddie's barrel.

Clara led them down, and in the dark Jill could pick out the wave-bladed sword, as it still glowed faintly. Behind her there was a quiet *snap* and then harsh light flooded them, throwing out long, dark shadows as Selene turned the flashlight on.

The stairs were concrete, chipped and cold, wet in places, and led down to a dusty cellar. Clara moved through the maze of exposed pipes and cardboard boxes, still with the sword held out in front of her, until they ran up against the back wall. Here she paused, and then began moving along it until they came to a large, metal cabinet. It had rusty corners, and one door was dented so the two didn't meet in the center, leaving an odd, grinning crack.

"Something tells me that ain't the way to Narnia," Selene said dryly.

Clara just grunted and, putting her shoulder to the cabinet, shoved it firmly out of the way. There was a horrendous scraping, and a sudden draft of cold, damp air blew out at them.

Moving the cabinet had revealed a dark, ragged opening in the concrete wall, like something had taken a bite out of the structure. Dark, wet wooden stairs were just visible down at least thirty feet when Selene cast her beam into the passage.

"I'll take point here, if it's all the same to you," she said. "Stay close behind me, Jill. This place has bad news written all over it."

* * *

It did not get bad right away. The woman had given him new clothes, as his own had been irreparably burned when he'd backed into the flaming wall. He'd had to hold them onto himself while the woman procured a pair of coarse, black cotton trousers and a sort of robe-like top with a hood—similar to the outfit her assistants wore—and offered them to him.

Flammard took the folded cloth, and as the woman made no move to give him any semblance of privacy he turned his own back and changed as quickly as possible. He pulled the robe on and tied it with the attached sash, being careful to cross it securely over his chest, and only then turned to face her.

"You *are* interesting," said the woman, her dark eyes glittering. "What is your name?"

"Flammard," said Flammard, resignedly. "Yours?" he asked.

A flicker of a smile. "You may call me Mistress," she said coyly. "Tell me, Flammard, surely you have figured out by now what is going on?"

"I have some ideas," Flammard allowed, narrowing his own eyes. He did not like the way Mistress was looking at him, like he was a dish of cooked veal and she was longing to eat him up. "You want . . . descendants of Loki. Specifically men."

"Sons of Fire," said Mistress, with a regal nod. "Like you."

Flammard sniffed. "And you want them for . . . sacrifices? You've got a piece of the eternal flame there. It could stand as a proxy for Loki. I can't imagine what you hope to achieve, though."

Mistress gave a crackling laugh. "It's true some of the sons have died. They were weak. But they allow me to capture more powerful specimens. I'm not *sacrificing* anyone, per se. I can't help it if they're not strong enough, or that the fire won't accept them. All I want is what, I think, all any child wants. I wish to meet my father."

The words rang in Flammard's ears like a gunshot, and he took a step back. "You want *what?*" he gasped.

"I wish to meet my father—your father," Mistress said, as if this should be the most obvious and reasonable thing in the world. "All my life I've had powers and abilities that set me apart from my fellow humans. It took me a long time to realize that it was because I was *not* fully human. You and I . . . we are also part . . . something else. Something ancient and powerful. So I gathered to myself other like-minded individuals, and we set about devising a way to meet the person responsible for our gifts."

Suddenly everything clicked into place, and Flammard felt his stomach drop.

"You're using the door in the fire," he whispered. Behind him, the burning wall flared as if in response. "The door in the eternal flame, the one that can open anywhere . . . "

"*Almost* anywhere," Mistress corrected him. "I can open it—that part was easy—but I cannot open it into Loki's prison. *That*," she said bitterly, "I eventually learned, can only be done by a *son* of fire. A *male* descendant of Loki." She sniffed disdainfully. "Patriarchal scumbags. But, that's where *you* come in," and she smiled, ever so sweetly. "The others didn't understand, but I think you do. You'll help me, won't you? You'll open the door?"

"*No,*" said Flammard before he could stop himself. It was a stupid thing to say, but he was horrified at the thought of opening up a door to *that* realm, the realm of gods and spirits and giant snakes that wrapped themselves around the world; the realm where a man's heart could be weighed against a feather—literally—and where, he knew, all the things that made him just a little more than other people came from. All the things he'd tried so hard to suppress.

"I mean, look," he said, backpedaling a little. "Have you thought about what it is you're doing? Never mind, of course you have. I mean, have you thought about *who it is* you're wanting to meet? This is *Loki* we're talking about. The god of mischief and fire. The one who killed Balder—for *fun*! He's not exactly the nicest guy, if you read the stories, and there's probably *lots* more we don't know about him. He could be a *lot* more trouble than you seem to think he'll be worth." *And*, he thought internally, *Mother never wanted me to meet him. That says more than anything.* "Besides," he said. "How do you even know he'll still be in prison? If he's managed to get out and seed all these descendants—not to mention you and me—chances are he won't be *there* anymore."

Mistress was watching him, her expression of scorn slowly fading into one of disappointment. Idly she went over to one of the tables and began pulling on a pair of elbow-length, black gloves.

"The exact circumstances of my conception are rather blurry," she said. "I don't imagine your mother ever described how *you* were conceived? No? I thought not. Loki is the cleverest of all the gods, don't you forget that. And his prison is the last solid recorded location I have for him. It is, at worst, a start; but I also believe it is my best chance. Now, I'll ask nicely one more time, since we are half-siblings: won't you *please* open the fire door to Loki's prison? Think of my request with a cherry on top, if it helps."

Flammard eyed the woman, who was now resting one hand casually on the lid of a clay jar. He gauged the distance between them, and the distance to the door, and made his choice.

He leapt, vaulting over the high-backed chair, and sprinted for the door. He heard Mistress shout something behind him, and suddenly his way was blocked by a large man in a dark, hooded cape. Flammard ducked the first reaching arm, imagined himself like a slippery fish or snake, and dove for the gap between the man and the wall.

He would have made it, too, had not something cold and clammy closed around his ankle, and he felt himself jerked roughly into his proper size and weight. He tripped, fell hard on the stone floor, and the pain of the impact was more immediate and intense than anything he'd ever experienced. It rendered him immobile as large hands closed around his shoulders and pulled him back into the room, and even after the searing pain had subsided and he'd caught his breath, he found to his astonishment and horror that he could *no longer cheat*.

"According to some texts," came Mistress's voice, sounding triumphant and a little smug. "Loki was restrained, in his prison, beneath the earth, by the guts of his son. Well, one of his sons. Now, you might say this could be a result of a mistranslation somewhere along the centuries. It turns out, however, that it is quite likely *true*. Because, and this is a fact that took me *ages* to find out, the lineage of Loki is adversely affected by the blood of its kin—and *especially* by their sinews and intestines. Put Loki in regular chains, he'd break them in an instant. Tie him up in the entrails of his child, and poof! Welcome to your eternity of snake venom!"

Flammard tried to curse, but it came out as a groan. He felt like he'd chipped a tooth, and there was blood in his mouth from where he'd bitten his cheek in the fall.

"Don't worry," Mistress said as he was carried bodily over to the stone. The stone that did not *belong* here. The stone from the spirit world. "I'll loosen them up enough so you can open the door, just as soon as we have you properly bound."

No, no, no, no, *no,* Flammard thought, and the thought trailed into verbal speech as he was laid across it, and another cold length of slimy organ used to secure each wrist to one of the iron rings on either side. He tried to thrash, to kick, and found his feet caught and a frightening twinge in his elbow.

"You can't force me," he remarked, leaning his head back against the cool stone and staring up at the ceiling.

"True," said Mistress's voice from somewhere around his chest. He felt her shadow move coolly across him, and realized she must be standing between him and the fire.

He considered craning his head down to look at her but instead kept staring up at the ceiling and tested his restraints. They held with surprising strength.

He was spread out across the stone and elevated so that he had to stand on tiptoe if his feet were to support any of his weight. His jaw ached. It was remarkably uncomfortable.

There was a tickle at his collarbone as someone fiddled with his robes, and that caused his head to snap up. Mistress had a paintbrush in one hand and was carefully parting his robes with her other, nails dragging lightly over his skin.

"Now, now, don't look so worried," she began, seeing the look of horror on his face. "*This* part won't hurt at all . . . unless you're ticklish. In which case you'll just have to lie back and think of . . . oh . . . "

Mistress had succeeded in pulling open the folds of Flammard's robe so that his entire upper torso was exposed, and she was staring at it with such a look of surprised confusion that it would have been quite funny, except that Flammard knew *this* was where things got *really* bad.

* * *

The stairs ended in a dirt-covered stone floor, and Selene stopped at the bottom of them, shutting off her light. Jill flattened herself to one wall, fearful of Clara and the unsheathed sword she carried. It was then she noticed that things were not as dark as they should have been: a faint, warm glow was coming from the rippling sword. Not enough to light their way, but enough to illuminate its bearer, whose face was pinched in concentration.

"Heard something," Selene whispered after a moment. "Think we better go silent for now . . . if we can't go completely dark," she added, with a sour look at the glowing sword.

"We're getting close," Clara said defensively.

"Yeah," said Selene. "I figured."

They felt their way forward from there on out, and as the tunnel widened Clara moved to walk at Jill's side, holding the sword pointed downward so as not to accidentally stab Selene in the back.

Several paces on, Jill heard what must have originally alerted Selene: a snatch of conversation, distant and broken, and now a low sound of someone moaning.

Beside her, Jill felt Clara stiffen, then relax.

"Not him," she whispered.

The passage branched before them, and after a moment where Clara swung the sword like a pendulum between the two, she indicated the right-hand passage. They took it, and after that the sounds grew faint again.

"Jill," Selene said out of the dark in front of them. "Just so's you know, this is probably gonna get ugly. When it does, I want you to drop and run."

"What if I can do something to help?" Jill asked.

"Only do that if it's safe," Selene warned. "Maybe think of helping *yourself* first, okay?"

Jill knew better than to argue.

"Okay," she said.

* * *

Mistress was laughing. Which was, on the whole, not the worst reaction Flammard had ever experienced. There was a manic edge to it, however, that made his hackles prickle and his heart pound. Someone who laughed like that was definitely capable of making things *very* unpleasant for him.

"I should have known," Mistress let out in a long wail. "I should have *knooooown.* . . . Why, it's obvious to look at you, once you actually *look.*" She prodded him with one nailed finger, just above the faded brown scar on his left side, and he flinched. "We're *even more alike* than I first thought," she said, grinning widely. Bringing her painted lips up to his ear, she hissed with bitter triumph: *"Sister."*

Flammard weighed the benefit of explaining what being transgender *actually was* against his continued chances of survival, and settled on rolling his head to one side so he could glare at the woman, and say, *"Not* your sister," through gritted teeth.

"Puh," said Mistress, and flicked his cheek. It stung, but not as much as her next words. "You can call yourself whatever you like, I don't care. It doesn't change *what you are* at the most fundamental level. On the level that counts for *this.*" She gestured at the burning wall.

And . . . yes, there was the rage, Flammard noted with detached interest. There was the indignation, the fury, and behind it all, a little bit of despair. And now . . .

. . . now Mistress was unhooking his arms from the iron rings, pulling him off the stone, binding his hands behind him, and giving him a shove toward the corner.

Flammard, dizzy and a little bit nauseous, took two steps and felt his legs give out from under him.

Time to take new stock, he thought dully. *Good bit: not on the stone any more. Bad bits: entrails seem to be sapping physical strength as well as magic strength. Emotions not as strong as they should be.* Unless that was a result of the stress. It was a phenomenon Flammard had noticed before, and even actively practiced in order to remain calm with difficult patients. Now, however, he had a feeling that only a sweeping, consuming emotion like hate or rage could cause him to draw up the energy he needed to break free, and while he understood he had a perfectly good reason to get angry, he simply couldn't muster up the energy. Which he needed to do, and soon.

The realization was enough to panic him, except he seemed unable to do even that. Fear and pain dulled as he pushed himself up and rolled over so he could look up at Mistress, who was standing by the stone looking stormy and disappointed.

Then, to Flammard's amazement, she gave a little sigh and her anger seemed to dissipate. "Well, of all the setbacks I've experienced this is the most . . . *twenty-first century*," she remarked with dry resignation. "Your organs might still be useful—worth a try considering you're still a *child* of Loki. But there's no hurry. I had one other I meant to try tonight . . . "

She was interrupted by the sudden appearance of two disheveled men in dark robes. They had someone held limply between them, and they were panting.

"Forgive the delay, Mistress," one of them gasped. By his voice, Flammard recognized him as one of the men who'd managed the room full of prisoners. There were more than two, total, he now realized, taking in the additional robed figures who had caught him earlier, now standing to either side of the door.

"What?" snapped Mistress.

"I don't know how they did it, but they were out of their cages. Took us a while to get them all rounded up again."

"They got *out?*" Mistress said, and she turned on Flammard, one eyebrow arched accusingly.

Flammard decided he didn't have the energy to answer that question, so he just shrugged carelessly.

"Did any get away?" Mistress asked.

"No, Mistress," came the dutiful reply. "We got them all. Though this one gave us the most trouble." So speaking the pair moved further into the room, and dropped the body they had been carrying on the floor.

It was Marcus, and he groaned softly as he curled onto his side. One wide eye darted around the room, lingered apprehensively on Mistress, then settled on Flammard.

"Hey, Leonard," he croaked.

"Hey," said Flammard.

"Sorry," the man mumbled. "Tried my best."

"Wish I'd done the same," Flammard said, feeling the bitterness like a vague cloud around his throat. If he'd led the men out when he had the chance . . . but even the regret was muted now.

Flammard was beginning to feel lightheaded as Mistress marched over and inspected Marcus critically.

"Yes, I suppose you'll do," she said briskly. "I have the patience for one more attempt tonight. And if this doesn't work I'm taking out my disappointment on *her*." She flicked a glance at Flammard, and then moved over to the table with the clay jars. Clay jars full of entrails.

"Marcus," Flammard said, forcing himself to focus. "Can you run?"

"Nggh," said Marcus. "Knee's all jacked. Can't even walk."

"Okay . . . " Flammard groped, mentally, for the desperation he needed in order to keep talking. "Look, whatever she asks you to do . . . just do it, okay? If you can, you probably won't even die."

Marcus rolled an eye at Flammard. "And if I don't? Or can't?"

Flammard thought of the screams, and felt disgust roiling in his stomach—but it was far, far below him, like a storm in a valley and he was stranded on an exposed mountaintop. "Definitely you die. And badly. Just . . . "

Mistress was coming back, swinging a length of wet intestine between her gloved hands. Briskly she cast a loop around Marcus's neck, and the poor man cried out.

Flammard watched in muted horror as Marcus was hoisted to his feet and marched—and he nearly had to hop to keep the weight off his right leg—over to the stone. His hands and arms were secured in the same manner Flammard's had been, though he was tall enough that he could rest his weight fully on his one good leg.

The men in robes retreated to the sides of the room, well away from the fire, and Flammard wondered randomly if they were even aware of their actions. Mistress had said they were also Sons of Fire, but perhaps they were ordinary men she had enchanted—just as she had attempted to enchant him.

Mistress returned, a small knife in one hand, and briskly cut Marcus out of his t-shirt.

"What the *hell*—?" Marcus began, then yelped as the woman took a brush, dripping in bright red paint, and started applying it to his naked chest.

"No unpleasant surprises *this* time," she said, glancing scathingly at Flammard.

Flammard frowned, seeing the figure she was painting take shape.

"But that's a *binding* rune," he said, dumbly.

"Of *course* it is," Mistress said. "I can't keep them wrapped up in entrails while they try to open the fire gate, can I? It stops *all* their powers, you know."

"I'm getting that," Flammard said.

"Right, now then, what's your name, son?" Mistress asked, giving Marcus a sharp pat on the cheek.

Marcus blinked down at her. "M-Marcus," he gasped. "Lady, I don't know what'chu think you're doing, but—"

"Hush," said Mistress, putting a finger to her lips. She stretched the end of the word out so it became a long, soft, "Shh-hhhh . . . " She tapped Marcus lightly on the nose. "Marcus, I'm going to take these nasty things off you, so you'll be in full possession of your powers, and you're going to open a door in that wall over there. The one that's on fire. Can you do that for me?"

Marcus gaped at her. Then his gaze flicked to Flammard, and understanding dawned in his eyes.

"Lady, I don't know how the hell I'm gonna do that," he said. "But you believe me, I'll *try.*"

Mistress smiled briefly at him. "*Good* boy," she said. "Now, concentrate on the *door.* It's already there, you see. All you have to do is *open* it."

Mistress yanked sharply on the length of intestine that secured Marcus's left hand, pulling it away, and Flammard saw his eyes widen in horror as he realized his arm was still stuck there.

Mistress only smiled, and removed the entails from his right hand, and the ones still draped around his neck. She coiled them in her hands, like someone winding a length of rope, and stepped back. Then, with a grand flourish, she tossed them into the fire.

As soon as the guts hit the wall of flames it exploded outward, the flames reaching into the room, washing over Flammard and obscuring his view. He caught a glimpse of Marcus's horrified face, mouth open, and a moment later heard the scream.

Then the fire banked, receded, and Flammard blinked down at himself to find his clothes steaming faintly, but unburnt. The guts securing his wrist smelled singed, but they still held when he tested them. The effort nearly made him throw up.

Then he raised his head and saw that a part of the fire had not receded. It was reaching for Marcus, gladly, and Marcus was doing his best to flatten himself against the rock.

The fire did not recognize him, Flammard realized dully. He had more power than any of the others, save himself and Mistress, but he was at least three generations removed from anything non-human. He might be able to open the gate, but he could not survive the fire.

"Marcus!" Flammard shouted. "Marcus, you have to open the gate!"

"What *gate?*" Marcus shrieked.

"The one in the fire. You can't *see* it. You'll *feel* it." He swallowed, gathering strength, before going on. "Marcus," Flammard said, desperately. "Marcus, have you ever had any time in your life where something *crazy* and *inexplicable* happened to you? Some *wild* coincidence that was too good to be true, but *was?* If you have, go back to that time. Go back, remember whatever *wild, mad energy* possessed you, and use it to *open that gate!*"

Marcus stopped screaming abruptly. His eyes were so wide the whites were showing all the way around his dark irises, and his eyebrows were encroaching on his ginger hairline. He blinked once, twice, and then shouted something.

It was not a scream. It was a wholly different sound. It was direct. It had *purpose.* It was like no word or words that Flammard had ever heard before, but it resonated in his body and he felt an answering hum from within him, somewhere around his ribcage. Somewhere deep inside him, he knew those words, and from the triumphant expression on Mistress's face, she knew them too.

The fire was blown back suddenly, letting out a soft *whoomphing* noise, and retreated to burn in a narrow line around the edges of the wall.

In its wake it left, not bare stone, but a dark, empty void that breathed out a foul smell like wet, decaying plant matter, and a cold draft that made Flammard shiver.

With a faint cry Marcus collapsed to the ground, his head flopping limply onto his arms, and lay still.

There was an astonished murmur from the hooded men, and they shuffled hopefully forward.

"No!" shouted Mistress, stepping up over Marcus's limp form. "You shall not enter his prison. I alone will journey there, and I will bring our father back to us."

Boots clicking on the stone, she stepped forward through the door that had opened in the fire, gathering a piece of flame into one hand and raising it high above her head.

With all the attention focused on her, Flammard managed to scoot himself backward so his arms were planted firmly in the little strip of flame in the corner, and there he waited while he felt the entrails that bound him blacken, smoke, and finally give out entirely.

When Mistress had disappeared into the darkness he struggled to his feet, casting the horrible things away, and into the full swell of all his powers—and emotions. Behind him, he felt the fire flare up in sympathy.

His first thought was to close the gate—Mistress and Loki, if he was indeed still in prison, certainly deserved each other—but then he caught sight of Marcus, and all his training took over.

Unthinkingly, he moved for the fallen man.

That jerked the hooded men out of their daze, and as one they came for him.

There was a strangled cry from the back of the room—one of both surprise and pain—and a black-robed body went hurtling through the air, smacked up against the rock, and fell to the ground.

Flammard raised his eyes, and thought for a moment he was dreaming.

Claymore was standing in the doorway, and in her hand was not Bellatrix, but Feuermann, and she held him blade down, his blade glowing white-hot.

The men were rallying, recognizing the new threat. Claymore swung her arm meaningfully.

"Flammard!" she shouted, and at her voice Flammard realized this was, in fact, no dream. He felt a mad grin spreading across his face.

"To you!" Claymore shouted, and flung the sword, hilt first, across the room.

It was a long way to throw a sword, but Claymore had always been freakishly strong—even for their extraordinary family—and the sword arced true, diving gracefully toward Flammard like an eagle returning to its handler.

Midway its blade burst into flame, causing the robed men to duck and roll, as it fell like a comet toward him.

Flammard hardly had to reach; just raised his right hand, palm open, and felt it meet the smooth hilt of Feuermann. With the contact the last of the nausea and light-headedness left him. He felt whole and grounded, yet weightless at the same time. He was the fire in the sword and the wall, and the material world was a thin film that he could push around with the merest nudge of his mind.

He breathed out, long and slow, and the fire kissed his breath and danced around his face.

The long, rectangular room was bright and hot and alive with moving bodies. Jill hung back in the doorway and let Clara and Selene dive into the fray. She heard Clara shout something and toss the sword—which caught fire in midair—to a small, red-haired man who was crouched by the gaping black opening ringed in fire. He caught it, amazingly, and stood up. He was thin in a spare, sinewy sort of way, dressed in a dark robe that had been pushed off his shoulders and hung around his waist. He had two old, curving scars, one under each lean pectoral muscle, and his pale skin was thickly freckled.

Standing up with the sword, he seemed somehow to enlarge—though he remained the same size—his presence filled that end of the room, and the hooded men who had been approaching him turned instead to Clara.

Clara, who had drawn her own sword and was swinging at them lustily. Jill caught a glimpse of her face and was surprised to see, instead of her usual stoic blankness, an expression alight with excitement and anger. Fury, almost. She lashed out at the men, and each one she struck fell and did not rise again. Selene snuck out in her wake, pulling back the hoods of the fallen men, revealing a mottled group of unconscious humans.

"Clara," she said sharply. "Clara, hold up a second!"

But Clara did not hear. She'd caught the last man by the collar of his cloak and held him, her sword raised. It gleamed in the light of the fire, but there was something dark and red dripping down its length.

"*Claymore, hold! They are human!*" the red-headed man with the flaming sword—Flammard, Jill guessed—shouted.

He had a surprisingly high voice for a man, very much like Clara's, but it rang out through the chamber and reverberated in Jill's ears.

Clara paused. The man under her hand struggled uselessly against her iron grip.

"Are you sure?" she asked.

"More human than me," Flammard said gently. "Thank you, Clara, you've done enough."

Almost regretfully, Clara lowered her arm, forcing the hooded man to his knees. Using the hilt of her sword she knocked back his hood, revealing a white, terrified face with a bloody nose.

"Are you going to give me trouble?" she asked him.

The man shook his head.

"Here, Clara, I'll take him," Selene said. She'd holstered her gun and deftly took the fabric of the man's robe and twisted it behind him so his hands were pinned together. She gave Flammard an odd look, and then turned away quickly. Too quickly. Jill wondered if she was missing something.

"Claymore, help me with him," Flammard was saying. He'd put his sword—no longer flaming—aside, and was kneeling on the ground.

Daring to creep into the room, Jill saw he was referring to another man, a large one with African-American features and improbably red hair. He'd been stripped to his waist, rather like

Flammard, and was lying in a heap on the far side of a strange, grayish stone.

"We need to get him away from the stone," Flammard was saying as Jill approached. "Be careful of his right knee—I think it's sprained."

"What happened?" Jill asked as Clara, after sheathing her sword, took the man gently under the armpits and dragged him slowly around the stone, away from the gaping black hole.

Flammard looked up at her, and Jill found herself staring into vibrant hazel eyes that seemed to catch the light of the fire— even though he faced away from the fire that burned along the wall. There was something about his chin and the expression on his face that reminded her of Clara, but other than that they looked nothing alike.

"They made him open the gate," he said, as if this would explain everything. "He's probably been burned, too. Lay him down here, Claymore—mind his head!"

For Clara had nearly dropped the man in her hurry to get up and look around.

"Is that *the* gate?" she asked.

"*Yes*," said Flammard. "The woman responsible for this mess just crossed over. We'll worry about her in a minute—I have to get him stabilized."

Clara gave a frustrated grunt and turned to Selene, who was keeping herself busy checking on the robed men and not looking at Flammard. What *was* going on there?

"Selene, it's not over yet!" Clara shouted, drawing her sword and striding toward the dark hole—which, now Jill thought about it, hurt a little to look at and breathed out damp, fetid air.

Jill saw Selene turn to follow Clara, and was about to trail after them both, when she was distracted by the clatter as Flammard tossed his sword away and cursed softly.

Looking down, she saw he was removing his hand from the unconscious man's face, while the other gripped frantically at his upper arm.

"No pulse?" Jill asked, remembering her first-aid training.

"Or breath," Flammard said and began arranging the man so he was lying flat on his back.

Jill, who knew what came next, abandoned any thought of following Clara and Selene, and knelt down next to Flammard.

"I know CPR," she offered.

"Hopefully we won't need that," Flammard said, gently straightening the man's head, pushing the man's chin down to open his mouth, and then placing one hand on either side of his lower jaw and pulling forward to open the airway.

And then he paused. He got a strange, inward sort of look, and then he leaned in, placing one hand gently on the man's chest, took a short breath, then sealed his lips around the open, slack mouth, and breathed out.

Jill saw the chest rise, faintly, and then Flammard was sitting up. He exhaled, inhaled, and then went back down.

Another breath, and a longer one this time. Jill could see the muscles on Flammard's back—also freckled—straining under the skin.

There was an odd kind of spark in the air when Flammard sat up this time. The fire on the wall flared, and Jill felt a heat begin to rise from the man on the ground.

"Marcus," Flammard said, quietly and intently. Then, a little louder, "*Marcus.*"

The man on the ground drew in a weak breath, hoarse and wheezing, then blinked his eyes. These were dark brown, but for a moment they too held the same kind of fire as Flammard's. Then the light faded, and it was a perfectly ordinary—if somewhat distressed—face that was gazing up at Flammard and Jill.

"What . . . " he began, and coughed.

"Hello, Marcus," Flammard said. "Try to relax. I'm here to take care of you. You might be feeling some acute nausea, so I'm going to roll you onto your side, okay? Tell me if this hurts your knee—or anything else. Help me lift his shoulder please, ma'am."

Working together they got Marcus, who was almost as big as Clara, over on his side, with his good leg bent to provide a brace so he wouldn't roll all the way onto his face.

"You don't seem badly burned," Flammard was saying. "So I'm going to cover you with my robe. You'll be going into shock soon, if you're not already. Just stay awake, and stay with me, okay?"

"Whah the *hell* happened, L'nard?" Marcus mumbled.

"You did great, Marcus," Flammard said, and he really seemed to mean it. "You opened the gate. Everything's going to be fine now, just try to relax."

"*What gate?*" Jill hissed.

Flammard barely glanced at her, and he smiled sadly.

"Go ask Claymore," he said. "Oh, and don't touch that stone, if you can help it."

Jill rose and wandered off through the bodies, some of which were beginning to shiver and moan. Per Flammard's instructions she gave the strange, gray rock a wide berth, and came around to the other side to find Clara and Selene standing at the lip of the hole, both with their weapons out, and Selene casting her flashlight into the dark beyond.

"*What,*" demanded Jill, "is going on here?"

Clara didn't move, but Selene spared her a short grin.

"You'll like this one, boss. It's a transdimensional gate. A big one, too. According to Clara, it leads somewhere *you* might have heard of."

Jill frowned into the dark. Selene's flashlight barely illuminated the first ten feet, and all she could see was a field of wet, lumpy rocks—similar to the one in the room behind her—with green slime clinging to the cracks between them. It was cold, and smelled of decaying water plants.

"According to Norse mythology," Selene said, "Loki, the god of fire and mischief, killed Balder, who was the favorite son of Odin and the god of purity and light and all that whaffery. Anyway, this pissed Odin off, so he had Loki chained to a rock in a cavern under the earth, with a serpent to drip venom on him, for the rest of time. Or until Ragnarök."

"I know what happened to Loki," Jill sighed. "Didn't he also have his wife there to catch the snake's venom?"

Selene nodded. "That's not so important now. The important thing is, somehow, someone's managed to open a transdimensional gate to *that* place. Loki's prison. *There.*" She jerked her head at the hole.

"Wait," said Jill. "So . . . *Loki's* in there?"

"Not necessarily," said Clara. "There are . . . conflicting records as to what happened next."

"Stories, you mean," Jill said. "There are *lots* of stories about Loki."

"Those too," said Clara. "They can influence people like him."

"*Someone's* in there," Selene said, cutting off Jill's next question.

Sure enough, there was a sound from beyond the gate. A faint voice, and fainter than that, a slick, sliding sound. Like scales over wet rocks.

"Oh no . . . " said Selene, and then there was a high, anguished scream.

Fire flared briefly in the dark, and by its light they saw the silhouette of something huge and snake-like. It was writhing down from the ceiling of the place, where scaly coils gleamed in the light of the fire. A shadow of a woman stood up from the rocky floor, one arm thrust out as if to ward the serpent off. It was undeterred. The long neck lunged, a huge mouth opened, and the scream cut off in a startled gasp.

There was a rumbling from within the cave.

"Get behind me!" Selene shouted, grabbing Clara's elbow and pulling ineffectually. "Jill, *get out of here!*"

All of a sudden a face appeared, lit faintly from all sides by the fire that ringed the portal. It was a wide, flat face, with a blunt, scaled snout and two weeping, yellow eyes. Venom sacks bulged menacingly at the back of its head, and it was currently in the middle of swallowing someone. Jill caught a glimpse of a flailing arm and a tangle of dark red hair, before Selene knocked her away.

"*BEHIND ME, CLARA!*" she roared, and fired at the giant snake.

She hit it squarely in its right eye. Jill saw the spurt of vibrant, red blood, and the snake withdrew, hissing.

Not before Clara, stepping boldly over the fire, reached up and grabbed the dangling arm.

The snake recoiled. Clara skidded a few feet, then caught a foothold and stood fast. Between the two of them, the body emerged from the snake's mouth and flopped to the ground. Clara grabbed it roughly by the shoulders and began dragging it—*her,* it was a woman—over the threshold and into the room, while Selene covered her with more shots from her gun.

No sooner had Clara set her burden down then the snake struck again. This time its head shot past Selene and into the room, trailing a length of thick neck covered in glistening yellow-brown scales. Its open mouth struck upon the gray stone, caught it, and crushed it.

For a moment the head retreated back into the cave, spitting chunks of rock, and then it returned.

This time, however, Selene and Clara were ready for it.

Selene shot it again, in the same place as before. And again. And again.

At the same time, Clara swung up and lodged her sword in its throat.

The snake hissed and flailed; its right eye was a pulpy red mess, and Clara's sword, when it was yanked from its neck, left a deep wound that began to bleed profusely.

The snake flailed, hitting against the edges of the portal and once nearly smashing into Jill. But it was a retreating flail, and soon the snake was once more a vague shape in the darkness behind the flames, and then it was only an anguished hissing in the shadows, and then it was nothing at all.

In the wreckage of the room, Selene and Clara stood, the former calmly reloading her gun, the latter breathing heavily. Between them on the floor the crumpled, wet remains of what had been a glamorous woman in a black dress and boots lay in a bleeding heap.

"Flammard!" Clara called, sounding a little winded. "We need you!"

Flammard looked up from where he was crouched protectively over Marcus. "I can't leave him!" he shouted back.

Clara shot him a distressed look. "We need to close the gate, Flammard. The serpent nearly got *out*. You know I'm useless at these things—*please.*"

Flammard looked torn. His searching eyes landed on Jill, and he gazed at her imploringly.

Taking pity on him, Jill picked her way through the debris and fallen bodies—she tried not to think too hard about whether they were corpses or not—and resumed her position at Marcus's side.

"I'll watch him," she said. "You go do . . . go close the gate."

Flammard picked up his sword and used it as a cane to push himself to his feet. Visibly shaking, he staggered over to Clara and Selene.

There was a dull moaning sound, and the crumpled heap on the floor shivered. Jill had to suppress a swell of bile in her throat as she realized the woman must still be alive.

"You . . . cannot close the gate. It is opened, and must remain, so that our father may come into this world."

"Wasn't he there, tied to the stone?" Flammard asked, a note of sarcasm in his voice Jill did not wholly understand.

"No . . . " admitted the woman on the floor. *"He has gone . . . "*

"I thought he might have," said Flammard. "Then I don't think he'll mind me sealing off his prison once and for all."

This was greeted with a broken-sounding laugh that was part gurgle.

"You cannot close the gate. Just as I could not open it." Now there was a note of bitter triumph in the wrecked voice. *"Only a male descendant of Loki may open or close that gate. And you are no man!"*

Flammard stilled and Selene looked aside awkwardly, but Clara bristled in rage.

"He is my *brother,*" she hissed, going down on one knee so she could hold the edge of her sword to what had been the woman's throat. "You will show him the respect he deserves."

"What's this . . . another sister? No . . . no you are not a Child of Fire. You are . . . something else. A half-sister, then. What will you do, knight errant? You cannot kill me, for I am already dead; the serpent saw to that."

"Then why are you still here?" Flammard asked. He sounded more annoyed than anything.

"Our bodies die . . . our spirits go on."

"Yes, so I've heard," said Flammard tiredly. "So *go on* somewhere else."

"Or you will do what? You don't have the strength to banish me, and your half-sister has not the skill to—"

"I can do *this!*" Clara shouted, throwing aside her sword. She grasped the body firmly with both hands and lifted it clean off the floor. Raising it above her head she rocked back on one foot, and then hurled it over the threshold and into the darkness. There was a wet, messy-sounding *thud* and then silence. Jill found she had to look away.

"That was unnecessary," Flammard said mildly.

"I didn't like her," Clara responded.

"Neither did I," Selene agreed. "She the one running this mess?"

"She was," Flammard said.

Selene sniffed. When Jill looked up, she found Selene was staring intently at the flames. She seemed to have a hard time looking at Flammard. "Hate to say it," she said after a while. "But she did sort of have a point. These gender-specific things are stupid as hell, but they're sort of anal about their requirements and . . . well . . . you're not exactly a . . . a . . . "

She trailed off. Clara had gone bristly again.

" . . . you might not be man enough for *it*," Selene finished cautiously. "Just . . . you know, *in this case*. Is all I'm sayin'."

Jill blinked. Her brain was processing many things at once, and only now were certain facts gelling into a firmer under-standing.

Looking at Flammard, at the smooth shape of his lean body, at his graceful profile and small, nimble hands—not to mention the old scars on his chest—suddenly the reason for Lalai's trou-ble with the police and the feeling that she was hiding some-thing, and Selene's odd behavior, became immediately clear.

And then the words of the dead woman came back to her and swept that realization aside.

"Wait, wait, *wait*," said Jill, breaking the tense moment. "*You're* a descendant of *Loki?*"

Flammard half turned to glance at her, and in the mixed light of the fire his face took on a strange quality: both ageless and genderless, it was both male and female, young and old. But mostly, it looked tired.

"You could say that," he said. "I'm his son."

Jill felt her brows knotting as she stared at the three of them.

"Oh, you people!" she cried. "You guys *have* read those sto-ries about Loki, right? I mean, if *anyone* is *not* going to have *any problems* with having a transgender child it's going to be *Loki!* So go—go *on!* I can stand not taking samples this time since that snake looks even worse than a vampire. *Go on!*" She flapped her hand at Flammard.

Flammard didn't move at once. He was looking at Jill with a sort of wonder. Then he shook himself and turned back to Clara and Selene.

"Give me space—a lot of space," he said. "I don't want anyone else getting hurt."

Silently, Selene fell back to Jill and Marcus, while Clara, after Flammard jerked his head at her, retreated a few steps, retrieving her own sword and holding it, point down, in front of her.

Flammard shrugged and turned back to the gaping hole. With an effort he raised his own sword. He seemed suddenly very small, and very delicate, and very, very tired.

The man named Flammard Nordstern faced the open gate and raised his sword. Feuermann rested in his hand like a warm assurance, and at this point that was all that he had going for him. Days of drugged sleep and the aftershocks of the magical binding and the stress in general had sapped him of all but his most dire supply of emergency energy.

And yet he needed to do this. For Claymore—because she was right and only he could—but also for Lalai, and the life he had built for himself. The life *he* wanted. And, also, a not insignificant part of him wanted to prove Mistress wrong.

Flammard was a little surprised at how certain he was that Mistress *was* wrong—Claymore's partner had made a good point, even if it had hurt. Yet he knew, deep in the core of his bones, that this was not only his power, but his right.

Taking a deep breath he opened all the little gates within himself, all the gates he so carefully kept closed most of the time. It was slow going, as some of them seemed to have fused shut, and by the time he had finished he was shaking. Not from fatigue, not anymore, but from the effort needed to hold all that energy in.

The fire felt it too, and rose up to greet him, as it had Marcus. But unlike Marcus, it found Flammard a friend, and he let out a sigh of relief as he felt the warm flames embrace him.

He reached out—Feuermann's blade began to glow—and drew in the edges of the door, and began to drag them shut.

It was hard going. The door did not want to be closed. It had been closed for a long time and now it was finally open it wanted to stay that way. More so, it wanted to rip wide, tear a channel between the worlds. Flammard shuddered at the thought of what might flow through that channel, and pulled harder.

Both of his hands were on Feuermann's hilt now, and he noticed only vaguely when his hair caught fire. Not ignited by the flames caressing him, but of its own accord.

We are our swords, he thought to himself with an inner shrug. And his sword was Feuermann, the fireman.

Slowly, slowly, the door shut. Flammard held it there, feeling the seams knit together, sealing it thoroughly, until not even he could tell where the handle of the door was. Then he took a step back, and surveyed the wall—which was complete once more, covered in flames as before.

It would not do to leave it like this, he realized. So, almost regretfully, he coaxed the eternal flame out of the wall and onto his sword, and then, weeping for the waste, he pushed the fire down, pulled it in, and extinguished its physical presence.

As the fire died, the strength in his arms abruptly gave out, and he heard a *clang* as Feuermann's blade hit the floor, cold as stone now. His hair went out, and darkness surged in around them—the only light coming from an electric flashlight someone had thoughtfully turned on and pointed at the ceiling.

A dull chill spread up his body, and utterly spent, Flammard felt himself collapsing forward, powerless to stop his own fall.

Only he never met the hard floor. Instead he was caught by strong, steady hands, warm under their soft, leather gloves. They lowered him gently, lifted Feuermann from his own lax hands, and Flammard felt himself pressed into a huge, welcoming body. Welcoming, even though it had odd poky bits. Claymore still wore the armor he'd made her. That made him smile.

The presence of the body retreated briefly, and then he felt the weight of a jacket being wrapped around his naked shoulders. It soothed the aching chill, and Flammard breathed in the familiar smell of clean leather and sweat that permeated everything Claymore owned.

He leaned his head forward and found her chest. Turning his face sideways he rested it there and took a deep breath.

"Claymore?" he mumbled.

"I'm here," came the immediate reply.

"'M tired, Claymore," he said. "Take me home."

Strong arms passed around him and held him. He closed his eyes.

Clara insisted on carrying Flammard back up to the surface, which left Jill and Selene to handle Marcus. He was marginally more alert now, but that didn't make things any easier.

"We can't just . . . leave," he groaned, when Jill explained to him what was happening. "There're *others*. They got put back in the cells. We can't . . . "

"We'll come back for them," Selene assured him. She had been searching the robes of an unconscious man, and stood up holding a folded piece of paper. Shining her light on it, she gave a little cry of satisfaction.

"Clara, hold up. I found us a faster way out."

It was a map, Jill realized. It was not such a surprise, now she thought about it. Just because you worked in an underground labyrinth didn't mean you could automatically find your way around.

"I can walk," Marcus said when they tried to get him up. "Y'ladies shouldn't haf'ta carry me."

"Don't give me any of that, son," Selene told him sharply, and had Jill get on his uninjured side. Selene took the other, and hoisted one arm over her shoulders, while Jill did the same. Like that they were able to walk him out of the room, while Selene held her flashlight between her teeth to light the way.

They went first, since Selene had the map, and Clara followed, carrying Flammard bridal style. The way they took this time was indeed shorter but involved a lot more stairs. That slowed them down, and every time they stopped to rest, Jill worried that more hooded, angry men would appear out of the darkness and attack them.

Nothing came of that, however, and the corridors and stairways were silent.

"Who built this place?" Jill asked, once.

"Probably lots of people, over the years," Selene huffed next to her. No one had the breath for anything more, after that.

The stairs ended abruptly in a flat, stone ceiling.

"Oh, no," Jill said, imagining them having to retrace their footsteps, and Marcus moaned.

"Let me," said Clara, laying Flammard carefully on the steps and squeezing past them. She felt all around the seam of the stone panel, tracing the lines with her fingers, and then abruptly slammed her fists into it. Once, twice, three times. A little shower of mortar fell from the ceiling, but the stone didn't move.

Undeterred, Clara spread both her hands flat across the stone, planted her feet firmly, and *pushed.*

The slab of rock came free, and Clara slid it aside, letting in a confusion of yellow light and the sound of people talking.

At first Jill thought they were speaking gibberish, until she realized she was listening to overlapping conversations in several different languages.

"Here," Clara said, offering her arm to Selene.

Selene came and gave Clara her knee, equestrian style, and Clara boosted her up through the hole. Then she did the same to Jill, who found herself thrust into a loud, glittering world— made even more confusing by the myriad reflections whirling around her.

She was sitting on dry pavement, and Selene was standing over her. Over them arched a swooping, curving ceiling made of mirrors, and around them was a confused gaggle of tourists in bright clothing. The mirrors came down to the ground on either side, but in front of her Jill could look out, and there she could see the familiar Chicago skyline, and the orange-gray night sky above it. The air was cool and fresh, and smelled faintly of wet grass.

Ignoring the crowd gathering around them, they both reached in and helped drag first Marcus, and then Flammard up out of the hole. At last, Clara hoisted herself out and crouched, glaring around at their audience as she carefully slid the lid back over the hole. Not entirely, so you could still see where it was, but enough so that someone couldn't accidentally fall in.

"Are you all right?" a concerned voice asked in earnest, if heavily accented English.

Jill looked from Clara to Selene, to the two prostrate men.

"Now?" she asked Selene. "*Now* can we call 911?"

They did, and Jill waited with Marcus on some nearby benches while Selene went to get Arcana. From there she could see the confusing mirrors were actually a gigantic, bean-shaped sculpture, and she realized they had come up in the middle of Millennium Park.

Clara, waiting a few yards away, still with Flammard in her arms, beckoned to her the minute she saw the ambulance arrive.

"We can't stay for this," she said gently. "They will take care of Marcus. He will tell them about the others. We must leave now."

Jill swallowed a lungful of protests and went back to where Marcus was huddled under the black robe.

"Listen," she said to him, fishing in her pocket. "I've got to go, but if you ever feel like talking about what happened, give me a call," she pressed her card firmly into his hand and gave him a pat on the shoulder. "I'm sorry about this. Good luck."

She left him there, but lingered on the edge of the plaza until she saw the EMTs find him. She saw Marcus trying to brush them off and pointing at the mirror bean, where the dark hole was just visible.

Satisfied that things were going in the right direction, Jill trotted off down a flight of stone stairs, to the red hulk of Arcana waiting by the curb—Selene, Clara and Flammard already inside.

Lalai was sitting at her tiny kitchen table, pondering the bottle of rum left over from making eggnog the previous New Year's Eve, and wondering whether now was a good time to try getting drunk, when she heard the sound of a huge truck turn onto the street, coming to a halt right in front of the house.

Hardly daring to hope, yet feeling a flutter in her chest, she went to the window and pulled aside the curtains . . . and there was the giant, dual-rear-wheeled red monster that the three odd women had driven off in earlier that afternoon. Its rear door opened, and Clara got out, followed by . . .

Lalai was out the door and pounding down the stairs the next second.

"Darling, what's wrong?" Gem asked, putting his head into the hall as she passed.

Lalai didn't answer. She was wrenching the deadbolt off the front door and flinging it open, hurtling down the path.

Leonard looked somehow smaller than before, but maybe that was because he was almost swallowed by the huge leather jacket zipped up under his chin. He was leaning heavily on Clara's arm, but looked up when he heard the door open. He had a graze on one cheek and he looked dead tired, but he was alive. He was alive and looking at her.

"Oh, my—*Leonard!*" Lalai screamed, and ran forward and grabbed him. She kissed him, trying to be careful of his scraped cheek but probably failing, because suddenly she was shaking and sobbing and clutching his head and *he* was shaking too, his arms settling weakly around her waist, and together they sank to the ground in the middle of the path, holding onto each other and gasping for air.

Only after Lalai had caught her breath did she think to ask any questions.

"Where *was* he?" she asked, sparing a glance up at Clara, who was towering above them with an unreadable expression on her face. "And . . . what *happened?*"

Something flickered across that blank visage, and Clara sighed.

"He was kidnapped by some *very* unpleasant, and rather crazy, people," Jill said, appearing from around the nose of the truck. "I got some fluids into him on the drive back, but he probably needs more. And food. He wouldn't let us take him to the emergency room."

"Yes, he's like that," Lalai said with a sigh, and pulled herself together. "Come on, Len, let's get you into bed. You can tell me all about it in the morning."

She caught a look, then, that bounced around the three women, too fast for her to make out what it was.

"What?" she asked.

"Yeah," said the dark one—Selene. "About that . . . "

*   *   *

It was on the news the next morning. A cult of religious extremists living in the sewers underneath Chicago had been exposed when one of their captives had miraculously escaped and been found, dazed and confused, on a bench in Millennium Park. Investigation of the network of tunnels had uncovered a chamber of injured men—some in quite bad shape and one who was still in a coma—as well as a horrific prison in which were held six more men who had previously been reported missing, and some truly disturbing remains.

"The victims look to have been burned alive and then gutted," the reporter announced with a blink of her perfectly made-up eyes. "Who was behind this operation, and how Marcus Bowerman escaped, is still unknown—though many of the suspects recovered have now been linked to an obscure group called the Sons of Fire, which until now was thought to be a harmless role-playing club based online. Quite an unsettling occurrence, and right under our noses here in the heart of downtown Chicago. More from this story as news becomes available, I'm Amanda Casey."

Lalai looked up from Jill's laptop, on which the reel had been playing, and stared at them.

"You," she said quietly. "You're how Marcus Bowerman escaped."

"I wanted to stay and talk to the police," Jill said primly. "There was more going on that . . . " she stopped. Leonard, from his nest of pillows and blankets on the couch, had gone white under his freckles, and Clara had stiffened ominously. Meanwhile, Selene took the more direct approach and mimed zipping her lips.

"What?" said Lalai. "What *happened?*"

Leonard looked miserable. "Lal," he said brokenly. "There's some things about me I haven't told you . . . "

"Flammard, don't . . . " Clara began, and stopped.

"Len," said Lalai, more gently. "You know I love you more than anything, and I've been worried sick about you this last week, but you can understand why I'm *curious*, right? Whatever it is, I promise won't be angry." She paused, and turned to Clara. "Why'd you call him *Flammard?*"

"Because that is his name," Clara replied blankly. "His true name."

"It's embarrassing," Leonard said, drawing a hand over his eyes. "It's a type of sword. *Flammenschwert,* they're properly called. Means 'flame-bladed.' *That* kind of sword . . . " he gestured to the sword with the wavy blade that was lying across their coffee table. He gazed apologetically at Lalai, and she could see he was nerving himself up to tell her something. It reminded her of the moment when he'd come out to her as trans—except then she'd already suspected as much. Now she not only had no idea what was coming, but it seemed to be weighing on him even more.

"The truth is . . . Lal . . . I'm . . . "

"Hold on a second," Jill interrupted, taking her laptop back. "Stop right there, please. Sorry Flammard—or Leonard, if that's what you prefer—I'm sorry but you *can't* go about explaining it like *that.* She'll think you're crazy."

"No, I won't," protested Lalai.

"You *will,* but you shouldn't, because he's not. So let me explain things the way I *wish* it had been explained to me."

"Explain *what?*" Lalai wailed.

Jill patted the back of her hand comfortingly. "Do you mind coming out to my truck?" she asked. "I've got some things to show you."

Lalai and Jill were out by Arcana for almost an hour. Clara could see them, heads bent over Jill's sample case, when she went to the window.

"What's she got in her truck?" Flammard asked from the sofa.

"Bits and pieces," Clara said. "Ashes from a summoning, notes on a dead unicorn, some demonic ectoplasm."

"Don't forget the vampire blood," Selene added. Selene, Clara noticed, was still acting a bit weird; she kept glancing all around the room without ever really looking at Flammard.

"Yes," she said. "And vampire blood."

"What on earth does she want with all that?" Flammard wondered.

"She's studying them. It. She's trying to make sense of the supernatural," Clara told him.

"And you're helping her?" Flammard asked.

"We . . . uh . . . work for her," Selene offered, staring out the window.

"Huh," said Flammard. Then he shot a twinkling grin at Clara, almost back to his old self. "I like her," he said, and leaned back on his pillows. "I think I'd also like to lie down again. Help me get into bed?"

Clara helped Flammard sit up. He and Lalai didn't have a bedroom, per se, but a loft over Lalai's workroom that housed a double bed and a long, low dresser. Clara boosted Flammard up the ladder, and stood on it while he got himself tucked in.

"Claymore," he said, once he was settled. "Loki wasn't in his prison. That's why the snake attacked Mistress."

Clara's face clouded over. "Then what the Book of Hecate said was true . . . "

"Not necessarily," sighed Flammard. "But I think it's worth noting for other reasons as well."

"Such as?"

"Well, consider that the freeing of Loki is supposed to precipitate the coming of Ragnarök."

Clara frowned, and nodded. "I will keep that in mind," she said. "Do you need anything? Or shall I go?"

"I think I need sleep," Flammard said. "Thank you."

Clara began to descend the ladder, when he spoke again, making her stop.

"I'm glad you came," he said quietly, and when Clara poked her head over the railing again he was smiling at her. "I'm sorry I . . . sorry I disappeared on you."

"You had things to do," Clara said, and glancing around the little apartment, she added, "It looks like you did them well."

"I still miss them," Flammard whispered. The fire in his eyes was banked, and they were drifting shut. "And you. You haven't heard anything . . . ?"

Clara shook her head.

"I also worry about you. Don't laugh."

"I'm not laughing."

The greenish eyes opened again, focusing briefly on her. "There's this saying," he said. "The fire department uses it in their training, to remind us that we have a duty to keep *ourselves* alive before anyone else. They call it *courage to be safe*. Clara . . . I won't ask you to stay safe, but have the courage, okay?"

"I'll try," Clara said. "You too."

"Thanks," said Flammard with a wry grin, closing his eyes at last. "I'll try."

Lalai was quiet and thoughtful when Jill led her back into the house. She went into the little kitchen and made herself a cup of tea. As she filled the kettle, she glanced questioningly at Jill and Selene. The former shook her head, but Selene said: "I could really appreciate a beer right about now—if you don't need me to drive tonight," she added.

"I think we have some left over from Gem's birthday party," Lalai said, going to the refrigerator and poking around in its doors. "And unless you guys have somewhere you need to be, you're welcome to stay as long as you want. That sofa folds out, and we have an extra futon around here somewhere . . . "

Selene raised her eyebrows and looked at Jill. "What did you *tell* her? She's taking this better than you did!"

Jill shrugged. "Just the truth: that we don't really *know* what's going on, only that strange things *are* happening and we need to find out more about them. I told her I'd take a sample of Fla—Leonard's DNA and see what I could find out from that."

Selene took the beer Lalai offered her, but didn't open it. She rubbed the back of her neck thoughtfully. "I dunno, boss," she said. "Demi-gods are tricky things. A lot of them don't look extraordinary unless they want to—or have to. It's a way of . . . like that protective coloration some animals have."

"Camouflage?" Jill suggested.

"Yeah," said Selene. "Just like that."

"How convenient," Lalai said dryly, pouring her tea. She turned around and leaned back against the counter, gazing past Jill and Selene to the door of the back room. "So if Leonard's the son of Loki," she said, thoughtfully. "What does that make you?"

Turning to look, Jill found that Clara had appeared in the doorway, ducking her bare head to pass into the living room.

She stopped at Lalai's question and got an inward, considering expression. Jill was suddenly very conscious of how little she really knew about Clara's family, and how many questions she'd carefully left unasked, for fear of offending the woman.

Clara didn't seem offended now, however, just uncomfortable . . . and perhaps a little sad.

"We share a mother," she said after a pause in which one could hear a pin drop. "All three of us do. But we have three different fathers. Schiavona and Flammard . . . well, you know about Flammard now. Schiavona made me promise not to tell, but she is also what you would call a demi-god. And I . . . " she gave one of her inverted shrugs. "We do not know."

"Surely your mother knew who your father was," Lalai said.

Clara's mouth twisted unhappily, and she went and sat down on the little sofa. Her knees came up almost into her chest, but even trying to make herself small she seemed to loom in that little room like a giant.

"I think mother knew, but she never said," Clara sighed at last. "I always got the feeling though, that I wasn't . . . well, I wasn't an *accident,* but I wasn't exactly part of the plan, either. I don't know. Flammard and Schiavona both had—both *have* fairly potent powers, whereas I . . . " she shrugged. "I'm just *me.* I don't know. I am the daughter of Dana Nordstern, and that's always been enough."

She looked miserable though, and Lalai looked as if she had more questions. Frantically Jill cast about for a means to change the topic, but since many of the questions she imagined Lalai was going to ask were ones *she* wanted answers to as well, this was proving difficult.

Selene came to her rescue, in a way, when she rolled her head to look at Clara and said, in her driest, long-suffering voice: "Jill wants to take samples from your brother."

"Only with his consent!" Jill added hastily, throwing her hands up in defense of the glacial glare being leveled at her. "And then only some hair, at *most.* Fingernail clippings would do, if that's easier. *Maybe* some saliva."

"He's *sleeping,*" Clara said, stonily.

"Then we'll wait," Jill said. "Lalai has invited us to stay. I can write up my report for Okedo, and, uh . . . can I buy you dinner?" she asked their host.

Lalai chuckled. "We usually cook our own food," she said. "But you can wash the dishes."

This was, more or less, how they passed the afternoon. Jill found herself chained to the sink, while Clara intercepted the string of visitors that began starting around noon. Most of these were Flammard's co-workers from his shift at the fire station and took some convincing to go away again. Eventually Flammard woke up and stumbled out into the living room, still wrapped in his blanket. Clara set him up on a throne of pillows there, where he received the remaining guests, while she towered over him like his personal bodyguard. The little apartment became quite crowded, and Selene disappeared sometime in the middle of it all, though that hardly made a difference in the crowd.

Lalai finally emerged from the kitchen and ordered everyone out so Leonard could get some rest. No, they weren't filing charges and he'd be back to work in two weeks. Out.

"*Now* we can eat," she said, closing the door behind the broad back of a firefighter. "Can someone tell Selene we're having dinner now?"

Since Jill was still elbow deep in dirty dishes (some of which she was washing for the second time that day), Clara was the one who got sent out. She went, looking like she was carrying a raincloud around her shoulders.

Clara found Selene sitting in the back of Arcana, sipping at a now-warm beer. Clara told her dinner was ready, and the woman nodded.

"Aye," she said. "You go on and eat. I'll be in inna bit."

Clara hesitated on the sidewalk, then she hoisted herself up next to Selene and dropped a small, cloth-wrapped object into her hand. Selene's eyebrows went up as her fingers closed around it and she realized what it was.

"You're giving me his ring back?" she said, uncertainly.

"He gave it to me," Clara explained, a little tightly. "When he . . . left. I gave it to you. I needed it to find his sword, which I needed in order to find him. I am returning it now."

"I just thought . . . after what I said . . . you might not want me to have it," Selene admitted, staring down between her knees.

Clara did one of her inverted shrugs. "I thought about it. Then I talked to Flammard. He's not angry. I thought if anyone has a right to be angry it's him, so I am trying not to be angry."

"Sorry anyway," said Selene.

Clara nodded, but didn't leave.

Selene took a deep pull from the bottle, then said: "It's just . . . there's this obvious, insensitive question I wanna ask, and if you keep sittin' there I'm gonna ask it."

Clara's face shuttered, but she didn't move. When it became clear she really wasn't going anywhere, Selene took a deep breath and began to speak.

"What was it like for you, growing up with that? I mean, how did you handle it when this person you *thought* was a woman, female, thing—everything that implied and all—was actually a . . . a man?"

To her relief Clara's expression cleared immediately. She almost smiled.

"Flammard came out to our mother when he was seven—a full year before I was even born. I never knew him as anything *other* than my big brother. It was the same for Schiavona—she was four at the time—but really, I don't think she noticed any changes except Flammard wanted to be called her *brother* now, and she was suppose to use 'he, his, and him' when referring to him. She got used to it. I didn't even have to. He was just *normal* to me, even after I found out most men *aren't* like him. He just . . . is." She rubbed her chin thoughtfully. "I don't forget that he's transgender, I just forget it sometimes makes otherwise good people act weird. I *don't* forget it makes him more vulnerable. He's my brother. My *only* brother. He's the only family I have left in this world, and I would lay down my life for him."

They sat together in silence, both looking straight ahead, for a moment.

"What did your mother think, when her seven-year-old daughter told her she was actually her son?" Selene asked.

Clara smiled wanly.

"She never talked about it. But Flammard told me she just shrugged and said: 'You come by it honestly, at least. Goodness knows, if the gods can get their genders wrong and have to swap them about then what's to be expected from poor, fallible humans?' And that was that."

Selene nodded thoughtfully.

"You know, Clara, I'd lay down my life to have a family like yours."

Clara sighed, settling down next to Selene to watch the sun set through the trees.

"I don't have a family anymore. Schiavona and mother are gone. It's just me and Flammard now, and . . . well. He doesn't want to be a part of my life anymore."

"Have . . . had . . . whatever," said Selene. "Most of my family's still in *this* world, but they won't have anything to do with me—or I them, honestly. Do you know what *my* mother said when *I* came out to her? She told me I was sick and that I was gonna go to hell. Where I would burn. She went into a *lot* of detail."

"I am sorry," Clara said, and Selene could tell she meant it, in her stiff way.

"Thanks," she said. "Sorry if I was weird."

"Good people sometimes are."

"I got history, is the thing."

"I understand."

"You want to hear about it?"

"Only if you want to talk about it."

Selene drew in a deep breath, then let it out again in a long sigh.

"You know," she said, finishing her beer. "I think I've had about enough of history. Yours, Flammard's, and mine. I say, let's think about tomorrow. I mean, we're *in* Chicago! Is there anything you'd like to see?"

Clara still looked a little fragile, but she was also smiling.

"You know, honestly, I hadn't thought."

"Well get *thinking,* sister—oh crap. Is that, like, a bad word to use around you? You know it's just a word to *me* but . . . uh . . . "

Clara shook her head, smiling a little sadly.

"I don't mind. I find it endearing, actually."

"*Endearing?* Wow, you sure have melted. But that's good, right?" Selene chanced a nervous grin at her companion, who responded with one of her signature shrugs and a nod of her head.

"Yeah," said Selene. "I'ma call that good. Good? Good. Let's go eat."

They climbed down off the truck, and together, they went inside.

*

I'm gonna carry the light
I won't let go of my right
I'm a son of the flames
You don't need my name tonight

I'm gonna carry the fire
Gonna make love to your ire
Drown your rage in my bright conflagration
I'm a fireman

I'm gonna carry the fire
I'm gonna carry the light
I'm gonna marry your ire

I'm gonna carry the fight
I cannot be chained anymore
I'm gonna carry the light
Like nothing that you have seen before

C-c-c-carry
C-c-c-carry
C-c-c-carry
the fight

I'm gonna ignite my sound
Dig up my sword from the ground
Hold it right to the sky
Scream to heaven that I
am a fireman

Well I've got nothing to prove
But I can take it from you
That you want to see my fire
So I'll raise my sword higher
I'm a fusion

And I will carry the light
I'm gonna carry the fire

I'm gonna carry the fight
I cannot be chained anymore
I'm gonna carry the light
Like you can't find the strength to ignore

C-c-c-carry
C-c-c-carry
C-c-c-carry
the fight

Love is too cruel
To take me from you
The serpent is not the source of my pain and fuel
Spark in the night, turn to the sky
Stuck in the earth I am a slave to my birthright
So get to the ground when I spread my wings wide
I can't tame my flame with my doors all unlocked
I cannot hide

Now watch me rise
Ignite me and I will rise

And I will carry the fight
I will send up the smoke and the fumes
I'm gonna carry this fight
I'm a fire, I was made to consume

C-c-c-carry
C-c-c-carry
C-c-c-carry
the fight

I'm gonna carry
Carry
I'm gonna carry
Carry
C'mon, c'mon
The light, the fire, the fight
The fight!
—Carry the Fight/*Princess Die*

The Arcana crew will return in
"Dying to Live"

We conclude this issue of Apsis Fiction *with the second episode in the second season of* Professor Odd—*the eighth episode overall. "Chronostrophe" takes what has been largely an adventure across space and adds the element of time travel. Though it follows "The Dogs of Canary Island," like all* Professor Odd *episodes it can be read on its own. Its predecessors have all been published individually from Heliopause, and it was written in the final months of 2013.*

CHRONOSTROPHE

Prologue

THE BOY SAT ON A ROCK in the middle of a river. Of course, the river was not really a river, and the rock was not really a rock, but *he* was still really a boy. At least he felt like one.

He had scruffy brown hair that was just a little too long—and had been that way since he'd left home—a short, freckled nose and contemplative eyes. At one time these had been gray, but in this time they were blue. Deep sapphire shot through with bolts of cyan and indigo, they somehow managed to catch the light on the water's surface, and in his reflection they appeared to glow.

He wore a pair of faded blue jeans with fraying hems, bright red trainers, and a jumper with thick horizontal gray-and-navy stripes—just like he always had. The jumper had a scorch mark under the left elbow, but otherwise it was in pretty good shape. It was always in pretty good shape whenever he returned to this time.

The river. The river swirled and curled around his rock, lapping at the sides and leaving glossy wetness behind. If he looked closely, the boy thought, he could almost see past the water and the stone to what they really were. What they really *meant*. But it was difficult for him, one born in time, to look at it from the outside.

Something changed about the current. New water was flow-ing in from somewhere, mixing with the stronger patterns and slightly altering them. The boy watched the play curiously for a while, before deciding it was nothing to concern himself with. He was more worried about a leaf which had become trapped in a small eddy near the shore. A speck of yellow atop the murky brown-and-blue depths, it was tugged in a repeating cycle by the swirling water—never stilling, never breaking free.

The boy frowned. The leaf was moving faster and faster now, becoming a whirl of bright color.

The boy stood up. He looked around. The horse was gallop-ing toward him, feet working noiselessly on the air, her mane billowing behind her. The boy reached out his hand and grabbed hold of a free strand, feeling himself swept out of the time in place and into a place in time.

The boy and the horse plunged into the river and disap-peared.

Part One

THE LITTLE CAFÉ on the seashore next to the boardwalk was crowded with Sunday holiday makers, and its tinny, canned music was drowned out by the laughing and screaming com-ing from the roller coaster down the beach. Elo, wearing her service-dog harness, was looking distinctly un-servicelike as she lounged on the sandy boards, soaking up the sun. Professor Odd sat in the chair next to her, contemplating her cake and ice cream.

"I do wish," she said with a sigh, pushing her round dark glasses up her nose. "That I really could have my cake and eat it too."

"I HAVE NEVER UNDERSTOOD THAT PHRASE," Dave said. His panvironment suit barely cleared the tabletop, and he was visible only as a small blue dome peeking out above the pink-and-white checked tablecloth. "TO EAT A CAKE AT ALL SURELY YOU MUST HAVE IT. I HAVE CAKE; I AM CUR-RENTLY IN THE PROCESS OF DIGESTING IT."

"Yes, but that's different," said the Professor, plucking the red maraschino cherry off the top and swinging it back and forth like a pendulum. "You *had* your cake, and you ate it. You do not have it any more, not in the form of *cake* anyway. You can no longer eat it."

"ONE CANNOT EAT WHAT HAS ALREADY BEEN EATEN. THIS IS TRUE," Dave admitted.

"My ancestors did," Elo said. "And cows, you could say, eat things twice."

"*That's* different," Alister said, scraping the crumbs off his plate with his fork. "*Are* you going to eat that, Professor? It's really good."

"I'm sure it is," Professor Odd said cheerfully. "That's *why* I was saying I'd like to have this cake and eat it too. Have it, as in have it ready and waiting to be eaten, but still be able to *eat* it without losing the perfect, as-yet-uneaten cake that I can then look forward to eating in the future."

"In other words, you want it both ways?" Alister suggested.

"That's what *seconds* are for," Elo said, grinning. "Think of *all* the possible cake that exists in your future. All the cake you have *yet* to have."

Professor Odd wagged her head from side to side, as if sloshing this idea around. Then she nodded and finally picked up her fork and sliced into the chocolate frosting and vanilla ice cream.

And then things *changed*.

Alister was sure they did. It felt like a subtle shifting of the light across the boardwalk, as though a cloud had passed over the sun, even though the sky was clear. He felt a slight dizziness, then a tingling in his stomach that threatened to make him ill, and then it passed as mysteriously as it had come and he was blinking across at Professor Odd in confusion.

Professor Odd, however, was anything but confused: she was *furious*.

"My *cake!*" she cried, gesticulating at her plate. "*Look* at it— ruined!"

Alister blinked and lowered his eyes to the table. Sure enough, the chocolate cake and ice cream was gone, replaced by a wedge of what looked like a green gelatinous pie with a slice of lime stuck in a healthy dollop of whipped cream on the top. There was no ice cream.

"Looks like that fruit pie," Alister suggested. "The kind they make in Florida."

"Key lime pie?" Elo said, scrambling to her feet and sniffing at the Professor's plate. "Smells good."

"How did it change?" Alister asked.

Professor Odd lifted the plate, pie and all, to eye level and examined it closely. She ran her finger around the rim and sniffed experimentally. Then she set it down and stood up, staring around at the boardwalk.

"Do you notice anything else . . . *different?*" she asked sharply.

Staring around, Alister had to admit that he couldn't. Unless . . . was the couple sitting two tables down always wearing matching red jackets? Alister rather thought they hadn't. And there were other things, too: the pattern of the tablecloths was different, and even the sound of the roller-coaster had changed. Just subtly though: it was loud as ever but running more smoothly.

"Professor . . . " he said timidly. "What is going on?"

Professor Odd sniffed the air and shook her head. "Either someone's learned how to pull probabilities in conventional universes, or . . . or . . . "

Alister had to resist the temptation to scream 'Or *what?*' and pound his hands on the table.

"THIS IS MOST INCONSIDERATE," said Dave, the lights on the front of his suit flashing. "SOMEONE HAS BEEN INTERFERING WITH THE SPACE-TIME CONTINUUM."

"Space-*time* continuum?" Alister repeated, to make sure he'd heard right. "Do you not mean . . . *time travel?*"

"Asynchronous spatial-locked time travel," Professor Odd said, her voice quiet and awed. Then, like a bird of prey bursting from its perch she swept up Elo's lead and said: "Back to the Oddity, and quickly."

"Why?" asked Alister, but he was already getting to his feet. "What's gone wrong?"

"Nothing yet," said Professor Odd, then looked down at her plate as though it contained a live crab. A live crab wielding some sort of weapon. "But things might *become* wrong."

* * *

Alister leaned back in his chair and folded his arms across his chest. "I'm afraid I still don't understand," he said. "How did you *not* know it was one of them temporally flexible universes?"

"Because it's *not*," said Professor Odd.

They were back in the Oddity, but the Professor hadn't detached them from the world with the surprising key lime pie. She was sitting in the Oddity's cockpit, hands moving swiftly and assuredly over the bank of colorful glowing circular buttons, looking at an amorphous blob of green-and-blue lights on the screen above. She frowned, tapped some keys, and then looked closer. Across the aisle from her, at the opposite console, Dave had climbed clean out of his panvironment suit and lay plastered across the other bank of keys.

Green and shimmery from the wetness, he looked like a fantastical Halloween decoration, with his ten octopus-like arms and the one huge, gaping eye like a yellow-and-orange pinwheel. From beneath the main, roughly dish-shaped portion of his body (from which the ten arms extended like spokes of a wheel), a fine mass of yellow feelers could just be seen, poking out and dipping into the crannies between the buttons. They were shiny and wet too, not from the saline solution of his panvironment suit but the natural slime Dave secreted in order to communicate. That slime could do more than communicate, Alister knew; it could make you feel drunk or happy or angry, depending on what Dave wanted. It could also, it appeared, allow Dave to connect directly to the Oddity.

A tentacle flipped outward, felt its way over the lip of the open panvironment suit (a barrel-shaped thing with a dome that rotated open), and dragged the whole thing close enough so it could dip inside. It felt around a bit, and then with a buzz of static the slime-to-audio translator spoke:

"IT IS A FRACTURED BLOCK UNIVERSE," he said through the translator, "WITH A LOW TOLERANCE FOR BRANCHING POSSIBILITIES AND NO SAPLINGS."

"In a *block* universe?" Professor Odd puzzled, scratching her scalp under her wig—sky blue today with streaks of pink and yellow.

"Could someone *please* explain to me what this means?" Alister insisted.

Next to him, Elo patted his arm consolingly.

"From what *I* understand," she said. "A *block* universe is a kind of temporally *friendly* universe—er, that is, it's a universe in which asynchronous time travel is possible—wherein the effects of the time-traveling objects or people are *built in.* That is to say, they've *always* happened. The course of history happens *because* there were objects or people that jumped about back and forth between the past and present. This is in contrast to, say, a *shifting* universe, which is more of a truly temporally flexible universe, wherein time travelers can *actively change* the course of events. To allow this, those universes must be able to hold within themselves lots of different possibilities."

"What, like those narrative worldtracks you told me about?" Alister said. "Where they're technically separate universes, but so closely related they can seem identical?"

"Sort of," said Elo with a sideways tilt of her head. "Only more all mashed together like."

"So what Dave means is . . . ?"

"Well," said Elo. "Sometimes a block universe will create other narratives branching off it—alternate histories and futures—that come into and out of existence depending on the point at which you're viewing said universe. Sometimes these 'saplings' as Dave calls them will grow alongside for quite a while before being reabsorbed. Sometimes they split off altogether and form completely new narratives. They're created by someone, say, going back in time and changing the course of history. Well, both histories can't be true in the same universe, and so it splits. Sometimes the changes are so small they don't drastically affect the course of events within a given universe, and so they slowly meld back together again. Sometimes *more* time travelers will come around and sort of nudge it back into position."

"Like," Alister suggested, "someone going back in time to assassinate a king or something—but then someone *else* comes back and stops them?"

"That's one scenario," Elo said. "It can get complicated if the second time traveler comes from the universe created by the assassination of that king, but it usually works itself out without it being a complete chronostrophe."

"You mean catastrophe," Alister corrected her.

"No," said Elo. "A *chronostrophe*. It's a . . . it's a thing. A bad thing. Sort of like a natural disaster in the course of time and space, rather than in space and time. They only happen in temporally flexible worlds, though, so I don't know much about them."

"Wait, hang on," said Alister, realizing they'd skipped over something, and now it was coming back to confuse him. "Aren't *all* universes just a little temporally flexible? I mean, we're *all* moving through time . . . steadily forward, you know."

"Yes," said Elo, a little tiredly. "But that's *natural* time flow. It's a little different for each universe—that's why there can be discrepancy build-ups when you hop from universe to universe the way we do—but they're all doing the same thing, pretty much. In a universe where *asynchronous* time travel is possible—that is to say: time travel back and forth and sideways—it's got to be a *special* kind of flexible otherwise it'd get torn to pieces."

"By chronostrophes?" Alister suggested.

"Something *like* that, yeah," said Elo. "Only chronostrophes can't happen because asynchronous time travel *can't* happen."

"*Except . . .*" this time it was the Professor who spoke, and she'd raised a finger for attention. Dave propped himself up on a couple of tentacles and gazed across at her. "It *does*."

"I'm afraid I still don't follow," Alister said.

"Look," said Professor Odd, beckoning him over. Alister came and stood behind the woman's shoulder, trying to make sense of the lumpy blue-and-green projection she was pointing at. "There are masses of time tracks, back and forth and all over. They seem to originate in the mid-twentieth century, and from there spread out all over the place. From ten thousand B.C. to . . . oh my, fifty thousand *A.D.* And there are fainter tracks too, cropping up mostly in the centuries leading up to mass extinctions—millions of years in the past *and* future."

"Hold on," said Alister. "How can you see what's happening in the *future* of that universe?"

"Technically, I can't," admitted Professor Odd. "I'm just looking for time tracks. I can tell you when they happen, but I can't tell you what's going on when they do. As to why I can even do *that*—well, let's just say having the Oddity located in its own special time stream allows us to get a sort of bird's-eye view of the whole thing."

"And this is wrong . . . how?" Alister pressed on.

"Well, because there's none of the usual markers or coping mechanisms," Professor Odd said, waving her hands expansively. "I mean, *look* at it! No saplings, no narrative braiding, no closed loops—*nothing*. It's like a block universe overlaid on a shifting universe that somehow *hasn't* torn itself to pieces. Sure, it *looks* normal enough if you just take the current present, but when you look at the *big* picture . . . " she trailed off and whistled between her teeth. "It's a *mess*."

"What are those?" Alister asked, and pointed. On the screen, splotches of twisted black were staining the bright blues and greens, blooming into existence and then fading out again.

A slosh and a *click* as Dave slipped back into his suit.

"THOSE ARE CHRONOSTROPHES," he said. "LOTS OF THEM."

"Oooh . . . " said Elo, looking gravely up at the monitor. Then she perked her ears at the Professor and said, in tones of moderate alarm: "What are you *doing?*"

"I'm going to see one," said Professor Odd, tapping away at the keys. "They aren't *acting* like proper chronostrophes—the way they just *disappear* again, it's not right. *Something's* going on there, and I want to find out what. Oh, and hold on to something—this might get a little rough."

The boy landed hard on the cold ground, the wind pulling at his clothes and hair and whipping his bare skin. He had the Paradox Matrix, however, clutched tightly to his chest, and he scrambled to his feet and ran across the rocky ground, tripping over the ruts and holes. There was still gunfire in the distance, but it was becoming fainter now. Captain Burn must have found a way to force the Future Soldiers back.

He didn't have much time, even so. The Maker's ship was circling around, gliding low over the ground and bearing down on him. It wouldn't fire on him, not while he held the Matrix, but he could see the Maker standing in the open hatch he'd jumped out of, arms braced against the wall, clearly getting ready to jump himself.

The boy made it another hundred or so meters when he heard the muffled *thump* of the Maker's boots hitting the ground behind him, and the man's whip lashed out, catching the boy around the ankle and sending him tumbling to the ground. He didn't let go of the Matrix, however, even though the wires were digging painfully into his chest.

"Peter, Peter, my dear boy," said the Maker, his voice gone soft and smooth.

Peter just held onto the Matrix and refused to meet his eyes. If he didn't look at the man, then he could resist for that much longer. He shut his eyes against the tearing wind, heard the engines of the ship directly above him, and expected to be locked in a tractor beam any second.

"What did they call you?" the Maker was saying. *"Lucky* Peter, wasn't it? Where's your *luck* gone now?"

The sound of that name—the name *she* had given him—sent a thrill of anger through Peter's body. The Maker had no right— no *right*—to call him that.

Surging to his feet, Peter rounded on the man, just in time to see a large barrel-shaped object drop out of the sky, bounce off his shoulder, and knock him to the ground.

Peter stared.

The Maker was sprawled, clutching his shoulder and moaning in anguish, while the barrel-shaped object put out a metal tentacle and shoved itself onto one end. It had a band of tractor treads around its midsection and a blue glass dome on top. Something like a satellite dish whizzed along a track that ran around the base of the dome, and appeared to focus on Peter.

There was a *whish* and a *thump*, and a person in an olive green overcoat and a wig like a blue-and-gold macaw dropped to the ground next to the barrel and the Maker's fallen form. She inspected him briefly then turned to face Peter.

"Hello there," she said in a bright, friendly voice. "Can we *help* you?"

Peter stared at them uncertainly. "Where did *you* come from?" he asked. "No, I mean, *when* did you come from?"

"Just now, and *up there.*"   The woman in the green coat pointed. Peter looked, and saw an access hatch on the bottom of the Maker's ship had been propped open, and within he could just glimpse a cavern lit by blinking, many-colored lights. His mind tried to make sense of this turn of events, and failed.

"Was he *bothering* you?"   the woman asked, indicating the Maker. "As far as I can tell he's part of the chronostrophe, but *you're* not. Though you're holding a pretty big piece of it."

"He is the Maker," Peter said uncertainly. "I knew him . . . well, I knew him when we were younger. He built a time ship, then went back in time to give himself the plans and got an army from the future and is trying to conquer the world."

"STOP RIGHT THERE," said the barrel in a harsh, artificial voice. Peter found himself jumping backward at the sound. "THAT IS A PRIME PARADOX. IT CANNOT BE CONTAINED WITHIN A SINGLE UNIVERSE WITHOUT DESTROYING IT."

"He built another machine," Peter said defensively.   "He called it the Paradox Matrix. It lets him do things like that. It's what's keeping this reality, well . . . um . . . *real.*"

"Oh dear," said the woman. "That's not good at all. Is there any way to turn it off without causing this universe to implode?"

"That's what I was *going* to do," Peter said, a little impatiently. Carefully he unwrapped his arms from the Matrix and showed it to them. "You see, I have it here."

The woman came forward and gazed at the device in awe. Out of the corner of his eye, Peter saw the Master on the ground behind her, struggling to sit up.

"You . . . " he began, "cannot—stop—*me*. Hand it—over!"

Peter felt the pull of his voice even now, and the woman straightened up to look over her shoulder at him.

Then the barrel produced another tentacle and gave the Maker a sharp *thwack* across the back of his head. He fell to the ground once more and did not get up.

"HE WAS UTILIZING AN AUDIO-OPTICAL SEDUCTION GENERATOR," it said. "I DIDN'T LIKE IT."

"I hope you haven't *killed* him," the woman said, a little reproachfully.

"I HAVE NOT," responded the barrel, which Peter was be-ginning to suspect was a robot. "BUT IN A FEW MINUTES OF LOCAL TIME HE WILL CEASE TO EXIST." The robot turned its satellite dish back to Peter. "WILL YOU DEACTIVATE THAT DEVICE, OR MUST I COME OVER AND DO IT FOR YOU?"

As if he'd been released from a spell Peter dropped to his knees, setting the Paradox Matrix on the ground before him and carefully unscrewing the lid. He lifted the core out, felt it tingling against his palms, and then—very gently—he ground it together between his hands until it had sputtered out into nothing.

The body of the Maker, his ship, and the wind and the dis-tant gunfire vanished. They were replaced by a tall house over-looking the rocky path on which they stood, a clear blue sky, and the distant sound of breakers on the beach far below.

Peter got to his feet again, and found that the woman and the barrel-robot were still there. That was odd. He'd assumed they'd been a result of the paradox, but they seemed just as solid and real as ever—the woman's clothes hadn't even changed, though Peter's had lost the rips and tears he'd acquired on his latest adventure.

"It's over now," he said. "You can go back to . . . wherever it is you came from."

The woman looked at him, her face impassive behind her round, dark glasses. "Oh, no," she said, taking a step toward him down the path. "It's *far* from over."

"It is for you," Peter said. "You can go back to your regular lives. Forget you ever knew me."

He called his horse, and heard her hoofbeats echoing up the hours. He reached out his hand, ready to be swept along, and—

"Oh I *see!*" cried the woman, and leapt after him.

The door shut abruptly in Alister's face, and when he got it open again he worried for a moment that they'd somehow been thrown into a different universe: the storm was gone, and the land was no longer in ruin. Instead of looking out from the hull of a giant ship, the Oddity's door now opened from a vent in the attic of a tall house. He looked down and saw the bare cliff edge was now covered by the gardens of the houses that ran along it, with a gravel path connecting them. The sun shone down out of a clear blue sky, and on the path the scary looking man had vanished, leaving only the Professor, Dave, and the little boy with the spiky box clutched to his chest.

They were talking together, the Professor and the boy, but Alister couldn't hear what was being said. He was on the point of asking Elo if they had any rope they could throw down so he could climb out, when he heard Professor Odd shout, *"Oh, I see!"* and leap toward the boy. There was a *twinge,* like someone had plucked at the sheet of reality, and then the Professor and the boy were gone.

"Oh *no . . .* " Elo groaned.

"Dave!" Alister shouted. "What happened?"

Dave, in his panvironment suit, all his sensors trained on the spot where the Professor had last been seen, didn't answer. Eventually he turned and rolled awkwardly over the path toward the garden of the house the Oddity had anchored to. He reached out three of his arms and threw the gate open, letting it be caught in the rosebushes lining the path. He approached until he was directly under the Oddity's door, and then something on the bottom of his suit ignited and he shot up into the air.

"MOVE," he told them, when he became level with the door.

Elo and Alister scrambled backward into the Oddity, and Dave shot forward, turning sideways and rolling up the stairs after them using the tread around the midsection of the suit. A long tentacle arm reached out and shut the door behind him.

"Dave?" Alister prompted.

"THAT WAS INCONSIDERATE OF HER," Dave said, pushing himself upright.

"What just happened out there?" Elo demanded. "First we were in a ship—then we weren't—and the world looked *completely* different. And then the Professor, she . . . she . . . "

"SHE FOLLOWED HIM," Dave said. "I WOULD HAVE TOO, BUT I WAS NOT SWIFT ENOUGH."

"Followed him . . . " Alister repeated. "Followed him . . . *how?* Er, *where?*"

Dave had rolled over to the cockpit and was now fiddling with the controls. The Oddity made unhappy buzzing noises, and Elo stroked the panel of lights nearest in a soothing manner.

"THERE WAS A REALITY SHIFT: A CLOSED TIME LOOP CAME TO AN END. THAT IS WHAT HAPPENED," Dave said, apparently answering Elo's first question. "I AM NOW AT-TEMPTING TO LOCATE . . . OH. I SEE. IT IS AS I FEARED."

"What is?" Elo said, coming around to lean over the dome of his suit. She blinked, shook her head, and stared at the screen again. "What on Aratowan does *that* mean?" she whispered.

Dave pushed himself away from the console of lights.

"IT MEANS SHE HAS LEFT CONVENTIONAL TIME. SHE IS NOW EXISTING IN EPI-TIME."

Alister and Elo stared at the creature in the barrel-shaped suit with puzzled and confused faces. At least, Alister certainly felt confused—though the term 'epi-time' sounded familiar—Elo looked annoyed into the bargain.

Dave prodded at the screen with one metal-gloved tentacle.

"HERE," he said, as if to explain. "SHE DISAPPEARED FROM THE CONVENTIONAL TIME FLOW. SHE IS NO LONGER PRESENT WITHIN THAT TIME-SPACE CONTIN-UUM. SHE HAS PASSED INTO *EPI-TIME*."

"Yes, I'm getting that," Elo said, with, Alister thought, com-mendable patience. "We just don't know what epi-time *is*."

Dave turned his sensor dish toward them, and four arms protruded from the suit, the tips raised expressively, and then all at once they went limp, like someone giving up on explaining something.

There was a knock on the door.

They all froze.

Eventually Elo went down the stairs and cracked it open.

"Hallo!" cried Professor Odd. Her wig was askew and one lens of her glasses cracked, but she seemed otherwise unharmed. Alister thought she must have been standing on a ladder to reach the door. "Hurry up! There's a chronostrophe starting about two thousand years from now, and Peter's agreed to let us help him solve it!"

* * *

The pounding of hooves was all around him, and for a moment Lucky Peter thought he'd managed to escape the strange woman. Then a new cadence intruded upon his senses: another pair of feet were running along beside him, almost matching step and rhythm. When the horse left him on the bank, disappearing into the churn of the river, he looked around and found he was not alone.

Somehow the woman had followed him! She had fallen when the horse dropped them off, and her hair had been pulled to one side. She was gingerly putting on her glasses, which had come off in the tumble, and Peter saw one of the lenses was now cracked. She was panting and red in the face, but did not seem at all surprised to find herself there.

"So," she said between gulps of breath. "*That's* how you're doing it. A *time being*, beautiful. But . . . I have to ask, for professional reasons, as it were—*who* the dawkins are you?"

Lucky Peter stared at her, not certain what to do. It had always only been him and the river before; the presence of another person—and a very grown up person at that—rendered him almost helpless.

Almost.

"You need to go back," he said, pushing her away from the river and calling his horse as strongly as he could.

"I shall. Oh, I shall," the woman said, refusing to budge an inch. She was tall and thin, and a little willowy, Peter thought, but even so her body felt as immovable as a stone under his hands. "First, however, I really must insist you explain what is going on! Your universe is in a very precarious state, you know, and I'd like to help if I can."

Peter stopped shoving to stare at her, dumbfounded. Adults never talked to him like this. It was always "Oh, you poor boy!" and "Let me help you find your parents!" They never saw what he was really doing. Not *really*.

Now he looked, however, it occurred to him that this woman was not the ordinary sort of grown-up. She was too colorful, for a start, and the way she bent almost double in order to talk to him did not seem condescending or superior; it was as though she were simply exerting an effort so she could talk to him face to face. Her own face was pale with a greenish tinge and thin pink lips, but her eyes were still hidden behind her round, dark (and cracked) spectacles. It made Peter feel like he was being inspected by a particularly colorful owl.

"Who *are* you?" he asked, his voice a whisper.

"I'm Professor Odd," said the strange woman, her voice equally quiet, like she was confiding a great secret. "I'm a trans- universal traveler. Who are you?"

Oh. That made things easier. Peter sighed and held out his hand. "Call me Lucky Peter," he said. "And I'm a *time* traveler."

"Lucky Peter," repeated Professor Odd. She reached out and grasped his small brown hand in her thin pale one. "I am so very pleased to meet you."

There was a *whishing* sound, and the horse arrived. Peter watched Professor Odd thoughtfully as the woman straightened up to get a better look at it. He wondered if she saw it the way he did: ten feet tall at the withers with fur like swirling blue clouds and a mane that fell in tumbles over its neck. Like always, the end of its tail was impossible to see: it stretched out toward the river and on into the uncomfortable distance that existed in this place. Peter couldn't see it, but like the ache of a sore tooth, he knew it was there.

As hard as it was to comprehend the horse's tail, its eyes were even worse: looking into them was like looking in the other direction of where its tail went. Whereas Peter thought its tail went on forever, it felt like its eyes were the end of everything. Like a piece of nothing from the end of the universe had been brought backward and was resting just behind its dark, graceful lashes.

Whatever Professor Odd saw she didn't seem frightened by it. She regarded the horse with her head inclined to one side. For a single, mad moment, Peter thought she was going to offer it her hand to shake, as she had done with him. But all she did was nod and make a small bow.

"I think I am beginning to see," she said, turning back to Peter. "This . . . where we are now . . . it's not really a place, is it? Not in the normal physical sense of the word."

Peter shrugged. "It's a representation," he said. "The best one she could manage. The river's not really a river, and we're not really standing on the ground. The human mind is not capable of comprehending the true nature of the Place Beyond Time, so she did the best she could using things we *could* comprehend. Like rivers."

"She?" Professor Odd said, with a questioning gesture toward the horse, who snorted in confirmation. "Oh yes, I see . . . I do see. So I suppose the river . . . that represents *time*, does it?"

Peter shrugged. "You could say so. Really, the river represents the *universe,* and the state of the river represents the state of time. Time itself is determined by the course of the individual water particles as they flow downstream."

"Molecules," said Professor Odd, a bit distractedly. "The word you want is molecules, I think. So, to put things in more conventional terms, would that be the past? Er, past-ward, should I say?" She asked this pointing upstream.

"Yes," said Peter cautiously.

"How far back does it go?" Professor Odd asked, sounding excited beyond all reason.

Peter shrugged. "Forever."

Professor Odd turned around and stared at him.

"*Forever?* Really?"

Peter shifted uncertainly from foot to foot. "Well, I suppose it does. I've been up it to the point where the river is just a tiny stream. Can't go any further than that—too small, and bushes get in the way. But I've never found an end."

"I see," said Professor Odd, and the really weird thing was, Peter thought she *did.*

"What about *that* way?" she asked, turning around and pointing downstream. "How far does it go that way?"

"Forever," said Peter simply. Then he amended himself. "Sometimes."

Slowly and steadily, as though her head rested on a set of gears, Professor Odd turned to look at him, her face a blank mask.

"What do you mean 'sometimes'?" she asked, and though her voice was still light and cheerful, there was a steely undertone to it that made Peter feel like there were knives hidden behind her words.

"The river . . . it changes," Peter said. "It doesn't always flow the same way. I'm not sure why. Sometimes you have a bad storm, and a flood happens. Sometimes a rock moves and opens up a new channel."

"A chronostrophe," Professor Odd said. "What happens then?"

"Sometimes there's a cliff," Peter said. "And the water just falls and falls and falls forever. Sometimes it ends in a pool with a sinkhole at the bottom. Once it was just a lake. A huge lake that went on and on in all directions."

"Once?" repeated Professor Odd. "It's not like that anymore?"

"Well, I fixed it," Peter said with a hint of pride. "That's what I do here. I fix things. All over time and space. So the river can keep flowing."

Professor Odd was frowning now. At the water. At the horse. Even at him. Not as if she were angry; she looked more frustrated than anything else.

"No, no," she said at length. "That's not what I meant: what *makes* the storm? What *makes* the rocks move? This isn't technically a temporally flexible universe; chronostrophes shouldn't be popping up all over the time. It would rip itself to pieces. Something's gone *wrong* with this universe, and I can't fathom *what*."

Peter went and sat down on a clump of moss by the side of the river and folded his arms across his knees. He looked pensively at the ground beneath Professor Odd's shoes (shiny black, like beetles) and wondered whether or not he should simply tell her everything. Telling her everything, Peter thought, might make it easier, but then again it might only make her ask more questions. Eventually he settled on an abbreviated version, which he hoped would satisfy her without causing him to pick over the sore parts of his mind where Sally had been.

"I'm not sure how it got this way," he began. "I think, maybe, it's *always* been this way, and I've *always* been here. I'm not sure. It's hard to tell, when you're outside of time."

Professor Odd was already shaking a finger at him, but in a kindly sort of way. "We're not outside of time," she said. "We're simply in another dimension of it. Else we wouldn't be able to have this conversation. But go on," she said encouragingly.

Peter sighed and dragged a hand through his hair.

"Truth is," he said after a while. "I don't think I'm even sup-posed to be here. I'm just trying to get home, really. I made a mistake—a bad one—a long time ago, and it changed things. Changed *history*. So when I got back, home wasn't *home* any-more. So I went out again, tried to put things back the way they were. But that only made things *more* different. I kept trying, but at the same time all these horrible things started happening all across history. I mean *really* horrible. World-ending horri-ble. Russia and the U.S. keep trying to start World War III at the end of the 20th Century, and I keep having to go in and tin-ker around to make it stop. But then I'll have to go back further to avert some *other* catastrophe, and that undoes whatever fix I'd put in before. So I fix it again, and *that* causes a catastrophe hundreds of years later. It's a never-ending nightmare, really."

There was a soft *tumping* sound as Professor Odd walked over the moss-covered bank to stand beside him. She was rubbing her chin with a long, thin finger and wearing the same concentrat-ing frowny-face as before.

"One big chronostrophe," she murmured, "*might* have been enough to push the timeline of this entire universe out of whack. The problems you're running into may be aftershocks. It *would* help me an awful lot if you'd tell me what it was you did . . . "

She trailed off suggestively, but Peter found he hadn't the heart. He was mustering the courage to explain how the time horse had first found him, when there was a deep *clunking* noise from the river, and a roar of fresh water.

"What was that?" Professor Odd asked.

"Boulder shifting," Lucky Peter said, climbing to his feet. "It's another turning—a bad one. Look, could you wait here and *please* not touch anything while I go deal with that?"

"Why should I wait?" Professor Odd asked. "Wouldn't you like some *help?*"

"I . . . er . . . " Peter stammered. He had gotten so used to being alone. He wasn't quite sure what to do with the Professor.

"Come to that," Professor Odd went on, "I've got some friends who might come in handy. We could go pick them up in no time at all. No time. Ha ha. Well, we'll have to take *some* time I suppose, but that shouldn't be a problem. Would you like that?"

Peter stared at her, dumbfounded. Eventually it was the horse who made up his mind for him. Coming forward up from the river it put its head down next to Professor Odd and made a happy *whuffling* noise.

"I . . . oh . . . oh, *all right*," Peter said, defeated. "But don't blame me if you wind up dead or dematerialized or *worse!*"

"I wouldn't dream of it," Professor Odd said, giving him a bright and toothy grin. Turning to the horse, she said: "To the cliff where we first met, if you please, not too long after we left it."

Leaning heavily on Dave's panvironment suit, Alister clutched his stomach and tried not to be sick. It had been confusing enough the way Professor Odd had suddenly reappeared, talking urgently about something that apparently wouldn't happen for several thousand years, but then there had been *the thing*. He and Elo agreed it had been vaguely horse shaped, but far too large and an improbable color of swirling blue. They had run along with their hands outstretched to tangle in its flowing mane (or, in Dave's case, twine an arm around a strand of tail) as the Professor and the grave-faced boy had instructed, but then something *awful* had happened.

To Alister, it felt as though for a moment every atom in his body was being torn apart. It was excruciating. Worse was the mental confusion he got from seeing the landscape disappear around him, replaced by a vast nothing that reminded him of the space between universes.

"Don't stop!" he'd heard the boy shout, and so he hadn't. He'd kept on running through the nothing, and eventually it gave way. Like rising to the surface of a lake Alister found he could breathe freely again, and that he was standing on the shore of a raging green-and-brown river while fuzzy, indistinct pine trees rustled far overhead.

He had his cheek pressed against the cool glass dome of Dave's suit, and he could dimly see a bright orange eye peering concernedly back at him.

"ARE YOU OKAY?" Dave asked, in what was no doubt meant to be a comforting manner, but because of the monotone of his slime-to-voice translator it came out angry and abrasive. The force of the noise also made the suit vibrate under Alister's hands.

Pulling away slightly he closed his eyes and waited for his stomach to settle down before answering.

"That was perhaps the most unpleasant experience I've had in my life . . . *including* the time I had your slime in my ears. Where in the world *are* we?"

"Ah," said Professor Odd, who appeared not to have suffered any ill effects from the journey. She was intensely perky and quivering with excitement. "That's just the *thing* Mr. Alister. Just the thing *indeed.* We're *not* in the world. Not rightly so. We've sort of stepped off to the side, as it were."

"WE ARE OUT OF THE TAPESTRY," Dave announced, and began to roll toward the river. Alister let go, having no wish to get any nearer to the rushing water.

"Sorry?" said Elo. "Could we have that again, not as a metaphor this time?"

Dave stopped, and slowly his sensor dish turned to focus on them.

"A METAPHOR IS ALL THERE IS. WE HAVE PASSED OUT OF TIME ALTOGETHER. WE ARE NOW IN EPI-TIME. YOU CAN *ONLY* PERCEIVE THIS UNIVERSE IN METAPHORS BE-CAUSE YOUR BRAINS ARE NOT EQUIPPED TO HANDLE THE TRUE NATURE OF THE INFINITE TIMELINE OF A UNIVERSE WHEN VIEWED FROM THE OUTSIDE. IS THAT CLEAR?"

"What he's trying to say"—Professor Odd leaped in—"is that we're *outside* the native timestream now. We've moved on into the *next* dimension of time. In order for us to exist here, things that we *can* understand appear as representations of what's really going on. Thus, what we perceive as time *now* is actually epi-time, the time beyond time, and *time* as we're used to seeing it is represented as space. Example: that river over there."

"THAT IS NOT A RIVER. IT IS THE TAPESTRY," Dave in-sisted.

"Your brain, er, *brain-equivalent*, might be coming up with some slightly different metaphors than ours," Professor Odd suggested gently.

"I'm sorry," said Alister. "I still don't quite get it."

"I think I do," Elo said, going over to stand by Dave. "If what we see as a river represents *time* as we normally experience it, then *upstream* must be the past and *downstream* is the future. Am I right so far?"

Professor Odd nodded encouragingly.

"So, it follows, since we can *move around* in space irrespective of the flow of time or *water* in the river, that means we can travel back and forth through time. This is how time travel works in your universe, then?" she asked the boy.

The boy, who looked to be maybe eleven and wore rumpled blue trousers and a jumper with wide blue-and-gray horizontal stripes, shrugged. He had a messy mop of dark hair and large, sad blue eyes. Alister thought he looked like the weight of the world was resting on his scrawny shoulders.

"It's how we do it," he said heavily.

"YOUR TAPESTRY IS UNRAVELING," Dave remarked, rolling back from the water's edge. "THIS UNIVERSE HAS BEEN WRITTEN OVER SO MANY TIMES, THE INK IS BEGINNING TO SHOW THROUGH."

"I think you're mixing your metaphors now," Elo chided.

"I AM DOING THE BEST I CAN," Dave began.

"Yes, yes, I *know*," Professor Odd cut in. "Peter and I have already discussed this. He thinks it's because of a great big chronostrophe he caused when he left his native timeline, but *I* think it was because of an *even bigger* chronostrophe that happened in *epi-time*, a long *epi-time* ago. But I can't be sure, for obvious reasons."

"It looks like it's getting worse," Elo remarked, as the water level rose.

"*Yes*," said the boy—Peter—crossing his arms impatiently. "I *told* her. There's a chronostrophe starting up in a couple thousand years. And since we've let it alone it's getting *worse*."

"Hold on," said Alister. "If this is *time* travel, and your chronostrophe doesn't happen for another two thousand years, what's the hurry?"

"You're still thinking of it as a one-directional spatio-temporal event," Professor Odd explained, but quickly, keeping an eye on the height of the water. "Like a regular *catastrophe*. A *chronostrophe* is a catastrophe *in time*. It ripples out all ways. And those ripples can disturb things far away from the epicenter of the event. This one, it seems, is causing a flood."

"It's thousands of years in the future from where we left conventional time and space," the boy Peter explained, making a nervous gesture with his hands. "But as far as the universe is concerned, it's happening *now*. And since we can only go forwards at a fixed rate in epi-time, as you're calling it, if we're going to fix this, we have to go *now*."

"Yes, how *do* we fix this?" Elo asked.

Peter gave an aggravated sigh. "We go to the beginning and *see what happened*."

"How can you tell where the beginning is?" Alister asked.

"I can't tell," Peter said. "But *she* can." He pointed. They looked.

Out in the center of the water, standing above the waves as if they were a solid bank, stood a horse. It was far and away the most remarkable horse Alister had ever seen: tall as an elephant with a flowing blue mane and tail and a coat to match. Subtle patterns of swirls and dots decorated its coat. The tail flowed away in the direction of the river, and Alister could not see its end. The horse's eyes looked like flat, black pools, and made him shudder.

"Another metaphor?" he asked nervously.

"You could say that," said Professor Odd. "Time beings aren't corporeal, but they do have some control over how they are perceived. Ready everyone? Peter, we'll follow your lead."

This time, when they ran, Alister was able to keep his head about him. They each caught hold of the horse's mane as it trotted past, and were then dragged back out into the river. Instead of sinking, however, whatever mysterious force was keeping the horse afloat was now affecting them as well, and they ran down over the frothing water for quite a while, before abruptly plunging into its depths. He had to close his eyes.

It was not so bad this time: there was a ringing in Alister's ears and then they both popped at once, but other than that he felt fine. A wave of warm air hit his face, and the cold strands of hair disappeared from under his fingers. He gave a small sigh of relief.

Relief that quickly vanished when strong hands grabbed him by the shoulders and a bright light shone in his eyes.

"Arrgh!" he said, and batted at the hands.

"State your name, rank, and serial identification," came a sharp, authoritative voice from behind a hazmat mask.

"Bane," said Alister. "Alister Bane. Rank . . . *am* . . . student? I haven't got one of those serial numbers . . . "

The hands released him sharply. Alister blinked and looked around.

They appeared to be in a small, sterile chamber made of white plastic blocks. A few feet away Professor Odd and Peter were receiving similar treatment, while another suited person was approaching Elo warily holding a collar on the end of a stick.

"Don't you even *think* about it," she growled, and the person stopped in their tracks.

Two more figures had crowded around Dave, but seemed unwilling to approach him.

"Sir," said one of Dave's attendants. "This robot isn't like anything I've ever seen. I don't think they're natives."

"I AM NOT A ROBOT," Dave objected, causing all the suited people to jump.

"Look," said Peter, rising to his knees. "I think something's gone very wrong here—or something *will* go wrong—and I've got to try and fix it. It would help me loads if you'd tell me who you are and what you're doing here."

"Yes," said Professor Odd brightly. "And *where* are we, exactly?"

The suited figures stared at them. Then one—the one who seemed to be in charge—turned to another and said: "Put them through decon, I'll see them in my office at seventeen hundred. See if you can get a serial number off the robot."

"I AM NOT—" Dave began, but Professor Odd shushed him.

Alister felt hands grab him under the armpits, and he was lifted to his feet. The person in the suit behind him marched him, gently but firmly, through a door and out of the room. By the sounds of it, the others were experiencing the same.

Decon turned out to be less traumatic than Alister had feared. He found himself shunted into a small white room where his handler went over and turned some levers on the far wall. A thick mist filled the room, which stuck to all parts of him. He closed his eyes and tried not to breathe too much. This was followed by a stiff wind, which made him feel stripped and bare. Finally the suited person took a soft brush and brushed him all over with it, as though he were a dog. He wondered, absently, what Elo was making of her decon experience.

When his handler had finished they took the brush and held it under a blue-violet light in a little alcove in the wall. A green light flashed soon after, and the room made a happy *bing* noise.

A door opened in the far wall, and Alister was ushered out of it.

They emerged into a circular gray hall with piping down one side and little banks of monitors on the other. His guide pulled open a hidden panel, revealing a closet with racks of similar suits. Pulling a string on the side of their helmet, his handler pulled it off and shook out a fringe of blond hair. Clear blue eyes peered at him out of a light brown face that was sprinkled with a few dark freckles.

Alister was stumped as to whether the person was male or female, and they were giving him such an appraising look that it made him feel quite awkward.

"Hello?" he tried.

"Well," they said at length. "You're not a replicant, at least. Have you got any psychic powers?"

Their voice was light and husky, and gave absolutely nothing away. Alister gave up.

"Not that I know of," he said cautiously. "Ahm, who are you?"

"I am Corp Lib," said the person, unzipping their suit and stepping out of it. Underneath they were wearing a trim gray jumpsuit covered in pockets with an insignia like a comet blazed across one shoulder. "Seven eight zero five one nine. Give me your hand."

Reluctantly Alister stretched out his hand, and Corp Lib clipped a small metal bracelet to it. They pressed a button and turned on a green light along one edge.

"Green is clear," Corp Lib explained. "Orange means you're in a controlled zone. Red means you'd better have an escort or the cleaners come pick you up. Follow me."

Leaving Alister with his hand still partly extended, the person called Corp Lib strode away down the hall. Alister followed a little shakily.

It led a long way, gently curving the whole time, and there were no windows. It began to feel suffocating. Eventually Corp Lib ushered him into a disc-shaped room with a sterile white light in the ceiling and cube-like chairs scattered about. Alister assumed they were chairs anyway; Professor Odd and Peter were sitting on them when Corp Lib opened the door.

"Hello there," Professor Odd said brightly as Alister took a seat. "Maybe you could help us with something, er . . . " she trailed off at the sight of Corp Lib's androgynous face.

"That's Corp Lib," Alister told her, not bothering to elaborate. He trusted the Professor, with her greater experience of different gender norms across universes, to be able to handle the situation better than he.

"Corp Lib," Professor Odd swept on, and the person in question paused as they were about to turn for the door.

"I am not authorized to divulge any sensitive information to you," they informed the Professor blankly.

"Oh, I'm not asking *that*," Professor Odd said. "Not *yet*, anyway. No, what we were wondering, actually, is what today's *date* is? Because, if what Peter here tells me is true, this building *shouldn't exist* for another *thousand* years . . . " she trailed off hopefully.

Corp Lib's brown, freckled face went, if possible, even blanker. They were saved from having to answer, however, by another door opening and Elo being shown in. Her fur was spiky and standing on end, and she glared at the person guiding her, who was a young man with a neat black beard and the same light brown skin as Corp Lib, only he had brown hair as well. Comparing the two, Alister noticed how they both exhibited characteristics of multiple races, all sort of mashed together to the extent that he couldn't place them as any particular race he knew.

"Thank your stars you don't have *fur*," Elo said bitterly, sitting down next to the Professor. "I don't suppose anyone's got a hairbrush? A *proper* one," she said, glaring at her handler.

"What year is it?" Professor Odd asked the young man instead.

To Alister's amusement the man balked at this as well. He turned to Corp Lib and said: "What year *are* we at, now?"

Corp Lib's mouth pressed together into a tight, thin line. *"Jeryl,"* they said in a warning tone.

"Do you not know *either?*" Professor Odd asked, sounding unreasonably eager. "There are several ways to find out. I could help . . . "

She trailed off. Both Corp Lib and Jeryl had stopped paying attention to them, their expressions turning inward and their heads tilting slightly to one side. They looked, for all the world, like people who were listening intently to something only they could hear. Or they were both having strokes. Alister wasn't sure.

Then the light on his wristband began blinking red. Looking around, he saw the same thing happening to the bands around Professor Odd, Elo, and Peter's wrists.

"That's not good . . . " Peter began.

Corp Lib and Jeryl both jerked to attention as if coming out of a daze. They looked at each other, nodded, and then rounded on the little group. Corp Lib touched a button at their collar and said: "Backup to holding room seven please. Backup, holding room seven."

"What's going on?" Elo asked sharply.

"Sensitive information, probably," Alister sighed.

A few moments later one man and one woman wearing darker jumpsuits with belts studded with weapons walked in from yet *another* door. They were the same brown as Corp Lib and Jeryl, though the man had close-cropped, extremely curly red hair.

With their two reinforcements, Alister found his group marched out of the room and down another hall.

Rounding a corner, Alister—who was in front—found himself hit by a blast of cold air. Blinking, he gaped and stared at the sight of a huge blue horse, its head tucked down around its forefeet in order to fit into the little passage. Blank dark eyes gazed at them, and Alister got the uncomfortable impression that its tail was stretching out through the wall.

The reaction from their captors was astounding.

Far from being shocked, they immediately pulled their charges to either side of the corridor—though Peter made a determined effort to get away—and Alister heard the man say in calm, businesslike tones, "We have an incursion on floor sub three. Incursion on sub three. Type A."

The horse snorted cold air over them, then vanished.

"What was your *horse* doing here?" Elo demanded.

"What did you mean, Type *A?*" Professor Odd asked, rounding on the man who had spoken.

The man only glared back, and without a word the four of them took a prisoner each and dragged them back down the hall, the way they had come.

This time they were thrown into a bare rectangular room with no furnishings. A door slammed behind them, and they were left alone.

"What *is* going on here?" Alister asked.

"This place is in the wrong time," Peter explained, gravely. "It belongs *at least* another two thousand years forward."

"How do you know it's the whole *place*?" Professor Odd asked, curious. "Not just the people who are out of date?"

Peter sighed. "The people look like sixtieth century New Americans. The architecture of this place, and some of the building materials, is all sixtieth century. While my horse took us to somewhere in the forty-second century, A.D. It shouldn't *be* here."

"Sorry?" said Elo. "How can you tell?"

Peter brushed a hand across his face. "With the people, it's their race: they're all mixes. By the sixtieth century there aren't recognizable races in New America anymore. Everyone's a bit of everything. Also, that one that brought Alister in was a nether."

"A what?" asked Alister.

"A nether," said Peter. "A *ney,* you might call . . . er . . . *nem* I think is the possessive form. Nethers are just what it sounds like: *neither* male or female. The farther forward you go, the more often you find them. They didn't become really common until after the fiftieth century, though."

"And your horse," Professor Odd said. "They seemed to rec-ognize it. Type A, remember?"

Peter nodded. "That's troubling. Most people can't see my horse. Not until they've been outside the river."

"In epi-time, you mean." Elo said.

Peter shrugged. He went over to a piece of wall where there was a little writing in one corner, and peered at it. Then he took a multi-tool from his pocket and began working at the seam around the panel.

"Er, what are you doing?" Alister asked.

"I need to know what this building is doing here," Peter said. "It would help if I knew which building this *was*. Everything was robot-assembled in the sixtieth century, and the robots would have a code for the building that's usually—*ah!*"

The panel came away in his hands, revealing a glowing square beyond. Peter paid it no attention, however, and turned the piece of metal over in his hands. Peering at it, he frowned, and then put it back.

"Any luck?" Elo asked.

"Sort of," Peter said. He'd gotten a deep, probing look on his face, as though there were some pain in his body that he was try-ing to isolate and diagnose. "The code is 10B208C Manhattan. Now, 10, that means it was built for scientific research. The let-ter B stands for *floor*—don't ask me why—and 208 is the num-ber of them. C is the region in New America. Mid-east coast, I think. *Manhattan* though, that's odd. They didn't usually name buildings like that. But I remember a building called Manhat-tan. I remember hearing about it when I was in the seventieth century. But that was a long time ago—for me, anyway."

"What do you remember about it?" Professor Odd asked.

Peter looked up at her. "I remember it blew up," he said.

There was a *hissing* sound and a panel of wall slid away, re-vealing another room beyond a wall of transparent material. This one was comfortably if sparsely furnished, and there were people standing in it. They all wore jumpsuits like Corp Lib and Jeryl, only these were black with little patches of red on the shoulders. One, Alister guessed cautiously, was a woman, one was a man, and one he couldn't say. Probably a nether, like Peter had described. They were all more or less brown-skinned, all dark-haired except the man, who had a snowy head with a face like a walnut peering out from underneath and stringy, veined hands. He glared at them through the transparent wall, and Alister felt his hopes for the success of their adventure wither under that stare.

Professor Odd, however, showed no such reservations. She went right up to the wall—which wasn't glass, Alister was sure; there were no reflections, just a slight fuzzy quality about the air—and smiled sunnily at their captors.

"Hallo," she said. "I'm Professor Odd. This is Lucky Peter. Those are my friends, Elo and Mr. Alister. We've got another, Dave, who isn't here at the moment, but don't worry—we're here to *help.*"

This got a blank stare from the people on the other side of the barrier.

"*Go* on," Odd said, nudging Peter with one elbow. "*Tell* them."

"They won't believe me," Peter said dourly. "They never believe me."

"They will this time," Professor Odd said, and for a moment the cheerful expression cracked, and Alister caught a glimpse of how deadly serious she was. She jerked her head toward their audience. "*Tell them,*" she said.

Peter opened his mouth, but the white-haired man spoke first:

"I am Dr. Rakar," he said icily. "You have been taken into custody following your breach of the secure sub-level of the Manhattan Tower. If you cooperate you will not be harmed. Now tell us: What sort of machine is this?" and he stepped aside to reveal Dave.

Or . . . not Dave. Just his suit, Alister thought, judging by how quiet and dark it was. Also the lack of any sort of objection at being called a machine. Professor Odd put her head on one side and frowned.

"That's not a machine," she said carefully. "That ought to have our friend Dave in it."

"There was a parasite," offered the nether, who wore a white armband and gloves and seemed vaguely medical. "Bio-scans picked up a non-sentient life form, but when we tried to remove it there were . . . well . . . there was an accident."

"*What?*" cried Professor Odd, dropping all pretense at cheerfulness. She looked aghast.

"What did you do with Dave?" Alister demanded.

"Where *is he?*" barked Elo.

Peter flinched at the shouting, and the people on the other side looked confused. The nether seemed indignant as well.

"We did *nothing* with the parasite," they said, a little bitterly. "It discharged a large quantity of green-colored slime and got away. The slime seriously compromised the condition of the Corp handling the machine, and now the machine won't work. We're also quite worried about our Corp. Can you please tell us if that slime has any toxins or other poisons that might be harmful?"

Professor Odd shut her eyes and rubbed her face. "That wasn't a *parasite*," she groaned. "That was a *person*. His name is Dave. He is incredibly intelligent and clever and very, very different from us. That machine is his panvironment suit. He was probably terrified at being ripped out of it, and reacted accordingly. I wouldn't worry about your Corp—he probably used a mix of opioids and other nervous system depressants that should wear off with rest and rehydration—but you *should* be worried about the fate of this place. *Tell them,* Peter," she said earnestly.

Peter looked up at the adults in the other room, a little sulkily.

"They're not from this universe," he said, jerking his head toward Professor Odd. "I am, but I'm from another time. So are you, it seems. You're about two thousand years in the past of where you should be, and this building's presence here is wreaking havoc on the future of the universe—which is already pretty messy, let me tell you. The best thing you can do is explain to us exactly what happened to you, what is going on now, and then we can find a way to get you home."

"Also," added Professor Odd. "Why did you call his horse a Type A?"

There was a stir in the group of people beyond the barrier, and the women came and whispered in the ear of Dr. Rakar. He replied with a question, which was answered with a nod.

"Take the barrier down," he said.

There was a sort of flickering in the air and a *fizzing* noise.

Carefully Professor Odd put a finger through the space where the barrier had been, then her hand, arm, and finally she stepped over to the other side.

The white-haired man watched her warily, but didn't seem particularly hostile. He was frowning, though, his dark eyes wrinkled almost out of existence.

"You saw the horse," he said stonily.

"Yes, *yes,*" said Professor Odd, waving a hand. "We've been through epi-time, all of us . . . as have *you* . . . " she added, her focus sharpening on the man. "If you saw it as a horse . . . "

"We call them incursions," the woman offered. "Type A's are the ones that look like horses."

"You've seen others?" Peter asked cautiously. He seemed almost hopeful, and Alister wondered if he could look forward to seeing cat and dog versions of the boy's horse.

"Not since the original jump," said the woman. She looked questioningly at the doctor, and when he nodded she continued. "We term them Type B's. *I* only ever saw them in conjunction with Type A's, though sometimes they appeared on their own. They look sort of like *riders.*"

"Riders . . . " Professor Odd repeated, turning back to Peter. "Riders?" she asked.

Peter shook his head. "I've never ridden the horse. It seemed wrong."

"Yes, yes, but have you ever *seen* one?" she pressed on.

"No," said Peter. "It's just the horse. It's always only ever been the one horse."

Slowly Professor Odd turned back to Dr. Rakar. "I think you had better tell me *exactly* what happened to this place," she said. "And what you saw during this *jump* of yours."

"First you tell me what that Dave creature is going to do to my staff," he returned.

"Probably nothing," Professor Odd said, surprised. "He'll try to get his bearings, and then come and find me. He's not malicious, I assure you. Provided you don't try to hurt him. Oh, but he can't communicate vocally without his translator; he speaks through psychoactive slime. So if he tries to glom onto your head it's just because he wants to talk to you."

The man gave Professor Odd a skeptical look. Shaking his head he walked over to one of the benches protruding from the side of the wall and sat down. Professor Odd promptly folded her legs under her and sat on the floor so she wouldn't tower over him. After a moment Elo and Alister followed suit.

"You appear to know as much about time travel as we do," he said. "So you'll excuse me diving right in. I am Dr. Rakar, as I have said. These are my chief of staff: Professor Cove"—he nodded at the woman—"and Dr. Mero"—a gesture toward the nether with the white armband. "I don't know what *your* native time period is, but do you have any knowledge of the sixty-first century A.D.?"

"Not in this universe, sorry," Professor Odd said.

"Human expansion and colonization of Mars," Peter said cautiously. "The first terraforming missions to Alpha Seti are launched."

Dr. Rakar was nodding.

"This . . . *place*, as you so flippantly put it, is the Manhattan Tower, built to house and conduct research from those same missions. It was built on the site of an ancient, Old American city that had been one of those lost during the Oceanrise of the twenty-first century. Our basement incorporates much of that city's subterranean transit system, which was carved out of a huge hard rock deposit. Because of its size, the building was equipped with its own fusion generator—which is the only reason we've managed to remain functional for so long without access to our home time's infrastructure.

"You see . . . " Dr. Rakar hitched himself forward a little, so as to ease his back. "We're not sure exactly why . . . but this building has been . . . how to say . . . *moving around*? Not just in space but in time as well."

"Yes," said Peter. "That's why we're here. You ought not to be moving at all. In either."

Dr. Rakar gave Peter an arch look.

"*How* did you begin this . . . erm . . . *moving around?*" Professor Odd asked.

Dr. Rakar got shakily to his feet and began to pace. He was a tall, long-limbed man who clearly didn't feel comfortable unless a part of him was in motion. Professor Odd took to swiveling herself around on the floor to keep track of him.

"On January the 18th, 6081, at exactly thirteen hundred hours, twenty-one minutes, time as we knew it ceased to exist. *Time* of some sort continued, as our cognitive and biological functions were not compromised, but all our atomic clocks stopped at once. That's how we have such a precise notation of the time.

"At the same instant, all our external sensors went haywire, and reports from the observation corridors told us that we—and our entire building—had been transported. We were no longer at our site in the Husson Delta, but—as far as we could see—in a desolate landscape with only a few coarse bushes here and there. What was really unbelievable, however, was that the tower appeared to be standing in the middle of a *river*, and the water was flowing *through* us. Through our basement levels, that is, only our basement wasn't obstructing the flow of water. . . . " He spoke earnestly, but with a wary edge to his voice that suggested he still doubted, even now, that he would be believed.

"Yes," said Peter with a sigh. "The river is like that."

"It's not *really* a river, you see," Professor Odd explained kindly. "It's a physical representation of the course of time within epi-time."

Dr. Rakar looked amazedly at his staff, who were in turn staring at Professor Odd with expressions of mixed fear and hope.

"You *have* been there!" the nether gasped.

"How is that even possible?" Peter said. "*I've* never seen you there!"

"That doesn't mean they weren't in epi-time," Professor Odd said. "They could have come and gone before *you* ever set foot in there. It's called epi-*time* for a reason. Time *does* pass there," she went on, turning back to Dr. Rakar. "Exactly as you say. It's just not the kind we can measure by conventional means. But it *does.* That's how your brain was able to continue to process experiences linearly and your heart was able to keep pumping blood and you were able to put one word after another. Erm . . . what else did you see? Besides the river? Because your area of epi-time sounds a lot different than the bits I saw. It was all mountains and forests last time we were there."

A frown clouded Dr. Rakar's face, and the man paced nervously side to side. "You mean there was no sign of the war?" he asked.

"*War*?" exclaimed Peter.

"War . . . what war?" Professor Odd asked.

"When *we* were there," Dr. Rakar said, "there was a *war* going on. Between the two types of incursions. Our observation team reported seeing a battle take place on the banks of the river. It appeared to be fought by the horse-type beings—Type A's—and another set that were more humanoid—what we call Type B's. Sometimes the Type B's appeared *riding* the Type A's, and the staff took to calling them *riders* because of that. These carried spears and other primitive weapons, which gave us the misguided impression that they were themselves similarly primitive.

"While we argued about what we should do, the fighting outside increased. It got near enough that we could hear a booming like cannon fire. Our observation team reported seeing a structure like a trebuchet on the horizon. According to them it fired something in our direction. Then the whole building was hit by a blast wave of some sort—yet suffered no structural damage. All of us felt it, however, even the androids. The whole population was knocked out for a short period.

"When we came around, the clocks were working again, and time seemed to be passing normally once more. There was no sign of the horses or the riders or the battle, but we were not back where we belonged. Instead of the Husson Delta, we were in a desolate snowfield which we later deduced was in Siberia. The real shocker, however, came when we picked up signal from the technosphere and discovered we were in the year 3056— *three thousand years* in the past."

"Hold on," said Elo. "You said *thirty*-fifty-six? It's . . . what now Peter?"

"We are currently in the latter half of 4213," Peter supplied.

"If you arrived in the thirty-first century, and now it's well past the fortieth," said Elo, "what have you been *doing* for the past thousand years?"

Dr. Rakar was nodding, and lifted a hand for silence. "Yes, yes, well . . . that is the second part of our story. It's a bit hard to explain, you understand. The best way I can put it is . . . well . . . we've *jumped forward* a couple times."

"*How?*" pressed Peter.

Dr. Rakar sighed. "We don't *know,*" he admitted. "Professor Cove"—he nodded at the woman with curly black hair—"hypothesizes it has something to do with the anomaly, but that could be coincidence."

"Anomaly?" Professor Odd piped up.

"Oh yes," said Cove, all too eagerly. "About a year after we arrived in 3056—so, 3057 really—we had a massive transdimensional rupture in the herbarium sphere. We call it the anomaly for lack of a better term, but *I* think—"

Dr. Rakar cut her off with a wave of his hand. "We'll come to that in due course," he growled. "Put plainly, Professor . . . er . . . *Odd,* Mr. Peter. Every two or three years—of *standard, conventional time*—we find ourselves pushed forward, suddenly, by approximately four hundred years. In 3059 we jumped to 3360. In 3362, we jumped to 3825, and in 3828 we were pushed to 4210. Despite Cove's hypothesis we really don't know *why* it's happening. All we know is it *does,* and when it does we move to a different location. From Siberia in 3059 we moved to the Australian outback in 3360. From there in 3362 we jumped to Antarctica in 3825. It was a good thing by then we'd figured out how to cloak the tower, since we were deposited uncomfortably near the International Ross Research Facility. We've been very careful not to interact with the temporal locals, for fear of changing history."

"That's very . . . prudent, of you," Peter said with guarded approval.

Dr. Rakar tilted an eyebrow at him. "We may be out of our depth, but we're not *fools.*"

"So, where are we *now?*" Elo asked.

"Now?" said Dr. Rakar with a heavy sigh. "It's, as you say, 4013, and we're in the Mid-Sierra Demilitarized Zone.

Practically home again, except for the fact that New America doesn't exist yet."

"But you arrived in what? 4010?" Professor Odd asked. "You're due for another jump any day now, if the pattern holds." She turned to look at Peter. "Is *that* why we're here? To help them get *home*?"

"It would be a good start," Peter said. "You're running a great risk, bouncing forward in time like this. What if, next jump, you come through in a heavily populated area? You've been incredibly lucky, so far."

Dr. Rakar passed a hand in front of his eyes. "We are acutely aware of that," he said.

"And there are other concerns," Professor Cove dove in. "The state of the anomaly suggests the tower will not survive the journey at the present rate of expansion."

"*Yes,*" said Professor Odd, rising to her feet to face the dark woman. "Do tell me more about this anomaly!"

Professor Cove seemed startled at this intensity. She blushed, but went on energetically.

"It began as spontaneous explosion of plasma in the herbarium sphere," she said, fiddling on her belt and detaching a small black box. She flipped open a lid and pressed some buttons. Immediately a holographic display popped into life in front of her. It showed a huge room with plants growing on the bottom and up the sides, and little walkways crisscrossing the empty space above.

"Here is a re-creation of its advent," she said, and pressed another button. In the hologram a single point of impossibly bright light appeared and then suddenly expanded outward, making the whole image white out for a second. When the colors and shadows came back, the speck remained as a single point of light, tiny and hanging in the air.

"Amazingly, it did not damage our structure," said Professor Cove. "Since then it has existed purely as a ball of light. One which does not affect *any physical object* near it. We contained the area and did an atmospheric purge, but the anomaly remained unaffected. As time has passed it has evolved to the point where our sensors can't make head or tail of it. It was monumentally radioactive—or it was about as harmful as a lump of coal. According to our infrared sensors, it was about 3 degrees Kelvin, yet it did not affect the ambient temperature of the surrounding air." Cove shook her head. "It's also not adversely affecting the flora we have growing there, though we still don't allow people inside without containment suits. Now, the worrisome thing is *this* . . ." the woman tapped some more buttons on her box. "Here is a record of the anomaly's state before and after the jump from 3059 to 3360. Watch . . ."

In the hologram, the tiny speck of light flickered, then suddenly expanded. Alister guessed it was now about the size of a cricket ball.

"3362 to 3825 . . ." said Professor Cove.

Now the cricket ball sized globe of light quivered, and then suddenly blew up to the size of a beach ball. Or one of those silly rubber balls people used to do home calisthenics.

"And finally, 3828 to 4010 . . ."

The sphere of light pulsed, sending little ripples of light across the projection, and then sharply expanded to the size of a small hot air balloon. It filled the room and blotted out much of the hologram with its light.

"This is as it exists now," said Professor Cove. "It's taking up most of the free air in the herbarium sphere, and the bottom side has damaged some of the taller trees. That's the distressing part of it: even though the thing isn't giving off any detectable amount of radiation—in fact, it doesn't seem to react with outside material at *all*—it appears it cannot coexist with outside matter. It's shorn off the tops of the conifers, clean as a whistle. It rejects all states of matter, too. I've wanted to test whether it will reject atoms or their components, but we've agreed that's too dangerous. We're not sure what is setting it off—it could be the time jumps, or it could be something that just happens to coincide with the time jumps. And the thing is, by my calculations, the next time it expands . . . it's going to do *this* . . ."

A final button press. This time the hologram showed the sphere of light flare, sending up tendrils of fire, and then it enlarged again. The view from the hologram backed out sharply, passing through transparent walls until Alister could see the shape of the Manhattan Tower, like a long, narrow, boat-shaped building that rose in steeples and cliffs. The sphere of light, which was located in the center of it, swelled out to engulf the heart of the building, digging into the foundation and peaking above some of the lower towers.

"Now, I can't predict what effect the sphere will have on our infrastructure," Cove said. "But running a simulation of what would happen if the center of the tower was suddenly just— *poof*—gone, it doesn't look good. The area the anomaly encompasses includes part of our fusion reactor and . . . "

"Basically the building explodes," Professor Odd finished, looking down at Peter meaningfully.

The boy climbed thoughtfully to his feet. "Yes," he said quietly. "That's what I remember."

"You *remember* this building exploding?" Professor Cove asked in amazement.

"I'm a *time*-traveler," Peter said heavily. "I've been to your future. *Future* future. I heard . . . it was history then . . . about a building called the Manhattan Tower exploding. It was only in passing, though. I don't know any details."

"Do you remember when the explosion took place?" Professor Odd asked.

Peter shut his eyes and frowned. "It's hard. I was somewhere in the seventieth century—sorry, this was a long time ago—and I had to defuse a time bomb. One of the locals who was helping me made this crack about, if we didn't get the bomb defused, the building we were in was going to explode like the Manhattan Tower. Those were her exact words. As you can imagine, I had other things on my mind and didn't ask for details."

"We can still infer rather a lot from that," Elo pointed out. "Like, if she knew it *was* the Manhattan Tower, that suggests it *was* in its own time. Because if it exploded, say, sometime in the forty-hundreds, natives wouldn't *know* that was the Manhattan Tower. They'd just be like 'Whoa, big explosion!'"

"So you must find a way to get back to your own time!" Professor Odd said cheerfully.

The two doctors and the professor looked at her glumly.

"Yes, and promptly explode," Peter added.

"We'll figure something out about that," Professor Odd said cheerfully, waving a hand. "Now, I think we'd better go take a *look* at this anomaly. And see if you can get a message to Dave telling him to meet us there. I bet he'd like to see it. Oh, Elo, Alister, could you help me with his suit?"

They took a small tram to the herbarium sphere. Alister was grateful, since Dave's suit was heavy and awkward to push, even with Elo's help.

His mind was still spinning, first from the shock of *time travel*, and then the shock of finding himself in a building the size of a city. Then again, he reasoned, it was not so different from going into another world completely, and the inhabitants of the Manhattan Tower seemed, on the whole, like decent people. Overworked, stressed-out people, but not the sort to intentionally make their lives difficult. Also, having been put through some very strange experiences themselves rendered them more apt to accept Professor Odd and Elo. A little part of Alister's mind was still a bit worried about Dave, but considering that all the other times the creature had disappeared on them he had proved more than capable of taking care of himself, Alister tried not to fret.

Any lingering doubts that still lurked in the back of his mind were banished when they reached the herbarium sphere.

Perhaps because of the sound of its name, Alister had got in his head an image of a large metal globe with a door in one side. As it turned out the sphere was rectangular, like all the other rooms they'd passed through, albeit one that must have been several stories high and the size of two or three city blocks. And it was filled with plants. The tram they were on stopped at a platform on the ground, and their group stepped out into warm, gentle sunshine speckled with green shadows of tree leaves and branches. The whole place smelled pleasantly of earth and pine and other foliage, and the air had a tender, moist quality that soothed Alister's lungs.

There was a rustle in the branches above them, and Alister looked up. Immediately he saw two things:

The first was a giant disk hovering just above the treetops—and in certain places resting upon them. It was featureless and white, and though it appeared to glow, its harsh light didn't so much as stain the trees, which continued to bask in a sort of autumn twilight. It made Alister's eyes hurt to look at, and so he cast his gaze down a bit, and saw Dave hanging from the branches of a nearby oak.

"*There* you are!" Professor Odd cried, pushing past Dr. Rakar and going to stand beneath the tree. Standing below the dangling green arms she plucked off her wig and patted the top of her bald head, like someone calling a bird. "Come on, then," she said. "We have your suit, but I want your input on *that*," she jerked a thumb at the disc hovering above them.

To the consternation of Dr. Rakar and his staff Dave swarmed down the tree and onto Professor Odd's head, where he clung, wrapping two arms around her skull and draping the others gently over her shoulders. Alister wondered how much more of a fuss they would have made if Professor Odd had turned around and they'd been able to see her own tentacle, fleshy white and green leopard-spotted, protruding just above the neckline of her coat. On the whole he thought it was better they hadn't.

"Are you all right?" Elo asked, pushing her way through the crowd.

Professor Odd blinked, sniffed, and coughed a bit.

"Dave is fine," she said after a while. "The Corp who . . . *surprised* him should be given lots of water and a hearty meal of eggs and banana, and should make a full recovery in less than a day. Now, if you'll *please* be quiet, we were discussing your anomaly. Which isn't so much an *anomaly*, I might add, but something that's been *misplaced*. Almost as badly as you. Yes? Oh no . . . I don't think they have that technology." Her expression had turned inward, and Alister could tell she was now talking to Dave. "*Really?*" she said. "Well, that's *fantastic!* And actually makes sense. How long have we got? Oh . . . oh, dear. Well, that would be pretty upsetting, but remember, we're dealing with *time travel.* Yes, yes it's *dreadfully* important. What? No! No, I don't think it's *supposed* to explode, not actually. Yes. Yes, I think there was a war. A war in *epi-time*. Oh, you bet it did. *Lots* of incongruities. And now they're stuck in one that's grown into a chronostrophe. Yes. Well, it's worth a try. Oh, I'm not sure about that. Look, why don't we put you back in your suit and you can ask them *yourself*."

As she spoke Professor Odd was wandering toward Alister, who still stood with one hand protectively resting on the dome of Dave's panvironment suit. Dr. Rakar drew respectfully back, but Dr. Mero leaned forward, fascinated.

"Is it *psychic?*" they asked.

"Not really," Professor Odd said, bowing down to allow Dave to scramble in through the hatch on the side. "Dave just communicates on a different frequency than we do."

There was a twitch and whir within Dave's suit, and a few lights flashed. The sensor dish did a circuit of the dome and the gear around his midsection rotated.

"THAT'S BETTER," blared the robotic voice. "NOW, I HAVE QUESTIONS. THEN WE MUST ACT AT ONCE SO WE ARE NOT DESTROYED."

"First, however, I think I ought to explain," Professor Odd cut in. "There's something *much,* much, *much* bigger going wrong here than just your tower getting plopped in the wrong part of space-time."

"Do you *have* to explain to them about *that?*" Peter asked, eyeing the glowing sphere nervously.

"I think I should," Professor Odd said. "It'll help me understand."

"You see," she went on, turning to face Dr. Rakar and the other two. "This *entire* universe, like I said before, is in a bad way. Things are happening out of order, paradoxes come and go, and since it's got no way to split into *different* universes, it's basically tearing itself apart. Now, I *think* this might be the result of the battle you witnessed when you were in epi-time. A side effect is people like you getting torn out of your native time periods and plopped down any-old-where, which in turn is creating *more* problems. So . . . first thing we need to do is get you *back* where you belong . . . second thing . . . *what* is it, Peter?"

Peter had been tugging insistently on her sleeve, and now he raised himself on tiptoe to whisper something urgently in her ear. Professor Odd grinned and shook her head.

"Yes, but do you really think this building's *meant* to explode?" she asked.

Peter frowned. "How do you mean?"

"I mean, what *you* heard—in your past and *their* future—
that was from a point in epi-time when you *hadn't* been here
yet. You *hadn't* helped them get home. So the version of time
in which they get back to their time and then blow up is one
in which *you and me* didn't interfere. I actually don't think this
chronostrophe was created by the building traveling through
time—it's an incongruity, yes, but nothing more—I think the
chronostrophe happened *because* it blew up. *Is* going to blow
up, if we don't do anything. I think the Manhattan Tower is
going to be *very important* to this universe sometime later on.
Or one of your staff"—she motioned toward Dr. Rakar—"who
would otherwise have died, is. *Our* job isn't to get it home—
that'll happen as long as we don't mess about too much—our
job is to stop it blowing up when it gets there."

"But this chronostrophe is *new* to epi-time," Peter persisted.
"It didn't exist before, even with the building blowing up."

"Two things," Professor Odd said, raising the respective
number of fingers. "One, you could have changed *something else*
that makes it necessary for the Manhattan Tower or its inhabitants to exist in their native future. So in effect you created a
chronostrophe by solving one. *Or, two:* What if that future you
were in *was* the chronostrophe, you just didn't know it yet?"

Peter looked up at her, his eyes wide and dancing.

"For someone who's not a time traveler," he said, "you're aw-
fully good at thinking four-dimensionally."

Professor Odd gave him a sly smile and turned back to Dr.
Rakar.

"This is all very interesting," the old man said dryly. "I'm
glad to hear you are so invested in our continued well-being."

"I am, generally, in all things," Professor Odd said brightly.

"But how in the world do you intend to get us back to 6081
without triggering a massive expansion of the anomaly?"

"I don't intend to take *you* anywhere," Professor Odd said,
wagging a finger at him. "Someone else has already taken care of
that. In the epi-temporal sense. No, what I'm most concerned
about is your anomaly here. I believe Professor Cove was absolutely right when she theorized the expansions were linked to
the jumps forward in time. In fact, far from being a *result* of the
time travel, I believe they are the *cause* of it."

"How do you figure that?" Professor Cove asked, a touch of indignation in her voice.

Professor Odd opened her mouth to begin and then turned to Dave, who whirred a bit before saying:

"THE ANOMALY IS YOUR UNIVERSE'S SUCCESSOR. IT IS JUMPING FORWARD THROUGH TIME, SEARCHING FOR A POINT AT WHICH IT CAN SUBJUGATE THIS UNIVERSE AND TAKE ITS PLACE. IT IS TAKING YOU ALONG WITH IT BY ACCIDENT."

"That's why you've been moving *forward*," Professor Odd explained excitedly. "That anomaly is actually a *baby* universe. To be precise, it's the universe that *should* have spontaneously occurred following the destruction of *this* one. For some reason, it's come in a bit early and wedged itself in a part of *this* universe. Specifically, *in this room*. Vastly unlucky, considering how much empty space this universe has. Anyway . . . "

"IT IS ATTEMPTING TO REALIGN WITH A SUITABLE TIME FRAME," Dave continued. "TRYING TO REACH A POINT WHERE THIS UNIVERSE DOES NOT EXIST. AS A RESULT IT IS DRAGGING ITS SURROUNDINGS INTO THE FUTURE ALONG WITH IT."

"That is wildly unlikely," Dr. Rakar said.

"*Unlikely,* yes," Professor Odd allowed. "But not *impossible*. Tell him, Dave."

Dave twirled in place, bringing his lighted panel to bear on the team of scientists.

"THE INACTIVE ACTION OF THE IMPACTED UNIVERSE IS SPATIALLY QUARANTINED. IT CANNOT AFFECT YOUR UNIVERSE IN CONVENTIONAL PHYSICAL WAYS. IN FACT, THE TWO CANNOT EXIST TOGETHER AT THE SAME TIME. *THAT* IS NOT JUST A UNIVERSE WITHIN A UNIVERSE, IT IS A *HOLE* IN YOUR UNIVERSE."

"How is it not collapsing? Or swallowing us?" Professor Cove asked.

"BECAUSE THERE IS A UNIVERSE *IN* IT," Dave said, with hint of impatience.

"I'm afraid all this doesn't explain the expansions, not to me, anyway," Dr. Mero admitted.

Dave extended four of his arms and raised them into the air, letting the upper ends flop down so the tips curled above his dome. Professor Odd took his meaning, and swept in.

"Because universes *do* expand. Most of them, anyway. This universe is pretty much identical to *your* universe, so of course it's expanding as well.   If I'm any judge, I'd say its native timestream runs even a little faster than yours. So here, you've experienced a few years . . . while hundreds of thousands— perhaps *billions*—of years had passed *in there . . .* " she pointed at the great orb of strange light hovering above them. "It appears to grow in leaps and bounds because it's growing *along with* the time jumps. So every time it jumps forward *in* time it grows the respective amount."

Dr. Rakar's shoulders drooped, and he exchanged a morose look with his staff.

"So you're saying there's no way at all for us to get home without this thing swelling up to the size of . . . oh, this entire *tower?*"

"I'm afraid not," admitted Professor Odd. Then she grinned. "Not to worry, though, I have a solution for that. You *would* be out of luck otherwise, but as it happens I have the very *specific* thing to solve this problem. I've got to go *get* it, however, and for that, I'm going to need *your* help," she finished, rounding on Lucky Peter.

"*My* help?" exclaimed Peter. "What *for?*"

"Why, to transplant the *impacted universe,* as Dave so clinically put it."

"IT IS AN ACCURATE TERM," Dave cut in.

"How do you intend to do that?" Dr. Rakar demanded.

"Depends," said Professor Odd.   "Do the expansions take place before, during, or after the time jumps?"

"The actual expanding happens after," said Professor Cove. "However, we can predict an oncoming jump by measuring the microwave radiation being projected on the surface of the anomaly—er, universe."

"Excellent," said Professor Odd, rubbing her hands together. "You keep right on doing that. Now, I'll take Peter and be off— we'll see you after the next jump."

So saying she took Peter by the hand and trotted off through the trees.

"What *are* you planning?" the boy demanded.

"I'll explain when we get back to the Oddity," Professor Odd assured him. "Now would you be so kind as to call your horse?"

"*Oi!*" Elo shouted, running after them. "What do *we* do?"

"Yes, what *about* us?" Alister asked, alarmed.

Professor Odd looked up at them, her brows raised in surprise. "You're going to help Dave, of course!" she said, and grinned at them.

The next moment there was a pounding of hooves, a rush of wind, and a flash of something blue. It made Alister's eyes sting, and he turned away to rub them. When he turned back, Peter and the Professor were gone.

"Well that's just *great*," he sighed.

Elo turned right around and put her paws on her hips. "*Help* you?" she barked at Dave. "Help you with *what?*"

Dave's arms slowly retracted until he was a solid metal cylinder again. "I REQUIRE PHYSICAL ASSISTANCE," he said. "CONSTRUCTING THE ANCHOR." He turned to the three staff members, who were beginning to look angry and bewildered. "BRING ME YOUR ENGINEERS," Dave intoned at them. Then added, a little grudgingly; "PLEASE."

Part Two

THEY CAME THROUGH KNEE DEEP in the shallows of the river and Peter refused to take Professor Odd anywhere until she explained.

"You're *planning* something," he said accusingly. "You're planning something, and we're not going *anywhere,* or when, until you tell me what it is!"

The Professor looked down at him, her face a mask of innocent surprise. It didn't fool Peter; he'd had *ages* of reading adults' faces: it was about the only way, he'd found, to get the truth out of them. He ground his teeth and put his hands on his hips.

"Isn't it *obvious?*" she asked. "We're going to save the Manhattan Tower!"

"*You're* saving it," Peter said.

"Not without *your* help, I can't," Professor Odd corrected him, gently wagging a finger. "You see . . . " she said, wading over to the shore, "what we're looking at is the eruption of an impacted universe. Basically, one universe starts up inside another. Well, things can't go on like that for long, so one of two things happens: either the larger, older universe finds a way to shut down the new one—crushing it out of existence—or the new one achieves a sort of critical mass and blows the old one apart. An eruption. Doesn't happen very often. Not at *all* in my experience. Universes are generally pretty good about keeping their timelines linear. Now, *your* universe, its timeline is all *over* the place. It was heading for self-destruction, even *with* all the little fixes you and your horse have been shoring it up with. So along comes this *new* universe, to fill its place in the void. Only, *surprise!* Because of you this universe isn't quite done yet, and so the new one is stuck in the old one, with no choice but to erupt. Oh, it's sliding forward, naturally, just like water sliding off a duck's back, because universes don't *like* coexisting this way, and they will scramble time trying to get apart. But there's *too much* time. So . . . "

"It'll blow," said Peter. "It'll blow apart the Manhattan Tower. I know. I've been *in* that future. So it *can't* have destroyed this universe!"

"Perhaps," said Professor Odd. She went over and sat down on a nearby rock. "You have to remember, that was at a different point in epi-time."

Peter frowned at her. She sighed.

"Am I right to assume that, the point at which you first heard about the Manhattan Tower explosion, it was fairly early on in this . . . crusade of yours?"

Peter nodded, his throat gone suddenly tight.

"At that *point* in epi-time, things might have gone a little differently. Obviously, they did. Because *I* wasn't there that time—oh."

"Oh?" said Peter. "Oh, *what?*"

"I just had the most uncomfortable thought."

"More uncomfortable than the universe ending?" Peter asked, scathingly.

Professor Odd looked down at him, seeming not to have heard. "Me," she said quietly. "It's *me.* I am your chronostrophe. Because I wasn't *here* last time. Whatever brought the Manhattan Tower forward also found a way to shut down the erupting universe before it destroyed this one. But because I've left Dave and Elo and Alister back there . . . they can't help but interfere. It really is . . . all on me. On us." Then she smiled at him, brilliantly. "Oh well," she said. "Let's just hope we're the good kind of chronostrophe."

"*How* can you be the good kind?" Peter wailed. Professor Odd had begun stumping along the bank, upstream. She turned her head over a shoulder at him.

"A chronostrophe is just a turning in time, where it wriggles and twists and lays over itself," she said. "Mostly, things are worse afterwards. Doesn't mean they *have* to be. You've got a *time horse,* I've got an *Oddity.* You move up and down through time. I'm stuck flowing in one direction, but *I* can move side-to-side in *space.* My Oddity can cross between universes."

"How does that help?" Peter asked.

"What do you think I'm crossing, when I'm between universes?" Professor Odd asked.

Peter felt his eyes open wide as a picture began to form in his mind.

"You *can't* mean . . . ?" he began.

"*Now* will you get your horse to carry us the rest of the way?" Professor Odd asked. "Back to where I left the Oddity, if you please. This will be *some* trick."

Alister stood with Elo on the floor of the herbarium sphere, watching Dave's anchor take shape. As far as Alister could tell they had not helped much. The staff of the Manhattan Tower, once it had been explained to them that doing what the not-a-robot in the metal barrel said would facilitate them getting home, had proved to be all the help Dave needed. Which was just as well, since Dave needed cranes, forklifts, hundreds of feet of metal pipe, pulleys, chains, and more hundreds of feet of solid metal girders.

"It's pretty unlucky, when you think about it," Alister remarked.

"What is?" Elo asked.

"This whole . . . *thing*," Alister said, waving a hand at the eerie, glowing orb of the baby universe. "That it had to turn up *here*. I mean, of all the places in *this* universe, it had to be in the middle of a *building*."

Elo considered this.

"Actually, I think it's very *lucky*," she said.

"How so?"

"Because here we can *do* something about it," she said. "If it had been in interstellar space, for example, no one would have noticed anything. It would just go *boom*, and no more old universe!"

Alister thought about this, and decided it was not comforting. He wondered how many universes ended that way: suddenly, with no warning, because something had gone terribly wrong in a place where no one could see or do anything about it. To take his mind off it, he pointed at the crew of corps (apparently a rank and not a name at all) welding metal girders together, and remarked: "I wonder what he's building."

Elo scratched behind one ear and regarded the scene critically. The metal girders were being assembled at the far end of the herbarium sphere, where they could stretch from the floor to the distant ceiling without coming into contact with the baby universe. Two girders had been balanced upright, wide enough apart to straddle the universe if they had to, while a third had been laid horizontally between them. Little clots of people were clustered around the corners on either side where the horizontal girder met the vertical ones. From between their close-packed bodies little jets of sparks flew.

"I don't believe it," Elo said at length with a shake of her head. "If I didn't know any better . . . I'd have to say . . . he's building a *door.*"

There was a *clang* from high above, and a fourth girder was lowered into place from a gap in the ceiling. Dave was up there, the bottom of his suit glowing bright blue from the anti-gravity plates, instructing the corps how the pieces should fit together.

His voice could just be heard: a faint fuzzy crackle that sounded mildly aggravated.

Alister looked over at Elo, feeling his eyes bulge.

"No . . . " he said. "No *way* . . . "

"Professor Odd *did* say to make an anchor," she said.

Alister looked back up at the shape taking form at the far end of the sphere. It was roughly square now and could, with a little imagination, be considered a door frame. The metal pipes which had been run along the sides of the sphere were positioned perfectly above the outer edge, and it looked like the pulleys were being used to make runners that would slide along them, with chains hanging down to attach to the frame.

Alister looked back down at Elo, his jaw gone slack.

"But the Oddity's door isn't even that big!" he said.

Elo shrugged extravagantly. "*I* don't know. The Professor knows what that thing can do better than any of us. Come on, let's see if there's *anything* they'll let us help with."

The sun was setting on the cliff with the house where the Oddity was, but the ladder was still there and the portal undisturbed. Professor Odd pounded up the rungs and threw open the door, turning around to poke her head back out.

"Well?" she asked. "Come *on*. And bring the horse, we'll need them."

"Just *how* is this going to work?" Peter asked, climbing cautiously inside. The Oddity appeared to him to be a comfortable teardrop-shaped room, with a tangle of flickering colored lights at one end where a couple of swivel chairs were bolted to the floor. The middle bit was filled with a massive table, which in turn was covered in artifacts—he glimpsed a television screen and part of a bicycle—around which was arranged a set of wooden chairs with padded seats. Everything was warm and dim and vaguely soothing. It felt *safe* here, Peter realized. It felt *protected*.

"To be honest I'm still not quite sure about the *how*," Professor Odd admitted, buckling herself into one of the swivel chairs and pressing some brightly lit buttons. "I've never done this much temporal slippage before. Which is why I'll need your horse's help." She leaned her head around so she could see down the stairs and out the door, where the time horse was currently hovering—a nebulous shape of blue and twisting black. "Come on in then," she called to it. "I know you're not spatially locked to this dimension. You'll fit."

The horse swirled, swished, and eventually solidified enough to put its head through the door. Even though his eyes still had trouble focusing on it in this dimension, Peter couldn't help but notice how very *horselike* it seemed as it snorted and flicked swirls of blue, like ears, at the brightly twinkling lights.

"That's right," Professor Odd said encouragingly, and the horse came up the stairs with a rush of cold blueish air. Peter felt it pass into the place and make a quick circuit of the table, before coming to hover over Professor Odd's shoulder, the blue of its mane piling up like storm clouds near the ceiling. Its hooves made little depressions in the carpet there, and its shadow made the lights seem even brighter.

"You'll have to help me out here," Professor Odd said, barely glancing over her shoulder at the horse. Peter noticed she spoke to it in a matter-of-fact tone, as though it were an ordinary person. It was the same tone she used with everyone, he realized. From the director of the Manhattan Tower, to her friends, to *him* . . . Peter had become so used to people treating him differently, that he found this revelation unsettling. It should have been comforting, he supposed, but the way the Professor spoke to him, it was as though she considered him a fully competent adult—and the sudden responsibility of living up to that expectation weighed on him surprisingly.

While this bundle of thoughts tumbled through Peter's mind Professor Odd had been busy pushing buttons and pulling levers. The horse solidified further, arching its neck, patterned like the arm of a galaxy, to lower its soft nose to the Professor's elbow, where its nearly transparent whiskers could brush her hand.

"Yes, *yes*," said the woman, a grin spreading across her face. "*Now* you're getting it. Yes, just give us a bit of a lead . . . *here* . . ." she pushed up a large red lever and pulled a handle by her knee.

There was an almighty *jerk* that sent Peter careening into the table, where he just managed to prevent himself from slamming his ribs.

"Sorry!" called the Professor.

"Will there be any more of that?" Peter asked.

The light from the doorway had vanished, and now the stairs led down into murky darkness. Professor Odd pressed some more buttons, and the lights of the Oddity dimmed. The horse relaxed, releasing its physical shape and spreading out to hover over the bank of buttons. Their colored lights stained the swirls of white in its blue depths green and pink and gold, making it glitter like diamonds in sunshine.

"So . . . the good news is it's *working*," Professor Odd said, spinning around and unbuckling herself. "Bad news is, since we're not taking the *river,* this is going to take a bit of conventional time to get there. Which isn't so bad, really. It gives us a chance to catch our breath." She gave Peter an expectant look, and when Peter just stared back at her across the corner of the table, she sighed.

"Are you hungry?" she asked. "Do you need to use the bathroom? The Oddity's got a very nice bathroom."

Peter slowly shook his head.

"I mean, I could," he said. "Eat. Use the bathroom. I just don't. I don't *need* to, not any more."

"*Really?*" said Professor Odd, getting up and stretching. "That must be convenient." Her tentacle worked its way out of the collar and did a sort of undulation, like a cat's spine. Peter found himself fascinated in spite of everything.

"Have you got bones in there?" he asked, pointing.

Professor Odd put her head on one side, her mouth quirking into a smile. Far from being offended, she seemed pleased at the question.

"No," she said. "It's all muscle. Like an octopus arm, but with my skin, so it doesn't dry out."

"Farther in the future," Peter said, "I've met people with animal grafts. Claws and fur and stuff. Is it like that?"

Professor Odd shrugged. "A bit, actually. But it's not a *graft.* I grew it myself." She sounded incredibly proud of this, though Peter couldn't imagine why.

"Are there others like you?" he asked.

Professor Odd shook her head. "As far as I can tell, I'm the only one of me."

"Ah," said Peter, and sucked in a breath to ask the obvious question. "*What* are you?"

Professor Odd grinned at him, showing her white, square teeth. "I'm Professor Odd," she said, her mouth clicking shut behind the words like a steel door.

Peter let out a breath with a shaky laugh. "I'm sorry," he said.

"Not at all," said the Professor and wandered off around the table toward the back of the place, ducking her head to pass under the nebulous form of the horse. "It's just rather complicated. And, to be honest, I'd rather talk about *you*."

"Oh," said Peter, feeling his chest tighten up. He'd learned by way of many hard lessons that it never worked to *explain* things to people, least of all adults. But the Professor wasn't *like* all adults. She *expected* things of him. Peter coughed, as if that would help untangle the mess of feelings in his throat.

There was the sound of running water and then a *hiss* of steam. Professor Odd came meandering back down Peter's side of the table carrying two steaming mugs.

"Sorry, we're out of milk," she said, shoving a typewriter and a globe of an unfamiliar planet aside to make room for the mugs. She hooked a chair with one leg and pushed it out to sit on, offering one of the steaming cups to Peter.

Peter took it and wrapped his hands around the comforting warmth, but did not drink. If he started drinking, he started getting hungry, and even though he knew he didn't need to eat, it was still an uncomfortable feeling. He frowned through the steam at Professor Odd.

"Why do you do this?" he asked. "Travel around? Help people?"

Professor Odd sipped her tea and shrugged. "Why do *you* do this?" she returned. "Saving the world over and over again . . . changing things. Tweaking things. What's in it for you?"

Peter frowned at her. The tight feeling in his chest was back. Worse, he was beginning to feel hot and twisted up inside, like crying but he couldn't. "Isn't saving the world reason enough?" he asked defensively.

"It's a *noble* one," Professor Odd said. "I fancy, however, that it's not the reason you started. What happened, may I ask? *How did you meet the time horse?*"

Peter carefully set down his tea. He closed his eyes and clenched and unclenched his fists, feeling torn apart by the desire to tell her *everything* in the hope that—maybe—she could fix him . . . and the crushing weight of knowing that she couldn't.

After a while he reached out and deliberately tipped over one of the chairs.

Professor Odd watched him patiently.

A few moments later he went over, lifted the chair up and put it back. He sat down in it.

"You're lucky," he said, resting his head in his hands. "You're lucky to have a home."

"I know," said Professor Odd. She didn't sound patronizing; she sounded like she meant it.

"I lost my home," Peter said. "I ran away because I had a fight with Sally. A stupid fight." His voice sounded thick to him, and a bit wobbly. *Was* he going to start crying? He hadn't been able to cry in ages . . . but now he had to keep talking he didn't want to. So he swallowed hard and went on.

"Home was this big farm house surrounded by fields with a barn and horses and a cow named Daffodil and five cats all different colors," he explained. "I ran away across the fields, just meaning to hide in the wood until sundown. Give Sally a fright for ignoring me. Only . . . only I found the horse. And it was marvelous and *exciting*. And it took me away. We had terrific adventures . . . saving princesses and steering ships. That sort of thing. I was so young, I thought it was all a dream.

"But it went on and on and *on*. And when I finally got back to my home . . . it wasn't my home anymore. The farmhouse was gone. The fields were gone. I couldn't find Sally or any of the cats. It was just this . . . like a processing plant? With a whole bunch of unfriendly men in it."

"Were you in the wrong time?" Professor Odd asked gently.

"At first I thought I was," Peter said. "I didn't really understand how time travel worked back then. I really *was* as young as I look now. But I've been back several times, to the *right* time. Each time it's a little different. Each time it's *not* my home."

"That's what you're looking for?" Professor Odd said. "All these changes. All these adventures. You're not just trying to fix this universe. You're trying to get your *home* back."

Peter raised his face, and found Professor Odd had taken off her glasses. She had unusual eyes: very dark with wide pupils. *Like a cat's,* Peter thought.

"I know that's a stupid reason," he said bitterly.

"Not at all," said the Professor. "I think it's the best of reasons."

She looked at him then, very kind and very sad; her dark eyes reflecting all the glittering lights of the Oddity. Something occurred to Peter.

"You didn't always have a home," he said.

"Not always," said the Professor.

"You had to find yours," he said.

Professor Odd nodded.

Peter took a sip of his tea. It was scorching hot, herby and a little sweet.

They drank their tea in silence while the horse drifted around, its breath blowing the pink frilly curtains and rustling a stack of papers on the far end of the table.

Eventually Professor Odd put her mug down with a *clunk.*

"Well, first things first," she said. "Let's get that tower sorted out, and then I'll see what I can do about *you.* No promises, mind." She got up and slid past Peter, toward the cockpit of blinking lights. Peter found himself caught up in the wake of her coattails. He still felt a bit hot inside, but not nearly so twisted. When Professor Odd sat down in one swivel chair Peter took the other, and when she didn't object, he buckled himself in.

"Right," she said, flicking a few switches and bringing the lights back up to full strength. "We're going to need to time this *very* carefully."

"Tell me how I can help," Peter said. Glancing over he found the Professor smiling at him.

"*Thank* you," she said. "I will."

*   *   *

They had barely got the frame hung when klaxons began going off. The white lights shifted red, and Alister—who was halfway up a ladder checking some cables—nearly fell off.

"What's gone wrong *now*?" he asked when he got back down to the ground.

Elo, both forepaws holding her ears down against her head, shrugged wildly.

Dave sailed past. "STOP THAT AT ONCE. IT IS DISTRACT-ING," he announced, and the klaxons went silent with a hiccup and a beep. The lights remained red, however, which made it easy to see the cold blue glow spreading out on the far side of the baby universe.

People were crowding into the sphere from all sides. Alister saw Corp Lib running past, carrying a strange-looking gun.

"It's an incursion!" they shouted as they went. "Double type!"

"Double *type*?" Alister echoed, even as he was swept along by the tide of people.

A strong clawed hand clamped on his arm, and he reached around to take hold of Elo.

"NO. STOP. STAY *BACK!*" Dave blared, but to no effect. A moment later he whizzed over their heads again, and then there was a truly horrendous *buzzing* sound, and it felt like the ground had been jerked out from under Alister's feet.

He wound up on his back with Elo partially on top of him— she elbowed him in the chest as she jumped off—and a ringing sensation in his ears. Sitting up he found the entire crowd had been knocked off their feet, Dave hovering near the bottom of the baby universe, and the blue glow so bright he had to shield his eyes.

Everything went suddenly quiet, as though someone had muted the soundtrack of the universe. In the silence Alister found he could see things with uncanny clarity, once his eyes adjusted to the light.

He saw a shape, silhouetted behind Dave, like that of a huge, long-limbed horse. Its mane was stretched out to the side as if blown by an invisible wind, and its tail twisted away into the distance in a long, flapping arch.

The light, he realized, was coming from something sitting on its back. A brilliant white glow that, unlike the baby universe, washed the room and made sharp dark shadows appear behind everyone. As his eyes adjusted, Alister thought he could make out a shape to the light: it looked like a *person.*

"What do you want to bet that's a rider," Elo hissed in his ear, her strained voice loud in the silence. She was squinting fiercely and all her hackles were up, making her jumpsuit puff out around her shoulders.

It was certainly *riding* the horse. Alister saw now how its leg of light cut into the dark swirling blue of the horse's side.

The rider gave a little kick, and the horse reared forward, shredding into streaks of blue as it tore through the air above the heads of the crowd.

Alister felt the same tumbling sick sensation as he had before when Peter's horse had taken them into epi-time, but in this instance it was more big and vague, and then with an almighty *lurch* everything stopped. Slowly, sounds began to creep back into the world.

Now the horse and rider were at the opposite end of the room, near the metal frame. The rider had brought the horse right up next to it and was inspecting it curiously.

A slow wail of an alarm rose in the air, peaked at an ear-splitting pitch, and then faded away . . . only to return again a moment later.

"I *SAID*—" Dave began.

"It's the anomaly's activity sensor!" Professor Cove cried, disentangling herself from under a pile of corps and struggling to her feet. "It's gaining power for another expansion!"

"WHEN?"

"Right *now!*"

"NO, WHEN *ARE* WE?"

Professor Cove looked at Dave, her face wide and aghast. "How can I know *that*?!" she very nearly screamed.

The rider turned to look at them. Alister could tell because the light intensified, like a beam of concentrated attention. Putting his hand up to shade his face he tried peering around at it, just in time to see the air between the four sides of the frame go dark.

Not just dark—it went *black*. The thick, matte black of the Oddity's door. Then it gave a sort of flicker, and an image swam into focus beyond the frame that was so improbable that Alister had a hard time recognizing it.

It was the *Oddity*. But not the Oddity's door as he had seen it so many times. Rather, it was a view into the Oddity's main living space, as seen from above. Alister recognized the table and chairs and the wood pattern of the floor and the tattered carpet because he saw it every time he left his room on the second floor and looked down, but it was at a more direct angle now, as if Alister were looking straight down on it from somewhere far, far above from where the ceiling should have been.

"Oh good, you're here," Peter said, appearing behind him and helping him to his feet. Alister gazed at him, a little staggered. "Odd says she's got the spatial stretching at maximum, but she still needs people on this end to move the frame, whatever that means . . . "

"Oh, I *see!*" Elo said, almost yipping with excitement. "She's using the *attic vent* as a secondary portal mouth, but since there's no way for us to *move the universe* we need to *move the portal anchor.* Dave!" she shouted, but Dave was already herding people toward the line of ropes and pulleys that had been attached to the bottom of the frame.

"Where did *you* come from?" Alister asked Peter.

Peter didn't answer, however. With the mass movement of the crowd he now had a clear line of sight to the horse and rider, who were still standing next to the frame. Peter was staring, his mouth agape, something like fury building behind his eyes.

"You!" he shrieked, his young voice breaking, and took off at a mad sprint toward the horse and rider.

What happened next was so surreal Alister didn't think to even try to stop it until it was too late.

The floor of the herbarium sphere had been cleared of vegetation to allow the frame to be dragged across it, and so Peter was able to close the distance between himself and the horse and rider in a matter of seconds. Alister watched as Peter threw himself at the horse, grabbed the rider by its leg, and pulled it roughly off the horse's back. The rider was so surprised that it didn't try to fight Peter until it was on the ground.

It raised an arm as if to strike the boy, but its horse, after a moment of stunned stillness, surged into motion and knocked it over as it galloped away, fading into a streak of blue and the retreating sound of hoofbeats.

The rider remained, clutching at Peter's leg. Alister heard him scream.

Then the horse was back. Quite suddenly and all at once. It loomed over the rider, dark and stormy, and then it reached down and bit into the rider's shoulder, lifting it clean into the air and away from Peter, who scrambled away.

The time horse shook its head, shaking the rider in turn and making the light dance about wildly. Then it threw the rider to the ground and began striking at it with its forelegs. The rider flailed a little, then went still, but the horse kept stomping on it until the light dimmed and finally went out.

There was some angry shouting. Alister abruptly realized that the whole scene had hardly taken a minute, and that the corps were only just now beginning to drag the metal frame—now carrying the giant portal—forward along its rails. These would, Alister now saw, carry it neatly around the baby universe.

Except Peter and his horse were in the way.

Perhaps Dave couldn't see—and the rest simply didn't notice Peter—but everyone kept pulling, and the metal frame kept moving.

Alister saw Peter climb shakily to his feet. His horse bowed its head, and the boy reached up to tangle his fingers in its mane.

Then the lip of the metal frame came up against their legs, and slowly, they toppled over it and fell out of the universe and into the Oddity, where they were swallowed up by the shadows.

The horse dissipated into blue smoke around Peter as he fell, and the next instant he landed with a heavy *thump* on something soft and springy and smelling faintly of mildew. He blinked and looked up, and found he was staring out the ceiling of the Oddity and into the herbarium sphere where the baby universe was slowly being swallowed up by the Oddity's portal.

Professor Odd's head intruded on this view, looking down at him with a concerned crinkle between her eyes.

"I know," Peter wheezed, trying to get his breath back. "I think I just made things a lot worse. I just got confused. I thought the horse was *my* horse."

"I saw," said Professor Odd. "I don't think you were wrong."

"But my horse is . . . " Peter sat up slowly, using his elbows as props. His horse was hovering around the catwalk, peering down at them with concerned interest.

"Your horse is a *time being*," Professor Odd said. "I rather think the horse you just freed . . . *was* your horse. Just from an earlier point in *epi-time*."

Peter looked gravely up at the swirl of blue and black and white, but the creature's expression was, as always, impenetrable.

"Think again," Professor Odd said. "Why did your horse choose to take *you* away?"

"Oh gods," said Peter, the picture suddenly coming into sharp focus.

"It came to get you because it *knew* you'd be here. It had to get you here to free *itself*."

"That was the chronostrophe," Peter marveled.

"That's why it came on so quickly," Professor Odd said. "Because for you to do what you needed to do, *you* yourself had to be at a certain point in your own epi-time. Two points *needed* to cross, at just the right time for *both* of them. My, my." She gazed up at the horse, but instead of going away the wrinkle between her eyes increased. "And all because of the war . . . " she whispered.

"The war?" repeated Peter.

"The war Dr. Rakar and his staff witnessed. The one *you* briefly participated in when you dragged that rider off its horse," said Professor Odd. "I think I see . . . it was a bit like the Big Bang."

"Sorry?" said Peter. "I thought we were talking about *time travel*."

"Yes, we are," whispered the Professor. "I said it was *like* the Big Bang. Not an explosion at a *place*—there is *no center*—the time horses fought the riders in *epi-time*, so it affected the time-line of the *entire* universe. *Everything changed all at once*—just like the Big Bang." She gazed sadly up at the time horse, and then dropped her attention back to Peter. "All at once," she said sadly. "All over. Across an *infinite* span of time. Oh . . . oh dear, oh dear . . . "

Peter got the sense of an implication, huge and awful but not yet clear, building up behind the Professor's words. At the moment, however, they were distracted by an ominous *bonging* noise from deep within the Oddity.

Looking up, he saw the baby universe was now completely surrounded by the extended ceiling of the Oddity, floating like a white featureless orb above them.

Only not quite featureless: it seemed to be pulsing, cracks of brighter white tracing their way across its surface.

"That's our cue," Professor Odd said, her tone changing in an instant. She leapt across the table and scrambled into one of the cockpit chairs, pulling levers and pushing buttons before she had quite sat down.

From where Peter sat, he saw the image of the herbarium sphere (just visible around the edges of the universe) shut off abruptly, as though a black cloth had been draped in front of it. Now it was just the universe, still cracking, still pulsing.

"It's going to expand," Peter said tensely. "Can your Oddity handle that?"

"You know, I'm not sure," Professor Odd said, but she did not sound concerned. "The Oddity is to *space* much as your horse is to *time*. But I'm not going to push her limits just now. It's *far* easier to do *this* . . . "

There was a *clunking* feeling, and Peter felt all the hairs rise on his body.

Light bloomed behind the universe, but it was a distant light, and sort of colored—like the lights of the Oddity.

The horse swam down the wall and fairly cowered at Peter's feet, and Peter gazed up in astonishment as he watched the universe appear to *shrink*.

After a few moments, however, he realized what he was actually seeing was the universe floating *away*. The farther it got from them, the smaller it looked, until Peter could make out the sharp black outline where the walls of the Oddity stopped and . . . something *else* began.

It looked like a great blue-black void, pricked with distant, fuzzy lights. The universe they had just transported was quickly disappearing into it, becoming yet another smudge of light.

"I don't understand," Peter admitted.

"Like I said," said Professor Odd. "The Oddity is to *space* what your horse is to *time*. A universe *is* space. So I've taken that space and put it where it belongs: in the space *beyond* space. The place between worlds. Now watch, it should go for its expansion pretty soon, and I wouldn't miss it for worlds."

"Will we be safe here?" Peter asked, absently patting his horse.

"We'll be as safe here as anywhere," Professor Odd assured him. "Now watch. How often do you get to see a universe *begin?*"

So they watched.

For a while nothing happened. Then the baby universe shattered into countless points of light, and those points raced outward, like a firework. In their wake they left a faint glow against the velvety background, which in time faded into nothing. What remained was a swirl of blue and green with twisting arms—like a galaxy—reaching out to either side.

"Is it all right?" Peter asked, concerned.

"It's perfectly fine," said Professor Odd. "It expanded beyond visual space, that's all. There, that swirl? That's just a window into it. Like all the other lights are windows."

Peter looked out at the sea of universes. It took a lot to stretch his mind these days, but the thought of space spreading out in different directions, allowing countless universes to coexist, was enough to make his head spin.

Professor Odd had threaded her way back over to the cockpit, and after some judicious button-pressing, the aperture of the ceiling closed in, cutting off the view of the multiverse. Now it was just the plain dark dimness of the Oddity's ceiling, like the underside of a comforting blanket.

Alister and Elo sat in a corner of the herbarium sphere, a little ways from where Dave had hooked himself up to a water pump and was giving the contents of his panvironment suit a good flush.

"TRANSPLANTING UNIVERSES CAN BE STRESSFUL," he'd explained, and Alister and Elo hadn't bothered to ask more.

Though the operation had been a success from their end— the baby universe was gone, and the Oddity's monstrous portal was back to being an ordinary metal frame—the general excitement had not died down in the slightest.

"Did you catch what year we're in, now?" Alister asked.

Elo shook her head. "What I want to know," she said with a frown. "Is where that horse and rider came from."

Alister had wondered this himself, but reasoned that he was unlikely to get an answer anytime soon. He was scraping the back of his mind to suggest something for Elo to ponder when they were approached by the comparatively familiar form of Corp Lib, who looked a good deal happier than the last time Alister had seen them.

"Dr. Rakar wants to see you in his office," they explained. "That is . . . if you're available . . . " they trailed off, having seen the hoses currently connecting Dave's suit to the faucet.

With a regretful *squeak* Dave shut the water off and rolled away.

"THAT IS AN ACCEPTABLE INTERRUPTION," he announced. "I HAVE ADDITIONAL QUERIES."

"So does Dr. Rakar," said Corp Lib with a twitch of their face that suggested a repressed smile.

Dr. Rakar's office turned out to be near the herbarium sphere, but it took them a while to get there because of all the people crowding the halls. There were shouts and whoops and the distant sound of parties getting started.

"Does this mean you're back in the right time?" Alister asked hopefully.

Corp Lib made a sound like *"Eerf,"* and shrugged. "It's not quite that simple," they said. "I'll let Dr. Rakar explain."

Alister and Elo exchanged mystified glances as they were hurried through a pair of doors with frosted glass windows and into what would have been a comfortably spacious office except that it was crowded with people who were all talking at once. These seemed to be mostly employees of the Manhattan Tower, but a few of them wore uniforms of a slightly different style. Most importantly, however, Alister caught a glimpse of flyaway sky-blue hair streaked with yellow and pink somewhere near the center of the crowd, and he dove for it.

"Professor!" he shouted, elbowing a large person in a white coat out of the way. "*Professor!*"

"Ah, Mr. *Alister!*" Professor Odd turned, beaming at him, and extended an arm. She seemed entirely unharmed, and the boy Peter was standing wedged at her side, looking a bit flustered.

Dr. Rakar was there too, so full of emotion he looked ready to burst.

"What's wrong?" Elo asked. "What *happened?*"

"Nothing is *wrong,*" said Professor Odd cheerfully. "As I was just explaining to Dr. Rakar and Vanguard Brewer there . . . " she gestured at the large person in the white coat. "The tower has been returned to its native temporal area a bit *early*, that's all."

"What do you mean by that?" Alister demanded, and felt a steadying hand laid on his shoulder. Looking up he found himself gazing into the distant and benevolent face of Vanguard Brewer, who had a considerably darker complexion than most of the other natives, contrasted by particularly bright blue eyes.

"Today's date is February 4th, 6086," they explained gently.

"We've lost *five years!*" Dr. Rakar translated, looking anguished.

"Hardly!" said Professor Odd. "If we tally the time you spent between time jumps, in actuality you've *gained* about *four* years . . . because you spent *nine* years of your own relative time *in the past.*"

Dr. Rakar's eyes narrowed, and he gave Professor Odd a skeptical look.

"It's actually a pretty good deal," Peter said. "You're lucky to have gotten back at all."

"It might be difficult to re-integrate with your native timeline," Elo admitted. "But that's not a bad problem to have."

"Much better than getting blown apart by the expansion of a baby universe," Alister agreed.

"As it stands," rumbled Vanguard Brewer. "The tower is under quarantine until the Executive Office has had time to catalogue its status. And I will need to retain all of . . . " they cast their eyes over Peter, Professor Odd, Alister, and Elo before landing on Dave, " . . . you," they finished. "For debriefing."

Peter groaned.

"THAT WILL BE UNNECESSARY," Dave intoned, rolling over to a nearby cabinet and pulling open its door.

Alister glimpsed the interior of the Oddity's stairwell, but before Vanguard Brewer had time to respond—indeed, before anyone had time to do anything—he felt himself caught up in a cold wind, felt a pounding of hoofbeats reverberating in his bones, and in an instant he was tumbling toward the open cabinet door and up the steps of the Oddity, landing in a heap under Elo.

"Good timing, your horse has," he heard Professor Odd remark.

"She usually does," Peter replied from somewhere near Alister's foot.

"I ASSUME WE WILL DEPOSIT YOU IN A MORE NEUTRAL SPACE?" Dave asked, and Alister lifted his head to find the creature positioned in front of the left-hand cockpit, his cloth-covered arms hovering over the racks of buttons.

"Actually," said Professor Odd from the other side of the aisle. "I had something in *mind.* Hold fast, everybody . . . "

Alister writhed away from Elo's elbows, bracing himself against a leg of the table, but nothing particularly bad happened. The floor of the Oddity shook, a dull reverberation that tingled under his fingers, but nothing more.

A pale, uncertain light filtered in from the front door, and Peter gave out a small gasp.

"But that's the *river!*" he cried.

"WHAT DID YOU JUST DO?" Dave demanded, sounding closer to alarmed than Alister had ever heard him.

"I took the Oddity into epi-time," Professor Odd said casually. "Not so hard, really, what with the horse practically pulling us there already."

Alister pushed himself up and gazed around. Sure enough, there was Peter's time horse, floating nebulously by the upper catwalk. It dove for the open door, almost guiltily, and Professor Odd and Peter scrambled after it.

For his part Alister went to the door and stopped there—not wishing to leave the safe confines of the Oddity.

The portal had opened in a natural door made from the criss-crossing of branches of a shrubby tree by the side of the river. Looking out Alister saw the tall form of Professor Odd, her brilliant blue wig a contrast to the pale white sky, standing with her hands on her hips and facing down the huge blue horse—which was looking more solid and horse-like than ever. Its nostrils were flared, and its streaming mane billowed stormily above its head. Peter hovered nervously at its shoulder, seeming torn.

"Professor, what are you *doing?*" Elo asked.

"Getting a few things straight," replied Professor Odd, not turning her head. "I needed to talk to the horse in her native environment, that's why I brought you here. And I need to *talk* because I don't think we've got the whole picture—and it's important that we *do.* If only for poor Peter's sake."

"I told you I'm *all right,*" Peter protested.

"No, you're *not,*" Professor Odd said, but kindly. "You're homesick, and I can't blame you. Truth to tell, I think your horse is homesick as well, and that's why she's been doing what she's been doing."

"What *has* she been doing?" Alister called.

Professor Odd glanced at him, one flick of her pale alien face, unreadable behind her round, tinted spectacles.

"Trying to put things back where they were," she said softly, but still audible. The sound of her voice cut sharply over the distant murmuring of the river. "There was a war, you see. Here, in epi-time. Between the Riders and the Horses. Now I don't know why they went to war, all I know is that they fought each other. Viciously, brutally. The Riders would capture Horses and use them—*ride* them—have I got this right so far?" she asked the horse anxiously.

The beast nodded, one dip and bob of its giant blue head.

"Good," said Professor Odd. "I really don't want to get this wrong. Because I think that's why this all happened. The Manhattan Tower sliding back in time, the baby universe erupting within this one . . . and Peter. All because of this war. Which, because it was fought in *epi-time,* caused repercussions *throughout* standard time. Changed *everything,* all over. Changed things so much the universe couldn't hold itself together; so it began breaking apart, thus seeding a successor to take its place—the *baby universe* that cropped up in the Manhattan Tower.

"Only, something went wrong. Or *right*, should I say? Be-cause . . . because Peter saved *you*," Professor Odd took a hand from her hip to jab a finger at the time horse, who watched her implacably. "That was the big change. The thing that tied you to this universe long after all the rest of the Horses and Riders had been killed . . . or gone away. I do wonder what happened to them, but I don't think that's actually important. What *is* important here, now, is that you *stayed*. You went and grabbed Peter, before his existence could be eaten up by the disintegrat-ing universe and . . . "

She turned now to Peter, and though Alister couldn't see her face he could tell she was giving the boy her most intense gaze.

" . . . you started *fixing* things. The horse, because she is a *time being*, cannot directly influence spatial matters. Not to any great extent. But *you* can. You, dropped in at the right place and time, could *change things*. Fix things, I mean. It's what you've been doing. You're the reason this universe hasn't shaken itself apart. You're the reason this universe was around for the baby one to erupt *in*. You're even the reason the horse was able to save *you* in the first place! You are *everything* . . . " Professor Odd straightened up, taking in a deep breath. "You are *the* chronos-trophe."

Peter was shaking his head. He looked like he was trying not to cry.

"No," he said. "I'm not a bad thing. At least . . . I try not to be . . . "

"I never said you *were!*" Professor Odd laughed. "I told you, remember? Chronostrophes don't *necessarily* have to be bad. The word just means a sudden sort of *turning* in time. A twist. A shift. Now yes, a lot of the time that's a bad thing. But when everything is *already* broken and twisted up . . . perhaps, well . . . perhaps a big *turn* is exactly what it needs. Chronostrophes *change* everything, but who's to say you're not changing things for the better. I think you are. In fact, I think *you* are all that's holding this universe together at this point. You and your horse, running about time and space, trying to stitch together the gap-ing holes that got blown in it by the war. Who knows, perhaps that was even the rider's original function—after all, they were the one who moved the Manhattan Tower back to its native time—but somewhere along the line things went bad. Very, very bad."

"And now I'm all that's left . . . " Peter murmured.

"Yes," said Professor Odd, her voice going heavy.

"Trying to fix a tower while it's already falling down," Peter sighed.

"Oh, I wouldn't say it's *that* hopeless," Professor Odd said encouragingly. "You have already done a lot of good. The fact that the baby universe *had* a universe to erupt *in* is proof of that."

Peter smiled wanly. "But that's why I can't get home," he said, his voice like a hollow shell.

Professor Odd's shoulders drooped, and the horse bent its head to nuzzle at Peter's hair.

"Well, technically, I suppose you *could* just . . . stop," she said. "You *could* go back home. To whatever state it's in. You might even have enough conventional time to live out your life. But it won't be the home you remember, and the universe won't last. Without you to run about and fix things it will resume deconstructing. History will alter beyond recognition, paradoxes will occur, and eventually it will implode—or blow itself to pieces. All at once, across all time. A reverse Big Bang."

"As if it never existed?" Peter's eyes were wide with horror.

"In epi-time it will have existed," Professor Odd assured him. "There would always be a record of it. A dry riverbed, you could say."

Peter shuddered.

"No," he said sadly. "No, I couldn't do that. I couldn't just leave them all. I have to stay. I have to help fix things."

"You . . . didn't break this world," Professor Odd pointed out, hesitantly. "It's not your *job* to fix it."

"But if I don't then who will?" Peter burst out, going red in the face. "If I don't keep saving it, then all the people in it will *die*. Worse, they will never have *been!* Me included! All the undiscovered life in the universe, all the fishes and the dinosaurs and the future life I haven't seen yet—all *gone. Completely. Forever.* I can't let *that* happen."

Professor Odd looked down at the boy, turned so that Alister could see a sad smile toying about her lips. She seemed resigned, but also, he thought, a little proud.

"There is a chance," she said. "If you keep at it long enough, you might just be able to fix it. Permanently. So things really *do* go back to the way they were. This universe isn't temporally flexible—that's why it couldn't withstand the war in epi-time— but if you got it close enough to its original condition it should just snap back into place and *stick* there. So you can go home— to your *real* home. But understand, you are one person trying to counteract the effects of a huge and devastating war: you might be at it for a very, very long time."

Peter shook his head. "Perhaps it's better . . . " he said heavily, " . . . if I just gave it up altogether. Gave up trying to get home that is. If I can think of it as something I've actually *lost* . . . if I let it go . . . well, it still hurts just as much, but it makes concentrating on what I have to do a lot easier."

Professor Odd leaned forward and rested a hand on his shoulder. "But remember," she said softly, "your memories of your home are from before the war in epi-time. They are the only thing, likely, that remains of this universe, before it was so heavily damaged. I beg you do *not* give them up: they are, ultimately, what you're aiming for."

Peter looked up at her, his face so contorted in misery that Alister felt a mad desire to rush out and offer to switch places with him. *Peter* could go adventuring with Professor Odd—they seemed to like each other well enough—and *he* could stay behind and try to put the universe back together. But he knew it was a mad notion. This was Peter's universe, not his.

"It's just . . . " Peter was speaking very quietly now, so Alister had to strain to hear his words. "It gets harder. With every run. The memories become . . . memories of memories. It feels almost like an *idea* of a place I made up now. I mean, you say it'll take a long time. I've already been *at this* for a long time. So what kind of hope is there, that I'll even recognize my home if I find it again?"

Professor Odd straightened up, her face shuttered, considering. Then she turned to the horse and said: "Would you mind very much if I *borrowed* him for just a few minutes? I'll bring him right back."

The horse snorted uncertainly.

"Why?" replied Professor Odd defiantly. "I'm going to *refresh* his memory!"

"I don't understand," Peter said as Professor Odd punched buttons and flipped levers. "Where are we going? I can't leave this universe!"

"You're not leaving," Professor Odd said. "Not . . . *technically.* And certainly not for very long. As for *where* we are going? Well, do you remember what I said about the Oddity being to *space* as your horse is to *time*?"

"Yes," said Peter. "But I can't see how that applies."

"It *applies,*" said Professor Odd, "because in the vastness of infinite space, *anything* is not only possible, Lucky Peter, not only *possible,* but *probable!*"

Peter looked around, bewildered, at Alister, who just shrugged.

There was a wild shimmering of the lights around the Oddity's consoles, a flashing and dancing more elaborate than Alister had ever seen, and then a sharp plunging feeling, as though the Oddity had suddenly dropped several feet.

Bong, said the Oddity, deep in its core, and for the first time Alister wondered exactly *where* that was.

"We're here," Professor Odd said softly.

"Here . . . *where?*" Peter demanded.

Professor Odd took off her glasses and gazed up at him intently. "Your home," she said.

The door was cool, damp wood under his fingers. He didn't recognize it, but then, it *had* been a long time since he'd been inside his father's well-house. And that time, it hadn't been dimly lit by the diffuse colored lights of the Oddity.

Gingerly, Peter lifted the latch and pulled the door open. He stood there, just inside the Oddity, and looked out at rolling wheat fields, golden in the summer twilight, that he had not seen since he was *actually* eleven.

To his right, the fields ran up a gentle slope to where they stopped in the shadow of the deep green trees that marked the end of his father's lands and the beginning of Blues Wood. Night was already underway in between their trunks, though the topmost leaves still held a little of the warm summer light.

To his left, the fields sloped down to a cleft where, he knew, the canal ran up against the foundations of their house. This house was just visible in the gloom, the bright red sidings dim, and the comfortable brown shakes of the roof merging into the arms of the oak tree towering above it.

"I don't understand," Peter whispered. "What is this?"

"Your home," Professor Odd repeated. She was standing in the door behind him. "The one in the replacement universe, in fact."

"What?" Peter turned to stare at her.

The inscrutable woman just *smiled,* proudly.

"That baby universe we pushed out into the void?" she said. "We're *inside* it now. Well, all right, not really *inside* it. I didn't want to risk putting you into a universe where the native you is still alive—that can cause all sorts of problems—but opening a window and peering through? No harm in that. No harm at all. Now do watch—I tried to time this as best I could, but I'm not absolutely certain when—ah . . . "

Her voice trailed off, and Peter heard the rustle and crunch of someone making their way up along one of the paths hidden in the wheat. Then they hove into view along the rest of the rise, and Peter felt his heart catch in his throat.

It was Sally. Sally as he had remembered her, and *more.* Her hair was not quite as red: it was streaked with copper and gold—of course, how had he forgotten?—and her face was dirty and tired and not at all happy.

"This is the evening of the day you ran away into the wood," Professor Odd whispered in his ear. "The day the time horse came for you . . . in *your* universe."

Peter caught his breath. "But this isn't *my* universe," he whispered back.

Out in the wheat field, Sally was calling. She sounded upset, and annoyed, and a little angry, but it was *Sally,* and Peter ached to run out to her.

Then, as her calls were becoming less angry and more desperate, there was an answering rustle from the darkness of the wood, and Peter saw *himself* walk out from under the tree branches. He was wearing the exact same clothes as he was wearing now, but there were a few more rips and tears, and his face was very dirty. He looked sulky, but Peter could tell he was secretly delighted that Sally had come out to get him.

Peter watched himself run down into the wheat field and throw his arms around his sister's waist. The two exchanged words, too faint for him to hear, but he heard their laughter a moment later floating up over the rustle of the trees as a wind blew over the field.

"There was no war in this universe's epi-time," Professor Odd explained. "There was no time horse to take you away. In this universe . . . you went home. You are living your life. The one you originally had."

"What happens in it?" Peter asked, and found himself breathless.

"I don't know," said Professor Odd. "I can't see the future. Maybe you grow up. Maybe you die in a terrible accident. Maybe you get married and have a dozen children. Maybe you make brilliant discoveries and inventions. They are *all* happening in the narratives of *this* universe. This is what I want you to understand . . . you haven't lost your home. You *can* get back to it—if you can remember, not only that it *existed*, but that it *still exists*—somewhere . . . *out there*."

Peter looked out at the gently drifting stalks of wheat, and the two dark figures now making their way down the slope toward the house, whose lights had come on, filling its windows with bright gold. The hot twisting unhappiness was still there—was worse in a way—but it did not scorch so badly anymore, and he thought he understood what Professor Odd meant. Even if *he* never got home, a part of him—a version of him—had never left. Peter hugged that thought to himself like a hot water bottle on a cold night, and felt the warmth of it flow out his arms to the tips of his fingers.

"Take as long as you need," Professor Odd said, and withdrew quietly back up the stairs.

Peter waited in the doorway until the light of the day was gone completely, and the lights of the house had flicked off. He would be in bed by now, lulled to sleep by the sound of Sally's reading. Or they would be having a pillow fight. He shook his head, fighting back tears.

Coming back up the steps into the Professor's home, he found her seated at the table with Alister and Elo and Dave. They looked like they had been playing cards.

Peter took a deep breath.

"I'm ready now," he said, and against all odds, he felt a smile blooming on his face. It was a hard smile, a determined grin more than anything, but it was still a smile. He added: "I have work to do."

Epilogue

THE BOY CROUCHED ON THE ROCK in the middle of the river. Of course, the rock was really a gap in time, and the river *was* time itself. And he was not just a boy: he was the great chronostrophe, the turning that shifted the course of time, and would continue to shift it, until it ran smooth and true once more.

The horse came, galloping down the hours. Lucky Peter stood and reached out a hand to catch her flowing mane. Not to pull himself up onto her back, but to run alongside. Feet pounding, he plunged into the river, felt time grab him and take him. Now, however, he felt like he was finally *going somewhere* as well.

Professor Odd will return in
"Star Walkers"

ESCAPE VELOCITY

Apsis Fiction 4.2: Aphelion 2016 will appear in July 2016. In it you can look forward to:

"Star Walkers"
"Abandon All ——"
"Dying to Live"
and
"The Hidden Road"

Find the entire library of *Apsis Fiction* issues at

heliopauseweb.com/fiction/apsis-fiction

Apsis Fiction is a Heliopause Production; written, illustrated, edited and designed by Goldeen Ogawa.

More from Heliopause

The Adventures of Bouragner Felpz, Volume I: A Study of Magic

Driving Arcana: Rotation One

Driving Arcana: Rotation Two

Professor Odd Novellas:
#1: The False Student
#2: The Slowly Dying Planet
#3: The Promethean Predicament
#4: The Elder Machine
#5: The Dragons of Geda
#6: The Monster's Daughter
#7: The Dogs of Canary Island

Coming soon:

#8: Chronostrophe, and
Professor Odd: The Complete Season One

heliopauseweb.com

About the Author

Goldeen Ogawa is a self-taught writer, illustrator and cartoonist. In her spare time she rides her bicycle and sings. She lives in California.

About the Text and Design

The body of this book was typeset in Elysium using LaTeX. Cover art and design by the author.